Books by Austin Clarke

Novels

The Survivors of the Crossing

Amongst Thistles and Thorns

The Meeting Point

Storm of Fortune

The Bigger Light

Stories

When He Was Free and Young and
He Used to Wear Silks

The Bigger
Light

The Bigger Light

a novel by

Austin Clarke

Little, Brown and Company
Boston — Toronto

The author is grateful to Segel, Rubenstein & Gordon for permission to reprint lyrics from "Both Sides Now" by Joni Mitchell. © 1967 Siquomb Corp. All rights reserved.

SECOND PRINTING

T 03/75

LIBRARY OF CONGRESS CATALOGING IN PUBLICATION DATA

Clarke, Austin Chesterfield, 1932–
The bigger light.

The third vol. of a trilogy; the first vol. is The meeting point; the second vol. is Storm of fortune.

PZ4.C5973Bi3   [PR9230.9.C5]   813'.5'4   74–17256
                    ISBN 0–316–14693–5

Designed by D. Christine Benders

*Published simultaneously in Canada
by Little, Brown & Company (Canada) Limited*

PRINTED IN THE UNITED STATES OF AMERICA

For Frank Collymore

Part One:

Ice Cream Castles

in the

air

BOYSIE BEGAN WRITING LETTERS to the newspapers to voice his opinion on matters such as pollution, urban development and high-rise apartments in the downtown area where he lived. He liked the downtown area, and had lived there all his life in this country. These were matters which affected him, he said, more than the problems of immigration which affected some other immigrants he knew. He chose not to waste his time writing letters to the editor about the racial problem in the city, or about police brutality. He was a successful immigrant. And he maintained that he had not experienced discrimination and prejudice, and that the police had never stopped his panel truck to harass him, when he came home late at night from his janitorial services in the business district of the city.

Dots, his wife, was very proud of his sudden expression of commitment. She clipped each letter that he had written from the Letters to the Editor page, and pasted them into the photograph album, at the front. When friends came to visit, they had to look at Boysie's very wordy and very formal letters before they saw the photographs of other successful West Indian immigrants, relaxing in various poses of exuberance and fat, shining with contentment and accumulation.

There was one letter which Dots favoured above all the

3

others. Boysie had written twenty-nine letters to the editor, but only three had been published. This letter, which Dots would show last, was framed onto the page of the album by a border of black satin ribbon. Boysie had written it to the paper on the event of Henry's death. It was a beautiful letter for the occasion that had so tragically struck him. Henry was his only friend. And it was a formal letter. In it Boysie had tried to compare Henry White, his best friend in this country, who had begun writing poetry just before his death, with another great poet who had died in the prime of his youth. He had recently heard about Keats and he knew that this new knowledge was significant. "I am going to compare Henry to Keats." *Although this man was born in a small island Barbados, far and distant from this country of Canada, yet Mr. Henry White the late demised poet, is like that other poet borned on an island, Mr. Keats, who loved nature and flowers the same as Mr. White.* This was the simple reference to John Keats, although Boysie did not know his Christian name was John. Dots thought the letter was magnificent. "You write that just like poetry itself, Boysie," she told him, when the letter was published. And Boysie had sat beside her, in a rare moment of such closeness, for her to read the letter; and especially he wanted her to see how his name looked in print. This was the first letter he had had published; and the pride of seeing his name printed in the largest newspaper in the country made him feel powerful, and made him think that for generations to come, anybody who wanted to could see his name "in the pages of annals," as he boasted to Dots who didn't see it this way; and that this was only the first of many letters he intended to write to the editor.

Henry's death, and Boysie's memory of it, and the meaning he attached to it, was nevertheless soon forgotten; and

4

writing letters to the editor about other civic matters soon became the biggest interest in his life. He did, for the length of sincere and proscribed mourning, think very much about Henry, and what his sudden death meant to him: that a man so young and not married a year yet to Agatha, the rich Jewish girl, should be dead without having left a scratch on the surface of life. And for the first few months, with Henry gone, it was like having been abandoned on an unknown lonely road, like having the pleasant, cheerful side of his nature ripped away from him. Boysie went into mourning in a way which found him depressed, and silent, and very difficult to live with. He began to hate Agatha, with the same force as his wife Dots had hated her, when she screamed and refused to believe, as the newspapers had reported, that Henry had committed suicide. "Suicide? Black people don't commit suicide in this country! They mean Agatha murdered him! That is the suicide they mean!"

Boysie hated, as Dots hated. And when the energy of his body was spent through the hatred, and his depression was at its lowest, he forgot all about Agatha. She had tried to keep the relationship between them going, after her husband's death; but neither Boysie nor Dots, Bernice, their friend, nor Estelle, Bernice's sister, could, with Henry gone, any longer accept Agatha's friendship or her presence in their company. And so, Agatha drifted out of their lives, in the same way as she had entered; and they did not even mention her name, not even to group her in a despising remark, amongst white people they had known. She was dead to them. In the same way that Henry was dead.

Dots adjusted to her life as a nurse's aide at the Doctor's Hospital on Brunswick Avenue; and it continued in a routine of long hours with overtime that was not paid for, and which was helped from its iron routine of eight in the morning until five in the afternoon, six days a week with one day off, only through her fortnightly trips to the bank, where she deposited one hundred and sixty-five dollars out of her paycheque, and kept back exactly thirty dollars for pocket money and streetcar fare. Boysie was earning quite a lot from his office-cleaning contracts. And he was thinking of buying a house in the suburbs. "Perhaps, up in Willowdale, 'cause they have too much o' we black people living in Scarborough and Don Mills already, man!," Dots used as her motive for moving. The house was in her plans for the near future, as it had always been in her mind from the day she landed in Canada. And so, with Dots occupied with work, planning her material success, and conscious always that living on Ontario Street in the low-rental housing district was making it impossible for her to hold her head as high as she would have liked, Boysie was left to himself all day long in the apartment, until it was time for him to go to work, at four in the afternoon. Dots's ambitiousness kept her busy all the time, and it was only on weekends, on Sundays usually, when she was off duty, that she got a chance to look Boysie in the eye. And every other weekend, they made love. It was the only time they each had, from their respective races after material success, to lie flat on their backs without having to watch the hour hand of the black-faced electric clock on the dresser beside the bed.

Boysie would spend the mornings reading the three Toronto newspapers, and thinking of which article he could reply to; and to which letter to the editor he should add his comments, or contradict outright. It gave him much pleasure to sit and sip his tea which he drank with lots of homogenized milk in it, and read his newspapers, and reflect on the state of the world. And what gave him the most pleasure was finding "a grammar mistake" in the *Globe and Mail* which was supposed to be the country's leading newspaper.

He did not believe that he had such mental resources in himself, this fastidiousness with grammar and spelling. For he had come to this country as an ordinary man, an ordinary immigrant from Barbados, an ordinarily educated man, who was capable only of understanding the road signs and other printed instructions which he saw around him, and not much more. "Man, Henry," he had said, long ago, "just to live in this blasted country, you don't know that a man should have *at least* a grade eight version of reading and writing! I had only a grade three version. But I does listen and learn and think for myself."

Boysie was now, therefore, very alone. And he would feel it most heavily in the mornings about ten o'clock, when everybody he knew would be at work. The only persons he would see from his picture window, high up in the apartment building, were old men, too feeble to work, and old women walking cautiously over the ice to go to the corner store, or to the Liquor Store to buy, perhaps, a half bottle of liquor to keep the cold from drying their bones, and, perhaps, to bring back memories to crowd their own loneliness.

He was always interested to see these old ladies, with their slow patient walk on the treacherous sidewalks which were not kept too clean in this poor district of the city, moving in pain and in leisure, assured through practised lack of speed that the Liquor Store would be there, no matter how long it took them to walk the distance of a half block. And from his height above them, he could see the winter wind striking them like uncertain sailboats with black sails; perhaps a black hat would fall off the head and expose the whitened hair, or the wind would flap the shopping bag against their defenceless bodies, like a sail let loose. But they would always walk on, and always would they come back, holding the small brown-wrapped bottle in their hand like a child trying to steady a breathing slippery fish. And if this view of mornings of boredom did not satisfy him, he would come down in the elevator and watch them from their own level of their movements, and see and feel the wind ruffle their enthusiasm and their determination. He could see their reddened cheeks, coloured by clotted circulation, or by rouge, and their thin legs that looked as if they had a layer of grey scales covering them, to make them bigger in a strange way, so that it looked to him as if the bigness was transparent white silk fat, and the leg itself just bone. He saw their condition from their own level, and he thought more deeply about his own boredom, seven floors above their heads.

And back up into his quiet apartment, seven floors above the "smallened" old ladies, as he called them, Boysie would stand at one of the four large windows and look out into the falling snow, or the rain sprinkling down like steel common-pins, and think of what to do, and where to go. He particularly liked to look out at the window which showed him the people coming up out of the subway at Sherbourne Street, and who seemed determined about some time and certain of some place.

It was at this window one morning that he first saw the woman. She was dressed in a long brown winter coat that was down to about six inches from her ankles, and she was wearing a white beret which was drooped at the back of her head. From that distance he could not tell whether her boots were black or brown. But one morning he spotted her coming out of the subway, and he ran out of the apart-

8

ment, up the short street and onto the main road, in time to meet her at the corner. Her boots were brown. He did not see her face, because he did not look into her face, and he did not wish to confront her with any suggestion of his interest. It was enough for him to match his morning tea with the colour and arrival of her boots at the head of the subway steps, and follow her through traffic and people, transparently through trees and trucks and houses, until she emerged again, walking like a brown saint upright, alone as he was alone, and disappear eventually among the untrimmed trees that had come through the summer like long hair, filled now with falling snow. He saw this woman from this distance and from this height, and he grew to know her. And as she came and went, with the mornings of idleness except for the writing of letters to the editor, Boysie grew to like her.

He measured her arrival at the head of the subway steps with the drinking of his tea; and when he measured time and coincidence more, he got to know that she reached that point between five and fifteen minutes to eleven. His day revolved around the sight of this woman, whose face he had dared not to look into; and he would do nothing significant, could in fact do nothing significant, as it turned out, until he had seen her, for that day. She became what morning tea is to some people: the motivation to begin the day. She came into his day and became many different persons, men and women; and he lived among them, among *her*; and sometimes, when he was thinking about Henry, and the thoughts became too heavy for him with their burden of saddened reminiscences, he would populate his quiet apartment with her presence. And in his mind see many versions of her. And soon, he began to talk to her. He promised that one morning he would go out and really talk to

9

her, ask her her name, where she was going, where she had to go each morning, Monday right through Sunday, at that same time.

Once he mentioned her to Dots, and Dots went on cooking breakfast (as Boysie talked and watched the woman walking along the street), and when he was finished talking, Dots said, "She's probably a whore, reaching back home, Boysie, boy. Don't worry yourself about her." And right there, Boysie began to look at Dots with a certain disapproval: for she had not even tried to understand what he was talking about, to be sensitive enough to be concerned. It was left to him, in his creative confusion, to puzzle about the woman and to be frustrated by the mystery of the woman's punctuality. It hurt Boysie very much and he wondered how his wife could be so cruel to the creation of his observations. How then did she really regard the letters he was writing to the editor? How would she regard any other venture he should suggest? Boysie looked at his wife and in his heart he crossed her out, erased her from his mind, and in her place, he put the woman with the brown coat and the white sloppy hat. And it was only then, only when his imagination had filled in all the details of this transposition, could he sit down and eat his breakfast that morning with Dots. He promised never again to mention the woman to his wife.

Boysie began to see things that he hated in his wife. Or so he told himself. He had lived with them for six years, as he had lived with her; and they had never been so important; he had never been very trusting nor confiding in her, nor she in him; and they had lived in their pragmatic cocoon of marriage, while at the same time going their own ways, and thinking their own thoughts. For six years it seemed, for him, she did not really exist. He had not even bothered to find out the colour of her underwear, had not even been concerned that she may be unfaithful to him, "horning him": he had not given her this amount of feminine individuality. But now, the neglect of not having thought about these things became serious, and like an electric shock of sudden comprehension of an obvious fact, he faced his wife and tried to understand her. He was wise enough to feel, at least, that he might be too late. And this realization rendered him almost numb. He accused her for her infertility: every West Indian woman he knew had at least two children. He had the money now for bringing up his children, but his wife could have none. "This woman can't even breed," he said to himself, "and she doesn't even *come!* I must be cursed now, for my past, or something. Christ! All she is interested in is her bank account and a down payment for a house in the suburbs. What the hell do I have for my old age when I can't screw anymore? A house?" He wondered how he would live in a childless house, with a wrinkled sterile woman?

He would look back over his life with her, from the very beginning when she supported him in every essential and material way, from buying his cigarettes to the prophylactics they used. He saw her in those years and he tried to know her now, in the frame of the picture window that looked northwards to the subway station. The perspective gave him the possibility of travel, of arrival and of departure. It showed him nothing about his wife. Perhaps he should disappear. . . . He saw a woman who was dull, perhaps had always been dull; a woman getting old through fat, and quarrelsome through wanting to own a large four-bedroom house in a Toronto suburb. And the only thing he could do to quell the upsurge of hatred that his thoughts forced upon him was to replace her with the woman in the brown winter coat. He knew, however, that wanting to replace her was the same as wanting to disappear.

Boysie watched the woman walking morning after morning. And he filled his life with her. It was painful and it was joyful. Once, when he looked out, he saw her walking with a small child. He became disappointed. Part of his fascination with the woman was that he imagined her to be childless just as Dots was childless. He wanted her to be alone, just as he was alone. In that way could he cope with his fantasy. But his disappointment faded that very morning, and all of a sudden the woman was Dots, and the child walked in the opposite direction. And never again did he see her with the child at her side. It was then that he speculated that Dots could be a good mother if she ever had the chance. The presence of the child by her side that morning became a child inside her womb, put there by him. He looked around his apartment, around his home, around his life, and there was no child. Not even a pet. Nothing was with him now, except Dots; and she was slipping away gradually by her own silence, by his own preoccupation with new things, with dreams, and with isolation and with letters to the editor, which she stopped reading now; and by his inability to focus on both the woman below in the street and the woman in his apartment, in the heavily breathing half of the bed beside him at night. He thought again of where he could run to and when.

He thought at first that it was her work. He thought it was her fatigue. He thought it was her snoring. And he found out, quite by chance, that all those nights when he lay beside her, when her body remained stiff beside him, when her body did not move even when he lay on top of her, when her body accepted him as a glass accepts water, he realized that in all this time, Dots was not sleeping. She was just lying beside him, like a dying patient would lie on top of a bed in a hospital ward.

"Dots?"

"Yeah?" Her heavy breathing stopped, as if he had wakened her.

"You sleeping?"

"Yeah." And she started to breathe heavily again, in a kind of beginning snore.

"You really sleeping, in truth?"

She turned over heavily, drew up her legs, extended them again, drew them up again, as if she was disturbed from a deep peaceful sleep, and said nothing.

Boysie remained quiet, lying on his side, facing her, with his eyes opened in slits. He too began to breathe heavily, and then he started to snore. Then he lay very still. He was looking for something. He was hoping that what he was looking for would not be there, that it would not be. Half an hour later, with the help of the glimmer of the electric clock, with its face like the eyes of a cat in the dark, Dots muttered, "This blasted man! I ain' got time for that!," scratched herself between the thighs, and turned over. When he got accustomed to the dark, he realized that her eyes were wide open.

But he became frightened still, for she might have been sleeping with her eyes open. All these years. And he could not ask her; at least not then. He did not sleep at all that night. And the same thing happened many nights after that.

"Dots?"

"Yeah, Boysie?"

"You sleeping, already?"

"Ah? Eh?"

Her body moves in the quiet bed, and she shuffles her legs, touching his as if by error, then she draws them up, and puts them safely out of his reach; and she holds over randomly and drops her hand, her heavy hand, and just as randomly it lands on his neck, and he can't say anything in protest because he is supposed to be asleep and because he is not sure, and then she rolls over and rests eventually far away from him.

"You sleeping?"

"Ah? . . ."

The punctuality of the woman arriving each morning, and the uniformity of her dress, bothered Boysie so much that it interrupted his concentration on the morning newspapers. He would find himself reading the words of the world news reports without understanding their meaning; and a part of his attention would be on the tip of the roof which touched in perspective the pavement of the subway exit; and he would wait to see whether she would appear in the same winter coat, or whether his concentration upon her arrival would change her appearance, and make her late. He was becoming miserable on these mornings. Dots was drifting away from him, and even though they went out each Saturday night, he did not enjoy himself, did not care whether she enjoyed herself, and he did not like the music. Sometimes he thought of changing his drink. "I wonder if I should change my brand?"

For years he had taken Dots to the Mercury Club downtown, where they listened and danced to calypso music, and mixed with each new batch of arriving immigrants. Now Boysie began to dislike their raucous behaviour and the bright colours they wore and the noise they made, even when the music was playing. He became withdrawn from them, and all the time he wondered why. He would sit in a darkened corner with Dots, far from the press of people, and watch them, and wonder why they did not change their ways when they came to a new country. And as he watched them, his Scotch became tasteless water. He was becoming tense in the company of these young immigrants. Watching them dance and throw their bodies and their backsides in such abandon to the music made him so uncomfortable and envious, like a man thinking of the loss of his virility, that the new rhythm of moving the body alarmed him, and made him hope that he was never like them. He was never like that. Boysie would sit, silently, in a dark corner and sip his drink without making too much noise with the ice cubes, and think that perhaps his presence in that bar, where he was the only black person, was a favour. But these young people, they were always laughing and talking aloud and dancing in the wildest manner, and even when he saw them on the street they were laughing like that and making it obvious by their laughter and their speech that they were newcomers, and the new owners of the country. Boysie detested their conspicuousness. And when he began to hear and then read in the newspapers that youths were snatching purses from old women in the subway, he wished he was a policeman sent to arrest all of them. "They are spoiling my image," he told Dots, during one of their infrequent conversations. That was all he said to her. Even this was too personal to talk too much about to her. And he added these "thieves" to his other griefs. And every youth that he had met in the calypso clubs and in the streets became a thief. When he happened to be passing them on the sidewalk his body was overtaken with spasms, and he clutched his wallet. He carried a lot of cash wherever he went. "There was a time when I could walk the whole of Yonge Street without meeting-up one o' them!"

Boysie lived four or five subway stations east from

Bathurst, and he was glad that he lived so far. He was glad that he did not have to travel to work on the subways with "these blasted thieves." He did not know what he would do should he meet one of them. And it did not matter to him whether the thug was in the act of snatching a woman's purse; it did not matter to him that he had never had one of them pointed out to him; he did not know their names, or their police descriptions, and one of them had never molested his wife as she travelled back and forth from the Doctor's Hospital. He was not concerned or interested in such evidence. The newspaper reports were enough for him to convict these "thieves" in his mind, and arrest them with his own hands, should he come upon such a young West Indian in the subway.

"They making things more bad for everybody," he told Dots on another occasion. "This country have enough jobs for everybody to get at least one. Look at a man like me. I come into this country, and I did truly and really suffer a little bit. But it takes a while to know the ropes. I know the ropes now: I have work hard as hell for what I have. I build a business. And be-damn, no blasted West Indian thief is going to make life miserable for me." He was thinking clearly now. He was finding words and a new language coming with an ease he did not know existed. And he was preparing his mind to commit these thoughts to the exercise book in which he composed the first drafts of his letters to the editor. He wanted the Canadian public to know that there were some, "Hell, man! Not just *some!* They must be thousands, perhaps hundreds upon thousands o' Barbadians living here who do not believe in no foolishness like thiefing. Barbadians is hard-working people. Law-abiding, too, Godblindyou!," that there were many Barbadians who did not come to this country to live off stealing, and gambling and betting on the races; and many other West Indians, too.

He stopped thinking of himself as a West Indian, and he became strictly a Barbadian. He began to have doubts about Caribbean nationalism, about the West Indies as a group of people distinct from any other group. He did not know too much about Africa, and therefore talk he had heard about something called "Pan-Africanism" did not bother him too much. And he wished that Henry was around to give him some support for his views; but after all, he was a man, and he was a Barbadian.

Boysie did not want to be known as a black nationalist either. He was simply a hard-working Barbadian. But he wished he was wealthy and privileged and very conservative. Conservative to him meant a very good life and excellent education and being a Canadian. In a short time, he would qualify to take out Canadian landed immigrant status, and "be-Christ, I am going to get that passport the morning after I qualify for it!"

This tension in him did not permit him to be comfortable any longer in places where they sang calypsoes, danced the Reggae and played rhythm and blues. His discomfort began affecting his drinking, and he moved from the calypso clubs to the posh drinking places, the street-level bars in the Park Plaza Hotel, on Bloor Street, a fashionable area of the city. He took Dots there once. The first time they were dressed as if they were going to a wedding. Boysie himself felt a bit uncomfortable, but he told himself he had to endure it. Dots was not sure. He would sit and sip and dream of how successful he was becoming, and wish that the bartender or the waiter would realize that he was serving drinks to a celebrity, that it was he who had written three letters to the newspapers, and had got them published in the Letters to

17

the Editor column. He would sit and sip and wait for this recognition. He would wait for someone from among this unknown crowd of low-talking self-assured young Canadian executives to see that the man sitting in their midst was, by his appearance and dress, not the same as those "blasted thieves" in the subway, snatching purses. No one ever recognized him in this way. Once, the bartender smiled, and said, "Cold enough for ya, buddy?" Boysie did not know what rejoinder to make.

He would think of those old ladies crossing the street, slowly, near his building, going down to the corner to purchase their small bottles of liquor (he bought his by the case these days), and he would think of the woman appearing at the same time each morning of the week from the subway station, and he would look at his wife, sitting equally uncomfortably at the table facing him, but not seeing him, not recognizing him, sipping her drink of gin and tonic, no expression on her face, just looking into the space between them, the space that was widening every day, and he would place this woman in the brown winter coat in the chair next to him, between him and Dots, and talk to Dots as if he was talking to that distant woman.

"Dots, do you know something?" he said one Saturday night, as they were sitting at the small round black table, which had become Boysie's favourite place in the darkened corner of the classy bar. "I've been thinking of incorporating the little business."

"Doing what?"

"Incorporating."

"What incorporating means?"

"Incorporating. Incorporation, you know. Incorporation and incorporation taxes. You read about it in the papers every day. The big boys do it all the time. Down on Bay

Street in the stock market, where I work . . ."

"You only cleans offices down there, though, Boysie!"

"Anyhow . . . I see this incorporation thing as the only thing that could save a man like me. The only thing to save me from paying so much taxes to the government. I see myself getting bigger and bigger. Seeing the light. Just because o' this incorporation thing!"

"What do you do with this incorporation thing, Boysie?"

"*Do?*"

"Yes, do! Yuh must be able to *do* something with a thing which you say . . ."

"I see myself buying a couple of apartment buildings. No black man in this country ever do that. Then . . . the stock market, and then, maybe . . ."

"A castle in the air!" Dots said, and laughed from the barrel of her heaving stomach.

"When I go to work on Bay Street, every evening . . ."

"You don't work down there, Boysie. You *cleans offices* down there."

He ignored her comment, and went on talking and dreaming, turning the matter over in his mind, talking not really about it to her, but as if he was already incorporated, and was trying to acquaint his wife with his new status.

"The idea of incorporation may look like a simple thing to you, but I have the opinion that it is a more serious thing than you making out."

"I tired as hell. I work all week in that hospital, and I want to get home to my bed."

Boysie swallowed his drink, and with it went a bit of his pride.

"Man, tek me home in this blasted old truck, do, lemme watch the Johnny Carson show!" She made him feel her full resentment by sucking inward with her breath on her teeth; and when she shut the door on her side, it was as if the truck had exploded. Boysie made a note to himself to print BOYSIE CUMBERBATCH CLEANERS, INC., on the sides of his panel truck. That would be the first step, he thought, towards incorporation.

Dots shifts her position in the seat, and prepares herself to get out. They turn into the street where their apartment building is, and they are blocked by taxis and cars parked all over the street, and the street is crowded with young people, boisterous and happy and some drunk, going to parties in the same building. Dots notices the West Indian men with their women. And Boysie notices only the West Indian men. "I gotta get outta this area," Dots says, while he struggles to park the truck. "I gotta get out!" Her tone and the voice of the turning tires are at the same irritating pitch.

"How did you like that girl at the piano?" They are inside the lobby now. Boysie selects the front door key from a bunch of keys. "She's a great singer, eh?"

"Open the door, man," Dots says. "It cold."

The elevator was climbing. Boysie asked her what she thought of the music, and of the place where they had been drinking. Dots heard only the noise of his words. She remained silent. She was far away from him. At any rate, there were other people in the elevator, and she hated to talk in strange company. She had learned how to stand beside him, or lie beside him in bed at night, and not hear one word he was saying. People would be in the elevator, or in the subway car with her, and she could wipe them out of her consciousness. In the elevator with them now were five other West Indians and three Canadian women. The men were well dressed, and the women looked healthy and young and vibrant in the way Canadian women just out of their teens look: legs strong and breasts full, and with a glow on their cheeks, like young willing fulfilling women.

Boysie remains quiet, more than being silent; for he feels uneasy being so close to these young West Indians; and he feels suddenly old and useless because of what he knows about himself and his marriage; and he sees these West Indians, silent, and baiting, waiting for him to say something (or even look) about their women, or about the way they are dressed; for they are young and strong, wearing mod fashions, pimpish and expensive, and in their manner is the cockiness of the university student, assurance in this cold elevator, of exactly where they are going in this country. This assurance seems to exude from them the closer they stand to the women and when the women touch them in simple loving gestures. Nobody is talking now. But the whirring of the unoiled movement up, some of them trying to ignore the movement, or to pretend that they are not bored and uncomfortable — the whirring is perhaps like the constructing of their individual thoughts.

"Imagine, leaving the West Indies to live in a place like this!"

It was one of the Canadian women who spoke. Her voice was like thunder it was so natural and so unexpected. Dots shot her eyes in the woman's direction, and the woman acknowledged it and smiled. Dots just looked off. Without changing her expression of boredom and discomfort, she felt the atmosphere become relaxed. Somebody sighed, or breathed more easily. And the boredom of watching the floor shift on the illuminated panel above their heads was less obvious.

"What would make people leave a nice warm place like the West Indies to come up to a place like Canada . ."

The elevator reached its stop, and they all got out. And

they were all going in the same direction, towards Boysie's apartment. As Boysie reached his door, he fumbled in his pocket, waiting to see where they were going.

"Goodnight."

It was the same Canadian woman who had mentioned the West Indies. Dots was taken by surprise. The shock opened her mouth, and relaxed her face; and she smiled and said goodnight. The young people moved to the next door and went in. Boysie felt very insecure having them so adjacently close to him.

"Nice kids," Dots said. She unlocked the door with her own key (Boysie was still fumbling) and walked straight into the bedroom, leaving the door wide open for him to close. Once inside, he was safe and soundproofed from them. And his protecting apartment soon made him forget them. From the bedroom Dots was saying something about West Indian young men. "Nice kids," she said, not really talking to her husband. And Boysie hoped to find more in her words than she might have intended, so that he might pick a quarrel with her. "Nice kids. And look so strong. And clean. They make me proud to see them behaving so."

Boysie took off his winter coat, and threw it on the chesterfield couch. Dots could hear him moving around, just walking and making noise, and she closed the bedroom door because she knew that should he continue walking around and moving around, she would have to answer him. He was like a lion, sparring. He sat down and spread his legs in front of him, and loosened his tie. He had become a man who wore ties almost everywhere he went; he had changed his manner, his manners, his appearance of relaxation and of leisure, in the same way as he had changed his hair style. He had stopped going to the Negro barbershop he used to like so much; had chosen the Black Nationalist barbershop with its flags and posters and colours of black, green and red, its heavy music of James Brown and Reggae and Afros and photographs of Marcus Garvey; but when he found himself becoming out of place among those who were more conversant in the new slogans than in the old black ideology, he stopped going, and went instead to the Italian barbershop just around the corner from where he lived. In the Italian barbershop, he didn't have to engage in serious conversation or discuss Black Power (the Italians spoke in Italian: and the only word he could understand was "soccer"); nobody talked to him about his race, and he didn't have to hide his conservatism on these matters, nor exhibit either a knowledge or a consciousness of them. In the Italian barbershop, he was not forced into becoming a black militant.

He was becoming tired because of all this change in his life. And he was trapped inside his new material success. He was determined now to live within the measure of that success, in proportion to that success. What prevented him was all the noise which he found around him. All this noise made him retreat into the frame of mind and of behaviour that had him now like a man without direction, without any light in his life, a man gone cold.

So much so that now, just past midnight on a Saturday night, he was sitting sprawled on his back on the couch, his necktie loosened, just as he had seen some of the men in the stockbrokers' offices loosen theirs, and he could think of nothing to make him happy. He thought of the stock market men, how they worked late at night as he moved silently around them wiping off the sweat of their labour and profits from their desks with the chamois cloth, as they counted millions of dollars on small writing pads and adding machines, as he admired and envied their relaxed posture. They did not make any noise when they counted money. He worshipped their secure movements, and he liked the way they could loosen their ties and still command power and respect in their employees. He was sure they commanded the same attention in their homes.

A Scotch-and-water was in his hand, and a filter-tipped cigarette was firmly between his lips, and Dots was inside the bedroom with the door locked and was moving around waiting for him to do something to release the painful pressure that was like a boil filled with poisonous inflammation on both their minds. He had put a record on, and was listening unattentively to it. "Both Sides Now," sung by Judy Collins. He had first heard this song about clouds on Bloor Street, and Dots was with him at the time. Now he was surprised to find this album among his collection. He had bought it and had forgotten it. Soon after Henry's death, he stopped playing calypsoes, and buying them. Instead he began buying records which were more quiet and peaceful. He even thought of buying classical music, and opera, but he never got around to them. He had not often played these "quiet" records, for he didn't know too much about their rhythms and their lyrics. He had come upon this music by chance, and had liked something about it. He did not know what it was, above and beyond the fact that the music was quiet. He leaned over now, and turned the record up a little more and settled back into the couch.

Dots appeared at the door.

She looked in his direction, not at him, not into his eyes as she would have done in happier days, but *on* him.

"I trying to sleep!"

"I trying to listen."

"What's wrong with you, eh, man?" she asked him.

Judy Collins was singing about clouds. There were clouds. Clouds were up in the sky, and Boysie was thinking of aeroplanes and the kinds of clouds he had seen from the plane coming at him with force, as if the clouds were about to change into a cloud with body and more force and destroy the plane. He saw these clouds years ago. Now there were clouds of snow falling down in front of his picture window. And he was thinking of incorporating, and of how very peaceful it would be, very peaceful indeed, he thought, to live in a cloud, while Dots remained standing in front of him.

"How could you sit down there on your arse like that, on a Saturday night, and listen to all this blasted *dead* music. I don't know, Boysie, but I swear . . . I see you ackking-up here of late, in a funny way. I can't tell what happening to you, 'cause you don't even talk to me, you always in some trance."

She talked in her Barbadian dialect with its inflections whenever she was really angry, or whenever she felt she was speaking from her heart. Sometimes, too, she did it to embarrass him: to tell him that she was through and through a real woman. She did it also to be superior. And it always affected Boysie the wrong way, and made him want to choke her. He tried never to speak in his Barbadian accent. On occasions when emotion got the better of him, then it spilled forth. Judy Collins was singing about *"floes and floes of angel's hair, ice cream castles in the air . . ."* Dots was standing over him. Boysie was not quite sure he understood what "floes" meant; he had never heard the word before. Still, it gave him an airy feeling, a sensation of relaxation, and one of great peace within himself. But Dots was standing over him, and he was uneasy. The woman at the piano, in the bar, had sung the same song; and

25

on that occasion, he had heard Dots's reaction to it. Why did she think it was dead music, when it was giving him so much peace?

"Turn the damn music off, please!" She had come round now, and was facing him, although she was not looking into his eyes. *"Feathered canyons everywhere."* "What the arse you listening to, man? You uses to be a strong black man. At least when I first met you, you uses to be a strong black man. And you mean to say, that you could now sit down in my presence and listen to a song like this . . ." ". . . *they rain and snow on everyone . . ."* Dots sucked on her teeth in a rasping exasperated way to show him how great was her displeasure.

Boysie got up because he wanted to avoid a fight. He did not know how to tell her she was oppressing him, and turning him away from the new life and the new light of peace he found himself exposed to; and she was replacing it with nothing, nothing at all, just criticising it; and for him to have opened his mouth to reason with her would have been like opening the restraining gates which had held back, for so many months now, the explosion of words and anger and water and tears which they both knew would have torn the skin off their marriage, and perhaps also off their bodies.

Dots used to be such a simple woman. This woman used to be such a simple, sweet, and very pleasant woman. He fixed himself another drink before he changed the record; and when he did, he turned it up very loud. Then he went into the bedroom. But there was no reason for going there. He slammed the door behind him, thinking he had slammed it on her, and that he was locked away from having to see her, or to listen to the full disturbing noise of her voice which was now unrhythmical and very reminiscent of the calypso.

26

Once inside the bedroom, he regretted that he had locked himself inside. He had not actually locked himself inside, he could always go back out, but to do that without having some motive in his steps and in his appearance, even to do that without some clearly understood reason (and Dots would have to understand reason and motive as clearly and as loudly as if it was written up on her shopping list above the sink in the kitchen before she would accept him), would be to surrender. And he could not surrender. His life now was on such terms of silent but very clearly defined warfare. He was the kind of man who could not go back outside into his own living room because his wife was there. She had, therefore, by her presence in the other room, turned his bedroom into a prison. And had she been in the bedroom, and he in the living room, that room which once was so full of life and noise, so cheerful with the anecdotes which their friend Bernice used to regale them with, had now become like an anteroom to some deep-seated dramatic moment.

The air is heavy. And there is a smell in the bedroom. He could never understand why Dots would never buy a cheap tin of air freshener and squeeze it all around the room. Her hairpins are always on the dressing table. There used to be just one dressing table, when they were poorer. He was carefree in those days. But now he is obsessed about appearances, like a man getting old, and fearing the stain and the untidiness by the zipper of his trousers. He would watch that spot every time he went into the bathroom, and particularly in public washrooms. Dots's hairpins are lying like killed stiff insects on the face powder she dusts onto her face; and her other pins she uses to put her hair up with are stationary now, like small road-building rollers. Bottles for making her face attractive are on the dresser,

27

which Boysie calls "Yours"; and she has many bits of paper with telephone numbers on them, and newspapers and a Bible and another book which she began to read enthusiastically two weeks ago, and has only reached page 5 in it; and this book lies with its back broken now, at the place of paused concentration, dead to her interest like one of the hairpins, with its spine broken into two, like a hairpin.

There is a smell in the room. Boysie tries to imagine what kind it is. He breathes in deeply, and tries to locate the origin of the smell. It could be the smell of Dots's lingering body odour. It could be the smell of unwashed, accumulated underwear, and petticoats; it could be, "Boy, I don't know what kind o' deodorant they selling these days! The more o' this blasted thing I rub under my armpits, when the mornings come, the more I sweating like a horse! Every day! And at work, too!"; just the smell of two bodies that are not quite dead yet. But he prefers to think it the smell of one body, her body. Her body odour is so close to other smells that he does not like.

He sits on the bed and turns on the television. He remembers to keep it low, because he is accustomed to keeping it low, because Dots would lie in bed and all of a sudden start snoring, and soon after would call out to him, "Boysie, turn down that damn thing! I sleeping." He would want to throw the television into the bed with her, and let it take his place beside her, but was always prevented from doing this. And he would continue to sit on the edge of the bed, and lean over to listen to the lowered volume, and after a few minutes, disgusted and frustrated that on a weekend he could not listen to his television after eleven o'clock at night, because his wife is sleeping, he would turn the set off, and fall noisily into bed, not beside her, although he was in the same bed with her. And he would lie awake most of the night, thinking how best to open a conversation with her.

He needs to talk to somebody. He wants to talk to some-body, soon. He feels himself becoming too silent, too in-grown, too philosophical, talking to himself too much: not only in the mornings when he waits with his unread news-papers for the strange woman to emerge from the subway; not only then, when one could understand that kind of mut-tering to take away the tension; but even at work, when there are other persons around, in his panel truck on the crowded streets, and in the Italian barber's chair.

One Saturday night he lay on his bed for two hours, waiting for Dots to come in. He wishes she would come into his bedroom now, and sit on the bed, and say some-thing about the television he is watching. But the same hos-tility which keeps his mouth closed hinges her teeth upon teeth, only the eyes in the head conveying the hard feelings that should be expressed, this same hostility which keeps her from uttering a word.

He is in his bedroom, and he feels he is in a coffin. His coffin. Perhaps her coffin, since she spends so much time in it.

Once, he wanted to kiss her, but something stopped his hand from caressing her. She was in the bedroom with him, and she was very uncomfortable with him in there, sitting with a drink in his hand, watching the world news and lean-ing close to the volume so that she wouldn't be disturbed; and when she found that he was not going to leave the room, she got up and undressed in front of him, and the blood surged through his body, and he wanted to pull her to him, and rub his hands over her thighs, and perhaps in between her legs, even to kiss her *there*, to feel the tough-ness of her hairs there; and this powerful cruel feeling welled up in his heart, and then it took hold of his stomach

29

and became like a tightening muscle, and he could do nothing but sit, and pretend that he was really engrossed in the plight of the Vietnamese, while the jungle and the water, the cataract and the waterfall, the bushes and the hedgerows stood there within the power and the brutality of his grip, and he was powerless to hold out his finger, even by accident, and touch the tip of her breast; even if he had to say afterwards, "Pardon me, Dots."

He wanted to wash his mouth out with warm water, and brush his teeth, but the sink was full of underwear. He was frustrated again. He was the more frustrated because he had made the attempt many times to tell Dots that he did not like to see her underwear; and he had made the attempt to touch her where the underwear covered: *"floes and floes of angel's hair and ice cream castles in the air . . ."* The bedroom door was opened. Dots was standing in the bedroom.

"You ever listened to those words? You know something? When I hear this song I can't help thinking of dead people, of somebody deading, dying . . ."

"Maybe." He did not think she should say this to him. He had seen something under her bed, under their bed.

". . . the strange thing is, that when I look through the window in the living room, I only see hell down there. Come and let me show you what I mean. Come."

"Okay."

"I don't mean that you should come right now, but sometime. Make a point o' looking through that window while that song playing. Maybe a next person, you or maybe through this window. Maybe a next person, you or maybe Bernice, or somebody, would see a next thing altogether completely different."

"Maybe."

30

"I never knew that this would happen to me. I never expect this. I lived and lived in this place, and I see many things happen. Things that could change the most strongest man. But if anybody had tell me that this very thing would happen inside my very own house. Well, I wouldda have to tell that person, 'You lie like shite!" — pardon my language."

"What do you mean?" He was not sure she was saying what she meant to say.

"That woman that they find in the underground garage. That's what I am talking about! The woman in the underground garage of this very apartment building we live in. And you cocking-up your backside, listening to some damn fool talking about clouds and ice-cream and feathered crayons . . ."

"Canyons, Dots. *Canyons.* A canyon is a place where . . ."

"You don't have to instruct me! You don't! Nor be blasted *rude* to me! Just because you write two or three damn letters to some newspaper and they pity you, and print them, it still don't mean that you can *instruct* me! You don't have to treat me as if I didn't went to school!" The waters were bursting now. "And look at you! A good-for-nothing bastard like you. You, a man who I sponsored into this country. Worked for. Slaved for. And now, good Jesus Christ, you have the gall! I stomached insult upon insult in your behalfs. And now, you come telling me what a canyon is. Boysie, let me tell you something. Let me axe you something, now. What in the name o' bloody-hell is the worth of a canyon to me? What do I want to know the meaning of a canyon for?" She was holding the newspaper in her hand, all this time she was talking. She dropped it on the bed, and shouted. "*That* is a canyon! That, that underground garage with that twenty-six-year-old woman, is a canyon! And you want to hear what makes that more of a canyon to me? Because that woman in the newspaper is a West Indian woman. Just like me. But the papers didn't mention that, though . . ." For a while she had nothing more to say, for she had oversaid, in the first place, what was on her mind. What she had wanted to say to him when he entered the bedroom was, simply, "Boysie, why do you lissen to that song, when there is more serious things happening every day?" And she had prepared herself for the argument he would put up, and perhaps outwit her into seeing his point; for she was tired, she was getting tired and just as frustrated as he. She knew he was tired and frustrated with her. But when she saw him lying on the bed (she actually thought, "On my blasted bed"), she found herself uncontrollable.

The newspaper spread itself on the bedspread. *A 26-year-old single nurse was raped yesterday afternoon in the underground garage of an apartment building in the Sherbourne-Bloor district. Police said a man who was hiding in the building's laundry room stuck a gun in the woman's back, forced her into a dark corner of the adjoining underground garage, ordered her to strip and raped her. He then scattered her clothing through the garage as he escaped. Deputy Police Chief Jack Ackrab today called for stiffer penalties for persons caught with weapons. He said it is difficult to advise women on what they should do in underground garages. There were 181 rapes in the city last year, an increase of 17.5 per cent over 1970. Seventeen women have been raped this year . . . when every fairy tale comes real, so many things I would have done but clouds got in my way . . . Ackrab said police are patrolling garages as much as possible. He said people can get in easily because garage doors remain open for quite a while after vehicles have passed through . . . I looked at clouds from both sides now, I don't know clouds at all . . . Detectives Harold Lambton and John Wells who took yesterday's victim to the Wellesley Hospital said a man wearing a stolen maintenance worker's coat grabbed the purse of Elvi . . .* Boysie couldn't read any more. The record had come to an end. The story had shaken him. He thought of the woman in the brown winter coat. He had seen her many times while he was in the heat of want and sexual need, and he had never thought of luring her into the underground garage of his apartment building; and since he had never thought of doing that, he wondered what it would be like should he do it; but the moment he thought of it, he became nauseated, and for a moment he almost fell out of love with the woman because the nasty taste of the imagined act almost brought vomit to his lips. But still he wanted to know how it would feel. The story was intriguing.

"One hundred and eighty-one?" He turned the pages of the newspaper to get away from the twenty-six-year-old woman in the underground garage. He was framing in his thoughts the exact words he would use in his letter to the editor. Should he begin by stating his own abhorrence at the act of rape? Or should he expose the despicable nature of the man who would rape a woman? "This isn't war," he said. "This is not war." He must always use the proper grammar: it was very important in expressing your ideas, he thought. "Only in a war, and even in that, even at that, a man would have to be a damn beast to rape a woman . . ." (Dots had screamed one night when he forced himself between her tightly closed legs, after he had turned her over bodily from lying on her stomach, as if her stomach was stuck to the sweating summer sheets. "Oh Jesus Christ, man, Boysie! Are you raping me? Are you raping your own wife? Are you so hard-up, that you raping me? Jesus God, Boysie!" But her screaming was part of her enjoyment and her sensual laughter. Then she said, "More, Boysie, man more!"; and then she laughed louder than she had screamed. And then there was only a deep satisfied exhaust of breath. And then it was quiet.) But that was different. Dots had been joking. So that was different. *Floes and floes of angel's hair, and ice cream castles in the air, everywhere, so that was different.*

"You still want to tell me what a *canyon* means?" she asked him. She had gained the upper hand now. There was no point in being hostile and bitter. She felt it would be too great a brutalization. It was at this moment, and at moments like this, that he realized what a kind person she was, deep down; but he did not often reach her at this depth of her humanity. "That is what *I* would call a canyon!" Her mood suddenly changed from one of compassion to bitterness. She said in her Barbadian dialect, "And list-ten to this next one, now!" Why was she doing this to him, he wondered. But in her heart, she was saying that she had to, because, he was nothing, nothing more than a poor-arse black man who she had to bail-out and actually put food in his mouth, for years and years. "List-ten. Tek this one with you. A woman, a mother o' three-four thrildrens got her arse beaten-in last Monday night! In another underground garage where they does park motto-cars. Up near Scarborough. And when that woman see that blasted beast, the purse-snatcher, well, the long and the short of it is that they had was to tek that poor lady, flat on her back, in a stretcher, in a ambulance, up in the Scarborough Centennery Horsepital. And the police sometime later lay a charge o' non-capital murder on the purse-snatcher. He was a man by the name o' Rose. Well, I tell you, Boysie, that in both o' them two cases, the one with the out-right rape, and this next one, I swear that both o' them two womens is Wessindian women. The newspapers in this place can't mention a person by creed, race nor religion. But something in this story, and the place that it happen and the name o' the woman who get beat-up, all this tell me that that woman is a black woman like me. I know she black. She black, Boysie . . . something in the name, Dianne Daniels, tell me so. List-ten again, to this piece from the paper . . . *Missis Daniels, who was separated from her husband, died of multiple fractures of the skull inflicted by a blunt instrument. Her purse containing about fifteen dollars, was stolen.* Them two facts is what I mean. Number one, Missis Daniels is a woman separated from her husband. The bastard. He must o' left her with four thrildrens in this hard city. And number two, she only had but fifteen dollars inside her purse. Now, do you understand now, Boysie, why sometimes I can't even as much as look you in the face, furtherless allow you to lie down on top o' me. That is what I want you to know is my meaning to the word, *canyon.* That is the canyon in my life!"

(Sometime later, it must have been a day or a week or a month, or even a few minutes after Dots had said all this, did Boysie come across the story about which she had been telling him. When he listened to it that night, sitting on the bed, he did not understand the sudden use of her dialect, nor the meaning of it. He thought it was used because of the way she reacted to *floes and floes and floes of angel's hair.* And she might have begun talking to him in this way, since she was capable of this kind of change, and had then veered off, talking about things that had nothing to do with floes; and if Boysie was not too arrogant to recognize it, he would see that whatever she was saying was to the point, in the sense that her reaction was *not* only about *floes and floes*

35

and floes of angel's hair, but about life itself. Boysie then read: *Police found a purse lying on the ground outside the apartment block when they arrived. They searched all apartments directly above where the purse was found, and a suspect was arrested on the seventh floor. Police seized a socket extension wrench. Mrs. Daniels died about 7 p.m. Doctors had given her 31 pints of blood, about three times the normal amount in the body, to try to save her life.*

Sundays used to be a day of drinking rum punch, noise and calypsoes in Boysie's apartment. Glasses and ice cubes, records and dancing, men and women crowded into the apartment, drinking and dancing and deliberately getting happy and loud and noisy, from their unacquaintance with the system (which they called "racism") from early in the afternoon right up until past midnight. Not many of the visitors and friends in those hilarious days, three years ago, had to get up early on Monday mornings to go to work. Not many of them were employed. Their collective glee and happiness, which was measured in the amount of food they would eat and Scotch they would drink at Boysie's expense, knew that they had to remain just above the pitch of soberness so as to face themselves and their lives in the country they had come to in the hope of making an easier living, not a million dollars as some of them might have dreamed about before they tasted life, but just an easier living, easier than they had hoped for back home: to be able to wear a new dress to a party, to be able to own four pairs of shoes instead of one; to be able to walk down the main street in the city with a few dollars in their pockets, to be able to return home once in every two or three years on a twenty-one-day vacation, paid for later. "We does return home only to show-off!" Dots would tell them; to display

36

to the less fortunate and the less daring, who had not emigrated, the glamour of being abroad, of living in a rich country like Canada: for to be able to return home with five summer suits and two hundred dollars in travellers' cheques (which many had never known to exist before), to spend it like water on friends and strangers in the newly desegregated night clubs and hotels which once catered only to tourists from North America, on strangers who became friends with free drinks, was part of the dream of success.

Now, here of late, Boysie rejoices that his life is no longer taken up in that swirl of appearances and in that hectic and expensive consumption of food and women. He is glad that he has changed from that way of living. But he is bored. Now, on Sunday mornings, he listens to church music and church services on the radio. The station he listens to is itself a measuring rod of his intellectual transformation. It is the Canadian Broadcasting Corporation, the CBC, the government-owned, or public-owned, radio which he first found out about from his old friend and employer, Mr. MacIntosh down in the Bay Street stockbrokerage area. Mr. MacIntosh always listened to the CBC when he worked late in his office. And Boysie changed from the popular radio stations with their twenty-four-hour acid rock and rhythm and blues programmes to the CBC. But the CBC was beyond his comprehension. He felt, however, that he was doing something educational by just listening to it. There were lots of programmes about world affairs, and he should, by merely listening, understand some of the discussions. But most was above his intelligence. Still, he persisted. Once he changed the station to which his wife was listening, and she abused him, and then wondered why.

"I wish that you could feel that by listening to the CBC you would improve your knowledge of world affairs," he told her. She did not listen to his words; she saw only that he was speaking to her in a distant, superior manner and voice.

"Man, turn back on the blasted thing!" she shouted. Her hair was in curlers. She was wearing some kind of outfit which she called a duster. Boysie regarded her as shabby when she wore this duster around the house. He wanted her to be well-dressed around the house.

"I just thought that you might want to hear something different."

"Boy, I don't know what happening to you! You uses to be such a easy man to live with, much more easier to live with."

"At least you could try to use proper English when you are speaking to me."

"Wait!" The vacuum cleaner handle hit the floor. It rang out on the hardboard. She waited until it settled and until there was absolute quiet in the room. "Wait!" She then tore the head tie off her hair. The curlers made her look very appealing and he wanted to be strong enough right at that moment to grab her by the hand and lead her into their bedroom and fling her on the bed and stand above her, and wait until she melted in his strong presence, and undress herself, and invite him onto her body, to be coaxed, to be loved, to be womanly and feminine and fragile and delicate and like a wife. Or he wanted to be able to look at her tenderly and with gentleness, and say quite simply, "I love you, woman."

"Who the arse are you talking to, man?"

He wanted to be able to tell her that he knew. He wished he had this strength which he felt Henry had with Agatha. He wish he could just reach out his hand and grab her, and beat her, and make her stop making him feel so inferior and so insecure. He knew he was going to do something to this woman. Soon. But he could not bear the terror of having to think about it, and to plan it.

"All right, Dots. All right."

"Be-Christ, it better be!" She took up the vacuum cleaner handle and went back to her cleaning. Boysie did not bother to tell her about the noise. "I invite Bernice over this afternoon. She coming round five. Three hours from now."

"But suppose I had to do something this afternoon, suppose I had to write a letter to the editor, or listen to the world news on CBC or . . ."

"Kiss my arse!"

"Or listen to my music . . ."

"Listen to what? Listen to *floes and floes and ice-cream hair?* Look, don't make me laugh." And she laughed.

"I really wish that you could see what I mean, Dots," he said, quite sadly, and no longer with arrogance. "I really wish that you and me, and I, could be able to sit down and listen to something sensible on the radio for a change. And learn something about world affairs and these people. See the way they do things, 'cause as you know, Barbados is no longer in my plans. Or in our lives. I am not going back there to live. I am not even going back there to spend a vacation. I am fixed here in this country now. And I really wish you would understand, Dots, that to live here in the best way, a man has to know what makes this place tick. That is why I tell you that I am not interested anymore in listening to a lot of damn West Indian noise, called music. And that is why I *done* going back to the Mercury Club and West Indian places like that." He was getting rid of the tension within him. It was almost impossible for him to say anything these days to Dots. He did not know now whether she was listening to the words he was speaking, or whether she was transfixed on the spot where he had caught her with his first outburst, and that she was now stunned into that position, forced to be bombarded by the noise in his words and by the sound of the words. He did not know whether she ever listened to anything he ever said to her. But he said few things to her.

"I am a different man now, Dots. You have to see that. It doesn't mean that I am a different man because I find myself with a steady job, that I have a little business cleaning out people's offices. That didn't make me a different person, Dots. You want to know what made me a different, brand-new man? You want to know? Well, I'll tell you." He was finding it easy to talk, and he was talking with his eyes held down into the glass he held in his hand. He was not looking into the glass. He was merely holding his head down as he had seen some of the speakers on the public affairs programmes on the CBC television do. They would talk and talk and never have to look the other man straight in his eye. They didn't do it. Their words were sufficient to kill the other man's arguments. He did not want to kill Dots. He merely wanted to make her listen. Language, he felt, could be more mortal than fists. He wondered again whether she was still transfixed into her place. And he did not even know whether she understood this language.

"It started out this way. I was down on Bay Street. And one night, a young Canadian fellow who was in the office started talking to me. We started up a discussion. I had a chance to listen to him. He was about nineteen or twenty. And it was the second or third night I had a chance to talk with him. He is a student, studying something to do with philosophy. He introduced me to something called language, Dots. This language is what I am trying to tell you about now. I don't have to tell you that I don't know anything about philosophy. And before I met that Canadian young fellow I had never even heard the word philosophy. The only philosophy I ever heard about was something Henry used to call the philosophy of life. But this young fellow told me that he was a school dropout. For five years. In that five years he went from one job to the next. Cleaning cars, delivering parcels in a panel truck like mine, for businesses down Yonge Street. A whole set of odd jobs, as he called them. And one night as he was dressing to go to a party with his date, something happened to him. And when they got to that party, all the young men and young women there were going to school, learning something, and using this new language. And he told me that he couldn't use one word o' this new language, because he didn't know what it mean. He couldn't join in the discussion of this language. They were discussing the war in Vietnam in a language he never heard of. Do you know, Dots, that there is a big war going on all now so, in Vietnam? Anyhow. He said he really and truly did read something about the war in the *Globe and Mail*, and while waiting for the late movie he had to watch pictures of it on television. But beyond that, the war in Vietnam could have been the price war on gasoline in Ontario, for all he cared. The date he was at the party with said to him afterwards when he tried to kiss her goodnight . . . and listen to this now, Dots. This is the punch-line. That girl turned her face away from the young fellow and said to him, "Nobody without a social conscience version of language can ever kiss me again." Boysie paused to allow Dots to feed on his words.

"Now when I heard that, Dots, I had to listen. So, the young fellow thought about it. And on Monday morning when it was time for him to go to work, he went instead and registered at George Brown College where they teach

41

this new language to school dropouts. After being there for a year or two, a new world opened up to him. Today, he is a fellow with a university education. He going through for papers in this thing he named philosophy. That was one of the things that made me change, Dots. I don't have the head to go through for this thing called philosophy, or get papers in it, but I decided to do the next best thing. And it is this. I intend to master this new language. I have changed, Dots. You do not know the amount of thinking I have been thinking lately. And you want to know why you don't know? You don't know because I don't rass-hole talk when I am thinking. I mean, I used to feel that as a black man living in this country there was a certain level of things that I could do. And that I could get out of this country. I used to think so. And I even helped whoever said so believe it is so. I was destined to be a cleaner. And I used to feel I could only be a cleaner. I don't know if I am explaining this as good as I want to. But there was something in me that didn't let me see things destined for me to see. You see what I mean? For instance, then. I would watch that man who owns the brokerage place on Bay Street. I would watch him like a cat watching a mouse. And I would always wonder how come he has so much money, and I have none. And when I look at the amount of sweat that he uses-up to make all that money, be-Christ, if you compare sweats, well, it is Boysie Cumberbatch who should be the fucking millionaire. That is what I mean. I was living a kind of life that somebody destined me to live. And only after that young Canadian fellow showed me certain things about his life in terms of this language-thing did I see what he was meaning in terms of my life. Not that he put me to sit down and show me these things. Not that, Dots. It was really like looking out through one o' them windows there in the living room, and seeing things every morning and every night, and still not seeing one damn thing. Until, bram! all of a sudden I see for the very first time that what I was looking at was nothing, not one-fucking-thing! The young fellow told me the name of that in terms of philosophy. But I can't remember what is the term he used. I know what he means, though. And you know, too. Because more than once I heard you use a word "sperspective." And I know that that word "sperspective," which is the same word that Mistress Hunter over there in Rosedale used to use, is the correct word to call this thing by. Now, I am going to tell you something, Dots . . ."

He took out a cigarette and lit it, and held his head back down. He inhaled deeply and the smoke shot through his nostrils and he went on talking. He knew he had Dots within the grasp of his listening. And if not actually listening to the words, she at least was there, had to be there, could not move, because of the novelty of the occasion. He wanted her to be there. To see and to witness the difference in his life that he was talking about, and which pleased him so much. It did not please him to talk about it, although he was pleased to see the change in his life; for talking about it was very painful to him. And it had taken a toll upon him. It was tiring to talk too long, and he was feeling the results of this exertion. He held the cigarette in his mouth and the drink in his hand, and he listened for Dots in the apartment. She had a certain special sound which she made when she was home. Not a sound that he could hear, not that kind of noise, just the knowledge that her presence went hand in hand with some sound. He listened to her sound now, as he would miss it and listen for it when he knew she was at work. The apartment was very quiet and empty and the space of the sound, or the sound of the space she possessed when she was present, was not there. He went on thinking of what he had in his mind: the long hours of loneliness in the apartment when he was at home; in the mornings reading his newspapers and waiting for the woman with the brown winter coat to emerge and pass; and the new thoughts which were crowding his head, and exposing him to a tremendous and frightening awareness. "Did you know that the war in Vietnam is the biggest racialistic event of American imperialism? Did you know that?" He had just learned it. He had memorized the language. It sounded good to him. He did not know exactly what it meant. But he had tried to show it to his wife once. She looked at him in the way she always did when he did or said something which surprised her. Her surprise was not based upon her not having expected such wisdom from her husband; not that she was shocked by the increase in his education and perception. It was merely that she was shocked that such words could ever come from him, even if he had such education and perception. Dots had measured Boysie's worth by the history of his unemployment during the early days he had come to this country. And nothing he could do would ever give her a better impression of him. She never told him that, to his face, but she thought it. That was why she looked surprised when he said something which she did not expect him to say. It was as if she dared him to remain everlastingly ignorant.

He was thinking: she would leave the apartment to go to work; and he would assume that after she left the house, she went straight to work; and when she came in, he expected that she would have come straight from work. He had found himself living in this routine of expectation with her. It was the same with meals and other things she did around the apartment. He expected she would cook. Would

44

wash. Would clean. He was surprised to see that she did not clean under the bed. How many other things had he taken for granted in his routine life with her? She left to go to work. She came home. He accepted that. She came and went. But suppose there was a surprise in this too! "I wonder if I should follow her once of these mornings, just to see if she really goes to work," he said. But it was really not necessary. And then he thought some more about it, and realized that he had been living with this woman for so many years and he did not know very much about her. He did not know how much money she made. He did not know what she had for lunch. He did not know where she ate her lunch. And with whom. And for the past few months, he did not know what was the colour of her panties, he had been so far from her. And caught suddenly in this trap of speculation, he went out into the living room to see whether she had changed, to see if grey hair was already showing in her head, to see whether she was putting on weight. He had never thought of these things before. All of a sudden, he wanted to look at his wife. And he wanted to learn to know her again.

In the living room there was no one. "Man, I must be dreaming!" It was impossible for her to be here and not make her natural sound. He searched inside the cupboards, in the small kitchen, and in the bedroom, although he had just come from there. And Dots was nowhere to be seen. Had he talked so long? Had he really been talking such a long time, trying to impress her with this new language, and she was not even there to hear what it was all about? All this change in him: and she had scorned him, and despised him so much that she could leave without making her sound, without listening to him? What other things about his wife had he neglected to watch? Could the new language be clouding his perception?

The apartment became very quiet, and he grew frightened for the stillness. Her sound had left the place. It struck him that if she was dead, if she was really dead, and he had wished her dead many times before, even this afternoon, and last night too, if she were dead, he realized that it would be a shock just like this, that the place would be so quiet, too quiet for him to spawn any further use of this knowledge. Not that he could not deal with the lack of her. For he remembered wishing her dead when he was talking. But he had made her dead according to the specifications of his own ability to face that kind of death.

He could not endure the way the apartment was quiet without her. And so he put on a record to play. He did it absentmindedly. When the volume rose, he was hearing: *floes and floes of angel's hair . . . and ice cream castles everywhere . . .* The apartment door was unlocked, and he heard her voice say, "That's what I've been telling you, wasn't I?" Her perfect English: someone must be there. "Didn't I tell you this very minute, not one minute ago, coming up in the elevator . . ."

Bernice was standing beside her. *Feathered canyons everywhere . . . they rain and snow on everyone . . .*

"Come down from the clouds and say How-d' to Bernice, please, Boysie!" He was not sure whether it was Dots or Bernice who had spoken.

Bernice always brought freshness into their apartment. She was still working as a domestic, for a rich family, the Breighington-Kellys of Rosedale. And the conditions of her work were such that she did not wish to change her job, or her occupation. Whereas Dots had left the domestic service for the hospital as a means of ensuring her independence,

46

and her social status, Bernice continued to use her status as a domestic, and the large savings account that went along with it in the Royal Bank of Canada ("Naturally, darling!"), as the measurement of her independence. She had saved quite a lot of money. Nobody, not even her own sister, Estelle, knew how much. She was very secretive in these matters. The amount of money she had spent on Estelle during her problems with work and to assist her with her child was forgotten now. Bernice had turned over a new leaf, so to speak. Estelle was still living with her in a two-bedroom apartment, but she had permitted the bonds of blood to be uncut, so that she ceased to interfere in Estelle's life. She seldom talked about Estelle to Dots. And Dots recognized this silence as a sign that everything was going well.

"Under control, child."

"Well, gal, I wish I could say the same 'bout my life!" Dots sighed dejectedly. Bernice understood. Boysie was in the bedroom, or the bathroom. "You looking good, though. This is the one you tell me about?"

"Costs too much, though."

"Nobody else is going to take care o' you, hear. And who you going leave your money for, when you dead?"

"But a hundred dollars? For one winter coat?"

"It is yours."

"Yuh know something? I couldn' help thinking that if I was still working for Mistress Burrmann up in Forest Hill, I won't have to spend a hundred dollars on one winter coat. On no winter coat, if yuh axe me! Mistress Burrmann wouldda given me one of her old ones!" And they both laughed heartily. Recalling the days when the condition of their employment carried with it such gifts and hand-me-downs always made them laugh. But they could laugh now because they had both passed through that stage.

"Sometimes, I wonder if I made the right move."

"You not happy, Dots?"

"I don't think in terms of happy or not happy, child. What is being happy? In my life, I find myself with the things that should make a person happy. But something like it happened to the arrangement o' these things in my life. Especially, *the thing* I have inside there!"

"Boysie?"

"Yes."

"Again?"

"Again, child."

"But why Wessindian men can't do with only one woman?"

"Them? Them, child?"

"Boysie fornicating, again, eh?" Bernice smiled when she said it. It was a new word she had learned. "I catch that word offa the woman I works for. She told me yesterday that her own husband fornicating. I had to find out what the blasted word meant, even before I could laugh, or be serious."

"Not Boysie. It is something more deeper, worse than that."

"What could be worse than that? What?"

"Bernice, my husband doing some funny things. Funny funny things."

"Like what?"

"You believe in psychiatrists, Bernice? I hear a lotta people at the hospital talking 'bout them. Almost everybody who comes into the clinic goes to one. Or is advised to go to one! But being I am a Wessindian, I never really put too much truck in one o' them."

"My people goes to one. He has his own one. And she

48

has hers. But they call them *shrinks!* How you like that word?"

"All this time you here and I haven' ask you to sit down, and have a seat. Take a seat, girl. And look, I stanning up here with your coat in my hand, all this time . . ." She put the coat down; then she said, "I am really getting doatish and forgetful. Do you know that this afternoon Boysie was talking to me, and I forget he was talking to me, although I was stanning up in front of him, probably listening too. And before that, I went into the bathroom and I was in there for almost five minutes, and still I didn't know why the hell I was in there! It was then that I went downstairs and waited for you!"

They laughed like they used to do when they both worked as domestics. It was a long time since they had laughed together. Boysie came out of the bedroom, and they stopped laughing.

"How, Boys?"

"Not bad, Bernice."

"You very quiet these days. Don't even call. Don't come-round, don't do nothing. Only killing yourself with that cleaning work, eh?" She patted him on his shoulder. "Oh, Estelle say thanks for the birthday present for the little boy."

"Well, no . . ." Boysie resented Bernice. She was talking now, it seemed to him, as if her job and her new circumstances were more important and impressive than his, as if she was somebody special. Dots had given him this same impression just as she started working as a nurse's aide. She had passed all her exams. She knew that Boysie had never passed an exam in all his life, had probably never taken an exam — except his driver's exam. His life in this country had never called upon him to sit any exam of any type.

49

Her careless comment at that time had hurt him so much that he vowed to improve himself with education. It was then that he got to like reading the newspapers and experimenting with the new language. Now Bernice went on to talk about a party she was at last night. Boysie tried not to listen, but he was in a way jealous of her happiness, and his resentment of her was not a very serious one. She had attracted him sexually many years ago, and he had been rejected by her. This memory came sometimes into their minds, and made them both violent to one another. He could not allow himself to be envious of her. He wanted his life to be hard, organized, clean in its aspirations: the ability to see clearly what was going on around him.

"Child, the music was so good! They played Aretha Franklin and calypsoes the whole night! I danced every dance. And with every man I could find." The noise again, Boysie observed. The noise and the parties and the drinking and the dancing. He wanted to change himself out of that suit of clothes. "The three o' we used to have those very nice times right in this very apartment."

"The same thing I was telling Boysie. He been tekking me lately to some place where all they do is drink and sit down and listen to a woman singing about *clouds!*" Dots laughed sensuously and sneeringly. Bernice knew it was directed at Boysie. "Blasted clouds!"

"Clouds? You making sport!" And then Bernice laughed too.

"Clouds, I tell you."

"Them things up in the sky?" She exploded now, and slapped Boysie on his legs. "Boy, you going crazy? I don't even remember ever seeing a cloud in the whole sky in Toronto. You, Dots?"

"My husband's head up in the clouds."

50

"That's the song you was telling me about?" The song was now playing. Bernice listened to the words, and smiled. *"Floes and floes of angel's hair . . ."* She sang along with the music. "I listen to this every day. My lady plays it almost every day. It must be her favourite, too." She hummed along with the music when she didn't know the lyrics. "I still don't like the kind o' music they call rock, though."

"What rock got to do with it?"

"I just telling you that I do not like rock music. I wonder if by rock, they mean like a rock-stone or rock, like in a rocking-chair? I don't see neither of the two o' them things in this rock music."

"I am talking about clouds, Bernice. And you telling me about rock music."

"Anything that is not jazz music, or blues, or calypsoes, child, is rock to me! My lady that I works for holds the same opinion. She is a very nice person, and I agree with everything that she says. She's very nice that way." Bernice considered the matter settled, that Dots didn't have an opinion to combat her knowledge, and she settled herself in the chair, and said, "I went shopping yesterday. You should see the things I bought on my charge card! I bought a nice maxi-nightgown such as I see in a fashion book. Mauve."

"What about a drink, Bernice?" Boysie was making one for himself. Bernice nodded.

"Yuh telling me 'bout the nightgown, gal."

"Scotch, please Boysie. On the rocks. I drinks strictly on the rocks. I got myself some shoes, too. You know the new ones, with the thick soles, well, them. As I was in the store, I decided to spend a few dollars on myself, and before I left that place, my charge plate was heavy to the tune o' three hundred dollars. Thanks, Boysie. I almost buy-out the whole blasted store. Got myself some new dresses for the fall, too." She was wearing a new dress now. It was new in style. Dots thought she herself was the one who set the styles and fashions between them; but now Bernice was taking over; and Dots watched her and looked at the dress, and complimented her, but she did not feel happy about it. Bernice moved about in the chair, fixing things on the dress to attract attention. "Child, guess what I bought yesterday, too. A hair dryer. You must come and see my place. I changed it right around . . ." (Boysie was thinking of his bed, and what he found underneath it yesterday; and he was looking around as Bernice talked to see whether his own living quarters were just as well furnished as Bernice's. Dots had not yet thrown out the plastic flowers which she kept in a shiny gold-looking vase on the coffee table; and there was one in the bedroom too; and another one on the dining area table. Boysie hated plastic flowers. He had never seen plastic flowers in any of the offices he cleaned, and they were merely offices, and not even homes. Once he bought a pot of flowers — he did not know the name of the flowers, but he liked them, liked their full strong colour of red — and brought it home, and in two days it died because Dots did not water it, was not accustomed to watering the plastic flowers; and she seemed to be glad that it had died, that it was no longer competing with her plastic flowers, which she cleaned and shone and rubbed down like an athlete getting his muscles polished after a very hard race; and when she threw it out, with the flower pot, the three vases of plastic flowers became uglier in his mind.) "There's a lovely florist near where I living and I got him to fix me a lovely bunch of red roses, and child, you should see how one simple thing like fresh and real flowers could light up a person's life! I watch Estelle sit down and look at that bunch o' roses for almost half day last Friday. As if she was remembering something. You know what I mean? It wasn't no simple thing like watching a movie, which you know is here today and gone tomorrow. Not that. Estelle was watching those red roses on my glass-top Italian modern coffee table as if she was looking into a mirror or a crystal ball that contained her fortune. And I got to tell you something, Dots. I was stanning up in the kitchen watching the steaks we had for supper, and I got a glimpse o' her face, and so help me God, I have never see my sister's face light up so pretty, and contain so much meaning, just by watching a simple thing like roses . . ." (Boysie liked roses too; and he first came to like them when Henry wrote a poem that talked about roses. Estelle had asked him to read that poem, the day Henry's death was reported in the newspaper. The poem was printed beside his photograph, too. Boysie remembered that he used to be a gardener back in Barbados, working from seven in the morning till six at night, at the Marine Hotel; and it was his job to keep the roses red and blooming; and in all that time he never thought he could pick one rose and give it to his mother, or to his woman; and he never liked roses then, for that reason. He hated roses, then. But it was Henry who brought him back to roses. Henry's poem went something like, *But was it really time that killed the rose of our love, was it time, and was it time to die, is it time, this rose? Time has no power over roses or something-or-the-other* . . . He was trying to remember it well, this poem about the roses; and he remembered clearly that it was Estelle who had asked him that Saturday morning when they looked into the newspaper and saw Henry's photograph, it was . . .)

"Estelle remembered the poem, then."

"What you say, Boysie?"

"Time has no power over roses . . ."

"Bernice, I ask you. What the hell is this man saying? Do you know? 'Cause I can't mek head nor tail . . ."

"You haven't make the drink for me yet, Boysie?"

And that was another thing. Orders. Orders orders and more orders. He had never given anybody an order in his life. In the large rose gardens of the Marine Hotel back in Barbados, there was no gardener below him, and he could not give orders to the roses. He was the head gardener. But there was no assistant gardener. And for weeks he wondered why that was the arrangement. Once he tried to give orders to the roses: one flower bed had refused to grow and blossom, and he yelled at it, and said, "Kiss my arse, then, if you don't want to grow! Water won't mek you grow, well tek this, then!," and it was his foot, trampling the rose garden; and the night watchman who lingered about the premises during the day because he was in love with the head cook, a woman, saw him and reported him to the day manager who fired Boysie on the spot, right in the middle of the rose garden. "I order you to leave this premises, and never come back. That is an order!" Boysie got another job at the Hastings Hotel, in the tourist district of the island; and although he was hired as Chief Gardener, there still was no one for him to give orders to, because he was the only gardener employed by the hotel. So he gave orders to himself, and this time he did not step into the garden beds, he merely stopped watering them as often as he used to water them at the Marine Hotel. It was a step downwards.

"Gimme some more Scotch in this drink, please, Boysie!" Bernice asked. It sounded like an order to him, but he gave her the Scotch anyhow. Dots was smoking a cigarette, so she couldn't get up to do it. She gave one to Bernice who handled it, when she lit it, less clumsily than Boysie had

54

ever seen her do before. Boysie could feel the change in her, too.

"I brought you something, Dots." She got up and went to her coat, and when she didn't find it, she went instead to the string bag in which she kept the shoes she wore indoors when it was snowing outdoors. She brought back a small parcel and gave it to Dots.

As Dots unwrapped the parcel, Boysie could see that Bernice was wearing both lipstick and eye shadow these days. "This old bitch, she must be pushing fifty!" He wanted her to be fifty years old, and therefore outside the pale of any sexual craving he might have for her; and he wanted his wife to hurry up and be old, be fifty too, for the same reason. He was getting tired. Dots was forty-two, pushing forty-three, but she looked (and sometimes behaved) younger than a woman in her late thirties.

"Thanks," she said. Bernice had brought her some expensive lipstick and eye shadow. ("This bitch wants my wife to be like her, or what?" Boysie thought, jealous and envious and feeling left out. He thought of the woman in the brown winter coat, and he tried to see her face close up, but he could not because each time he saw her he was seven floors in the sky; and he wanted her to be younger than Dots, but he would have to wait to see whether she was in fact younger. Nobody could really look younger than Dots, he knew.) And he watched his wife very closely as she sat down talking with Bernice, and he saw the firmness in her legs, her forty-three-year-old legs, and her breasts which had not yet begun to sag and her behind which was firm and warm as a pear not quite ripe, and he wondered why she didn't become pregnant, for he had tried every night for a very long time, a long time ago, and when he could not get her pregnant, he gave up; he stopped making love to her at all, and then he tried, only casually now, for the purpose and the fun of their lovemaking had addled so far as he was concerned. ("I wonder if this woman is on the pill?") Dots never mentioned those things to him, and he never thought of asking her; so funny now, without provocation, but only through speculation, that he should bother to think about this. He went back in his mind to the contents of her drawer in the bedroom, which he would glance through, not really checking up on her, but trying to find something very personal that belonged to her; something which would draw him closer to her, he thought, which would also make him know something about her that she did not tell him, that she did not offer to disclose, that he had not asked about. All he found, one morning, when the woman in the brown coat was late arriving out of the subway station, was a tube. The tube is white. It is about six inches long. One end of it is larger than the other. And it looks like a "pop-gun," which he used to make and shoot peas with, back in Barbados when he was a small mischievous boy killing lizards. This "pop-gun" thing did not take his interest long, for that was not what he wanted to find in her drawer. ("In her drawer! Heh-heh-hehhhh! In her drawer, in her drawers, in her . . . if Henry was still living, I could make a joke outta this and he might even know what this things is!" At times like this, he reverted back to Barbadian dialect, because he was close to himself; and because he had not really learned how to speak the new language which he felt would release him from some of his torment. He had to be satisfied with his dialect until the new language could express his innermost thoughts. Dots was the same way, too: she talked a formal, strained brand of English at work and when she had visitors — until she forgot — or if the superintendent of the building was talk-

56

ing to her; but when she was angry, or when she was really close to her husband, she talked in the only tongue she knew intimately. "In her drawers, yeah, heh-heh-heh. What a joke!") He had put the tube into his pocket that morning, and had forgotten it there for two days while he thought of ways he could ask the young Canadian fellow if the new language he was learning had any philosophical explanation for it. But something told him it was personal, the kind of question he could not ask a young man, and a stranger at that. So he brought it back home and absentmindedly put it in his own drawer. He thought of it now, and went into the bedroom, and took it out, after making sure that Bernice and Dots were deep in their conversation; and he opened her drawer, tried to remember exactly where he had taken it from, and when he found the nightgown, the long white one which Dots never wore (she wore it once on their sixth wedding anniversary night), he lifted it, and found another one. "Jesus Christ!"

"Boysie, what are you doing in there!"

It was Bernice calling. Her voice was beginning to take on the effects of the straight Scotch. He had never given anybody an order in his life. Bernice was calling him to join them. "Man, they got a first-class calypso band down at the Mercury Club now, boy! You shouldda seen me last night, and the Saturday night before that! I dance the Watusi — is that what they calls it? I dance the Jamaican dance, and after I had in a few watered-down rums that they served down there, you shouldda seen Bernice on that floor with a young man, doing the Reggae! I Reggaed for so! Why don't you take Dots down to the Mercury? That is where the action is!" The noise in her voice and the noise from the West Indians down there at the Mercury and the "pop-gun" thing in his hand, in his trousers pocket, and

57

Dots in the kitchen trying on the eye-shadow makeup, and Bernice drinking and smoking, her eyes becoming red, her new dress in place and fitting her properly, and her hair now streaked with grey and in the Afro style and making her look dignified and very desirable.

"Are you seeing mens, now?" Dots was in a good mood, and her voice was loud and sharp and it had that Barbadian edge to it. "You stepping out with mens? At your age, gal? And young mens, to-boot!"

"I can't tell you what a fool I was all these years! Working my arse off. Saving up money. And life passing me by."

"You at the age now, gal."

"When you miss it for so long, and you find it suddenly . . ."

"Oh, Christ!" Dots gave out her raucous sensual laugh. "I hope you are eating green bananas and drinking stout, gal. Young man does give old woman the belly!"

"Look, Dots, haul your . . ." And she held back, laughing, and Boysie got the chance to look down in her brassiere, and what he saw there did not belong to a woman who will soon be fifty years old. It made him very unhappy. It made him think of what he was doing to himself: he had deliberately tried to take the sensuality in his background out of his present life. His refusal to listen to calypso, his refusal to be happy in a West Indian way of wide mouths and winding backsides when dancing; his new desire to be quiet and intellectual, to listen to soft music which the Canadian young fellow called "civilized music," and which he heard a man on the CBC television call classical music, his distant closeness with the woman in the winter coat, and his growing fondness for *floes and floes of angel's hair with ice cream castles* . . . "Wait, Boysie, why you don't go on a diet? Child," she said turning to Dots, "Those people I

58

works for, well I tell you, they have changed my life. You don't know I stopped eating pork and things like that! Look how I look. You don't see I tek offa a lotta weight. Granola. No milk in my tea . . ." ("But iron in your arse, though!" Boysie snickered, in his heart; and immediately got sick at his own raucousness and crudeness.) ". . . and I not puffing and puffing every time I climb a stairs."

"I always telling Boysie that his belly looks like a manager-belly."

"It big like that," Bernice said. She patted him on his stomach. His trousers were almost hanging below his waist-line. "You looking old before your time."

"What I want a big-guts man for? They does get outta wind before I ready! Heh-heh-heh!" Boysie hated Dots for saying that. Once upon a time, she could say these things and they would not hurt him, in fact he would welcome them, because he was more sure of himself then; and when she said them and laughed at him, and he laughed with her, and her laughing became less derisory because he had made it that, he still felt like a man; and even if they were said in the presence of others, it didn't bother him. But recently, her casual remarks had more edge to them. The slightest comment she made was now taken as an accusation and even as a rejection.

He was secure in material ways. He could not understand why the mention of the size of his belly should upset him so. There must be a deeper reason.

"Child, the fellow I seeing nowadays, I told you about him, didn't I?" Dots found herself caught in this confidence, which she had never mentioned to Boysie; and so she looked sheepish, before she could give Bernice her ac-knowledgement. Boysie became alert now. He had not been seeing clearly lately. He should train his mind to listen more. There were things he had seen for years and they had not registered. For instance, the "pop-gun" tube. And Dots had replaced the one he had taken from her drawer. "Well that man is a man. He is as flat in his middle as Mistress Burrmann is on her chest, that bubbies-less bitch! . . . pardon me, Boysie, boy . . ."

"When you bringing your young man to meet me . . . to meet me and Boysie?"

"Anytime, girl, anytime! But he is so busy. All the time he busy, busy, busy, reading one book after the next. He going through to be a lawyer. Got six more months, and then, I will be buying long white dress! How yuh like muh?"

"I saw two young boys tonight . . . was it tonight? . . . no, last week! Or last month? Anyhow, I saw two young boys last month going up in the elevator with we. They looked so strong, that if . . ."

"I am investing in that man." Bernice said it quickly to avoid further embarrassment: Dots had made a slip. "I investing in he. I don't want to burden him, and I don't intend asking him for nothing. He don't even have to be faithful to me. Faithful? What I want faithfulness for from a man? All I does want, child, is a little regular . . ."

"Did he tell you I saw him one evening coming home from work?"

"I watching him with Estelle, though! Like a blasted hawk, child. Estelle *likes* man. She likes more man than what John the Baptist read 'bout. But this time . . ."

"Look, gal, let me get up offa my arse and fix something for you to eat. I cook already whilst I was cleaning. I only have to make the gravy now, and dish. Help yourself to another drink. Boysie, don't you see Bernice glass empty?"

"You ordering-'bout Boysie very much today, girl. I

could get my own drink, man." She laughed. She should not have laughed. Had she not laughed, Boysie would have taken it as a defence, as something in his favour; but she laughed, and made her words just another little game that they seemed to have been playing upon him. "You ordering Boysie . . ."

"What the hell you think he is there for? If I don't order him, if I can't order him, who you want to order him, then?"

And Bernice laughed very loudly, and got up, still laughing, plucked out that portion of her new dress that was stuck to her behind, looked Boysie full in his eye, and went into the kitchen still laughing.

It was ten o'clock and the woman had not appeared yet. Boysie had to get to the barbershop before noon, because he wanted to go to the bank and make his monthly deposit and then be back home in time for the one o'clock CBC news. They were going to have a special broadcast about the war in Vietnam. Richard Nixon the president of America was playing the arse, Boysie felt; and he was banking on the Vietnamese to throw some blows in Nixon's clothes. This is how he put it to the Canadian young fellow the previous night when they both took a break and drank a coffee from their work. Nixon was going to start bombing the North again, and Boysie wondered what the North was going to do. He was trying to follow the war, and at times he had difficulty deciding whether the Vietnamese were all Communists, or whether it was just the Viet Cong, and he wasn't sure if the Viet Cong were in the North; but he liked the name Viet Cong. "They sure sound like Giants to me! I like that name, Viet Cong. Sometimes, my wife make me feel like one of them, a Viet Cong!" He was anxious to hear what the radio was going to say about the Viet Cong. Waiting now for the woman to appear, he wondered if in the eyes of a real Viet Cong he would look small, be a fool to be waiting on a woman he didn't even know, and whom he had not seen close up; but he felt that the Viet Cong were patient people, and so he felt better when he thought of that. Yes, he must start behaving like a Viet Cong, and in that way, Dots would respect him.

It didn't matter that his stomach was bulging, he'd bet that there were some Viet Cong whose stomachs were bigger than his. "If Henry was here I would argue with him that a Viet Cong could have a big guts and still be a fucking gorilliphant!" He laughed aloud, as he used Henry's favourite word — *gorilliphant* — a gorilla that was a giant. "Henry was a fucking gorilliphant!" He walked around the apartment trying to take his mind off the woman.

He was dressed. From the first time when he realized that his life was changing, he had decided to dress more tidily and properly, paying attention to appearances as much as to quality. He had the money to afford both. This morning, although he was just going to the barber's, he was dressed in a three-piece suit of a dark grey material with a very conservative stripe in it. His tie was a darker grey, and he made sure that his socks were black as his shoes were. He had thought of changing to boots, as almost every man was wearing these days, but he had seen too many hippies and loud-mouthed West Indians wearing them, so he drew the line there. His topcoat was a fawn-coloured brownish material, cut in the military style. He remembered, whenever he wore this coat, that he had first seen it on Englishmen in movies during the war in Europe. His hair was cut short these days, and to look at him you won't think that he was going to the barber's today. But he had become so meticulous and so fastidious about dress that he decided he had to look trim always. The only thing on which he spent more time than shaving every morning was his newspapers. He looked very much like an undertaker this morning.

And he was impatient and nervous, walking from the window that looked out on the street, to the bathroom (where he passed water, even though he had done so just five minutes before) and back again. He went into the bedroom, in Dot's drawer, and felt under the nightgown for the "pop-gun" thing; and it was there. He had thrown away the one he had long ago when he discovered that Dots had replaced it. The record player was still turned on, so he turned the switch and the red light went out. A record was on the turntable, and he took it off and dusted it ("This blasted woman thinks that I am made outta money!") and put it back into its jacket.

Then he got the idea. It occurred to him in a very simple way, and he wasn't sure that that was what he should do; but it was a good idea. He searched through his collection of fifty-odd records, and picked out all the calypsoes and the rhythm-and-blues and steel band songs. He put them tidily into a pile. He then searched the jackets of the remaining records to see that the records matched the jackets. He picked up the pile of records he had placed on the floor, opened the door, closed it but without locking it walked to the elevator, waited ("Good morning, Missis Thorne. Nice day, eh? Not too cold today . . ."), went down with Mrs. Thorne his neighbour across the hall, and walked straight to the incinerator. He threw the pile of records through the chute, wiped his hands as if he had just got rid of something filthy, and went back up in the elevator. He opened the door, closed it and locked it this time, went to the window and leaned over on his elbows to wait. There were four records remaining in his collection. ("Wait till that woman comes home! If she opens her mouth to say one word, well . . .")

The woman was coming. She was coming, and he was getting very nervous as he saw the white floppy beretlike hat she always wore; and he wagered with himself that she would be wearing a coat of another colour, but she was in the same brown coat, and the same dark tall winter boots, and the same large tinted glasses so large that they made her face look like a timid animal's, and in her hand was the same white shopping bag, made out of plastic. It looked like plastic because it was shiny. He wondered what she had in it. She walked upright with no swagger, without incitement towards herself, without self-consciousness, without a swinging gait as Bernice did, and she walked out of his sight, and he remained at the window thinking that "I gotta see that woman close-up once of these days!" He was going down now in the elevator on his way to the garage underground where he parked his truck on the weekends. He had never given much thought to the safety or to the danger of these underground garages, probably because he had just seen his strange woman pass.

He got into the truck and revved up the engine. "This damn cold weather could kill an engine, to say nothing about a man, it is so damn cold . . . wonder why some places are so damn cold!"; and as he waited for the engine to warm up, he felt inside his coat pockets for his cigarettes and he pulled them out, and with them were the two clippings: women in underground garages where a *26-year-old single nurse was raped yesterday afternoon* but it is morning now, *in the underground garage of an apartment building in the Sherbourne-Bloor area,* "Christ, what some men won't do for a piece o' pussy!" *and a 36-year-old mother of*

64

four "A mother? Even a woman who is a mother isn't safe in this blasted country!" *who was beaten by a suspected pursesnatcher in the underground garage of her Scarborough apartment Monday night, died of her injuries last night in Scarborough Centenary Hospital.* "I wonder why Dots changed this second story to a different hospital when the paper says Scarborough. Did she really say Scarborough, when she read it out to me, or . . ."; the motor was ready now, and he drove out. Suppose he was parking his truck one morning early, about three, and he saw a woman in the underground garage, would he rape her, would he make a pass at her, would he make conversation with her? "Shit! what am I thinking?"

These thoughts disappeared as he emerged from the garage to meet the sun, and it was a bright day and very cold, and he remembered asking Henry many years ago how it could be cold with the sun still shining, but he couldn't remember what answer Henry gave him. "That bastard had an answer for every question." It was probably a philosophical answer, too. But he was by himself this morning and he had things to do. As he waited for the light, he saw the old ladies with their shopping bags coming from the Liquor Store, dressed in the same faces and winter coats as they wore to church every Sunday morning; and he wondered what exactly was in those bags. He was walking between an alley one night not too long ago, to clean one of his contract offices, just a laneway, and he stumbled upon three men, their faces red around the cheeks and their necks white like parts of a dead chicken, or like paste or flour dough, in black coats shabby around the elbows, ("Why do bums always wear black?"), drinking from the mouth of a bottle. As he passed, one of them hailed him, "Hey, buddy! Sir, just a minute, sir," and he

65

halted in his pace, for he was no longer afraid or scornful of confronting drunks either in elevators or in laneways; and the man came up to him, with the bottle of wine in his hand, it was something named "67" or "76" or it could have been "1776," it was so dark in the laneway; and he knew what "1776" meant, the independence of America, it should have been, could have been 1776; but this man said to him, "Could you spare a dime or a quarter?" Boysie stopped, put his hand in his overalls, fumbled a little and took out a thick wad of bills. "You buying coffee or you are buying wine with this?" The man's teeth showed and he was missing some in the front and some at the back, and the whiskers on his face bristled and he said, "Take a swig, sir. You're a goddamn gentleman." Boysie put the bottle to his lips, and when he took it away, almost half was gone. He gave the man a five-dollar bill. "You're okay, you're okay, you're from Jamaica, right? You're goddamn okay, mister!"

These old ladies were hurrying to cross the street with the light changing now from amber before he moved off. One of them, — there were only three crossing together, but not in the same company, not as friends, — wore a crucifix around her neck. He moved off, turning right onto Wellesley Street East, and he looked about him and saw all the derelict men and women, most of them past fifty and certainly older than thirty ("The Eskimos live to be thirty years old, ain't that a bitch, Mr. Cumberbatch? In my country, in *their* country really, 'cause it is theirs, but they live to be thirty and when I am thirty I will just be beginning to hit my highest earning power! What do you think about that, Mr. Cumberbatch? I am a Canadian, but they're the *real* Canadians!"), bulging in their bodies in places where you won't expect them to bulge, the women beyond the child-bearing age and child-bearing interest, walking heavy as if a barrel of water is suspended just below what used to be their waists; and the men, some of them thin and emaciated, some fat in a way that a woman is usually fat low around the hips, and their complexion like, like like what, Boysie? "Like what, Boysie? Goddamn, you never see one o' them bastards down by you on Parliament Street with their skin the colour o' putty?" Yes, their skin is like putty, and they always seem to be in a small hurry if they are not too slowed down with wine. He thought he must soon leave this area: for this was not the place to live when he was striving so hard for appearances, and grappling with a new language. ("If a king was living in a fucking pig-sty, what would you call him? A king, or a pig?" He and Henry were drinking one Saturday afternoon in their favourite bar, the Paramount Tavern, when Henry asked him this question; for Boysie had just described the area in which Dots had signed the lease for the apartment. Boysie did not know the city in those days; and to be living in the Parliament Street area or the Ontario Street area did not mean anything significant to him, except that "the rent is blasted reasonable. You are talking a lotta shite 'bout pigpens and kings, but I's a fucking unemployed man!")

He must prevent himself from getting mired in this pigpen area with the women and the men who all looked as if they had misused their bodies for the first twenty-five years of their lives. He was waiting for the light at the corner of Sherbourne (this woman from the subway must walk along here every morning: perhaps I should park here and watch her like a private eye, Ai-yiii-yiiiii!) and Wellesley, where the nurses are mostly West Indian and Filipinos, "I never had a 'Pino yet! Uh never had a white beef yet! A 'Pino beef is the sweetest beef in the whole ranch o' Wellesley Horse-

67

pittance!" Who said that? Not Henry again! Sheee-it! "Three Filipinos travelling through Afri-ka!" Who said that? The Mighty Sparrow, Calypso King of the World! "Three sweet 'Pinos travelling through Africa . . ." Why did he burn *all* his calypsoes? He should have kept "The Congoman," by the Mighty Sparrow, about the three white women travelling through Africa: he liked that one. He had burned all his music that had rhythm, and only three were left. The Judy Collins album about clouds and floes and floes, *floes and floes of angel's hair and ice cream castles in the air!" I like those words, though.* No matter what Dots say. I like floes and floes of ice cream hair . . ."

The snow was coming down, he hadn't noticed it before, and he was humming the song to himself, and his mood picked up and he was happy, and then he heard the blowing of car horns behind him, and he realized that he had been standing a long time after the light had turned green.

"What the fuck is wrong with you niggers, eh?" The man in the Oldsmobile thundered away before Boysie could get his window rolled down to call him a bastard.

The other two albums which he had kept were "I better check their names when I get back, you know I can't even remember the jackets!" He should have swerved into the middle of the road and ram the man, or take down his license or follow him; but it was such a nice day with the sun shining. "I'm becoming like a real Canadian, saying 'It's a nice day today,' when it is cold as hell!" He knew what he was doing talking in Barbadian dialect; he knew what he was doing. He was driving slowly, looking around enjoying the day, and didn't know that he had reached his barber's. Nobody was with him so he could talk as he liked, and that was why he spoke Barbadian.

"Hey! Mister Boysie! What you doing?"

68

Alfredo Cammillio, *Specialists in Scissors Clipping, Parking across the Street in the Esso Gas Statione,* greeted Boysie this way, with the same exuberance, as if Boysie was a long lost customer, every time he appeared in the barbershop. The barbershop was not special, and it was not an exclusive one. It was an ordinary barbershop. "Mister Boysie! Long time I don't see you! Why you no come to visit Alfredo, no?" Boysie was in the barbershop less than two weeks ago; but Alfredo had this exuberance about him. Boysie took off his coat very carefully and hung it on the rack, and then, just as carefully, he selected his seat. There were four others waiting before him. They were all Italian. And they were talking in their family dialect about the recent soccer match between Italia of Toronto and Santos of Brazil. Boysie had seen that game too. The game had been played about six weeks ago. But everybody was talking about it, because Santos, with the star Pele, had won the match, one to nil, through a free kick which resulted from a foul. The Italians in the crowd went mad, shouting and with tempers; and Boysie, who was sitting in a row of Italians, narrowly escaped being smashed in the head when two Italians started arguing about the refereeing. There were many West Indians in the crowd (West Indians and Italians were the two minority groups which supported soccer in Toronto), but Boysie had deliberately chosen to sit apart from them. When the blows started, it was in their direction that he crawled along the seats, and sat at the edge of a seat at the end of a long row of shouting West Indians. He felt he was safer among them, although he felt uncomfortable in their midst.

In the barbershop, the Italians were saying *scaremoparemo, madre-tutti-soccero-Pelito-issimo-que-passa,* and things like this; and Boysie listened very carefully, and loved their language and nodded his head when they looked in his direction, and regretted that for all the years in Toronto, visiting Henry in the Spadina area where the Italians lived, he had neglected to get close to an Italian, close enough to learn how to speak their language, " 'cause God-blummuh! not too long from now, is going be these same spaghetti-eating fucking Eyetalians who going be running this fucking town, you mark my word! You ain' see that one o' them is the biggest councillor on City Council already, Joe Pickinninni!" and Boysie listened very carefully to Henry's warning, then and later, as he saw droves of Italians walking the streets, owning the streets, spitting in the streets, digging up the streets, and congesting the streets with new apartment buildings, "And I ain't ever taste an Eyetalian meats yet, sheee-it! ain't that a bitch!" Henry knew all these things; and Boysie sat here, this morning, listening to men who might have been his brothers-in-law, had he been successful with conversational Italian phrases, most often used, and then successful with an Italian woman: "Whatssa matter for you, Santos win, I ask you Mister Boysie did Santos win? compadres," and arms and hands were flying about for emphasis and in the excitement and the love of argument, just like back home around the Bath Corner, when Henry and Boysie, Dots and Bernice, and children the age of Estelle's son would crowd around and talk and shout and laugh and curse one another's mothers in jest, just to make a point about cricket. "I wonder if the Eyetalians really own Toronto already?" Boysie surmised, as he was bombarded by the voices. Somebody's hands were blocking his vision of a black woman who was passing the street; and even though he got up to see better, to see the hips and the legs better, — "You like, eh? Nice-ah stuff, eh, Mister Boysie?" — she was gone. Everybody was disappearing from him; everybody was gone before he could get a good look, and everybody was giving him orders.

When his turn for the chair came, Alfredo said to him, very confidentially, and very much like a father, "Mister Boysie, why you don't change your car? A man like you. A man prosperous like you, look, the way you dress, you come in here and you look *grando, mucho grando*" (Boysie thought this was what he said). "I tell you. I put you on to a man, a fine gentleman who sell you new car. Good deal . . ." He was back in his thoughts again: did the Italians really own Toronto? And had the Mafia moved in yet? "I give you his card, *grand torino, felicimo* . . ." And then Alfredo talked about his trip to Boysie's country, and mentioned for the tenth time how many women he screwed (Alfredo once told Boysie how best to "screw the women, eh?"), and how much he liked black women, and Boysie listened, for the tenth time, trying to make up his mind whether Alfredo was making all this up to make his time in the chair more easy and bearable; deciding whether he should be insulted by this information; deciding whether he should tell Alfredo that he liked Italian women; deciding "I must get me an Eyetalian skins before too long, boy, 'cause a fellow tell me that there is pure mustard, mozzarella, garlic and olive oil underneath there, and you know how much I love garlic and mustard on my meats, Boysie!"; the Italian woman that Boysie craved to get was a woman with thick thighs who wore black all the time, who had a shade of a moustache on her top lip, whose lips were thickish like his, whose hair was black and who had just a faint smell of the odour of womanhood and strength about her, not a woman who wore deodorants and perfume and you could not smell the real smell from the smell of Helena Rubenstein: that was the thing Boysie wanted. Should he, "should I ask Alfredo here, palo-mio here-o, to get meo an Eyetalian woman-o? Sheeeeeee-yit"; oh Henry, Henry, Henry-o, Henrico, O'Henry . . . "Henry was a real motherfucker, a gorilliphant!'" And that was what he called himself.

"I give you the man's card, eh? You go and see him and make a deal." Alfredo dusted the clipped hairs off his shoulders where the dandruff ought to have been, flicked the cloth and made it sound like a whip, held out his hand for the price of the haircut and the one-dollar tip Boysie always gave him, and then he hugged Boysie and patted him six times on his back. "I love you, Mister Boysie. But, *please,* change your car."

Boysie thanked him, nodded to the other Italian gentlemen waiting, fixed his coat comfortably on his shoulders, a hair was biting into his neck, and just as he got to the door, with his mind on the same black woman who had passed, Alfredo said, "We go to the trots this week together, eh?" and Boysie left. Alfredo had not given him the card. Alfredo had no intention of giving him the card. Alfredo had no card. It was just his way of talking to Boysie. And Boysie liked him. If it was not inappropriate to say it these days in Toronto, he would have said, openly, that he loved Alfredo, as Alfredo had said he loved him. But Alfredo came from a place and a time and a space where men said "love" and the word passed for what it really stood for: in Toronto, with so many homosexuals — "Thirty fucking thousand o' them!" — Boysie could not expect that his language would span that time and place of precise meaning. Alfredo never went to the races with Boysie, or with anybody else. It was just his way. And Boysie had stopped doing those things for excitement and entertainment soon after Henry was buried. That part of him was buried too.

72

Now, what should he do? Where should he go? There was still lots of time before he had to go to work; and he would have time to change from his "business clothes" which he did not wear to his business, because his business was cleaning and he could not clean in clean clothes. "That is something, eh?" he told Dots one night, when he came home tired and soiled. "Imagine! Most men and women too, go out every morning to work, wearing business clothes, nice clothes. And I go to work at night, wearing old clothes, as if I am a blasted cockroach! You ever thought of it that way?" But wearing old clothes was no great difficulty. What was becoming difficult was all this night work, which made most of his day idle and listless and without enthusiasm. There was really no place for him to go: everyone he knew was at work. Dots was at work. He couldn't call up a friend and talk or drink, or do anything; and since he was now normally against gambling at cards or dice or at the racetrack, his ability to clothe and people his vegetating hours with anything creative was taking its toll on him. That was why he fell in love with the woman in the brown winter coat, because he knew he would never see her, never want to see her, and never should, since he had despised those kinds of complications in his life. Brigitte, the German mistress he had had for about three years, was far away now, in Western Germany, and there was no real person, no person in the flesh, just the imaginations of a liaison with the strange woman that was on his mind, and that was not a threat: infidelity was not a problem in Boysie's life these days.

He entered the parking area of the Esso gas station to find the manager and the man who pumped gasoline standing beside his truck. They had been talking. And as he drew closer they changed the tone of their manner. Boysie walked

73

up to the truck and unlocked the door.

The manager's face changed from annoyance to wonder. "You own this?"

"I think so. What's wrong?"

"Well it shouldn't be parked here!"

A year ago, this would have been the signal for Boysie to explode: you son of a bitch, you goddamn racist bastard, who the hell are you talking to, who you think me for, this is a fucking free country; and only after he had said these things would he size up the situation, depending upon the manager's counter-attack, and then explain his reasons for parking the truck in the Esso station. He had spent too much energy, for years, exploding, and he was tired. But most of all he resented always having to lose his temper in order to gain, or to contain, his pride and his dignity. He was changing into a different person. He was dwelling on appearances. And he wanted to be respected as a man: he wanted his treatment to match the clothes he was wearing. He did not wish to disrespect his clothes, nor abuse them.

The manager waited for his explanation, and Boysie saw that he was waiting. In a neutral voice, without hostility, and really without overweening and informative feeling, he said, quite simply, "Just came from Alfredo's barbershop."

"Oh well, that's all right," the manager said. "I'll be goddamn if I thought a man dressed like you would be driving this goddamn old heap." And he came to the window, and rested his hand on the door of the truck, and smiled at Boysie. "What're you trying to prove? Are you a hippie lawyer, or some radical university professor? Dressed like that, the way you do, and driving this heap?" And then he slapped the truck, as a man would slap the rump of a horse going out to face the starter.

Boysie drove off. He had things on his mind. While wait-

74

ing for his turn in the barber's chair, he had leafed through the latest copy of *Chatelaine* magazine, a journal published monthly, which dealt mostly with women's lives. In it he had seen an article about black women in Canada. Otherwise he would not have spent too much time on this magazine. The article bothered him. It said that black women were very lonely; and he didn't want to read the article too carefully, for reading about these things, about police brutality and police harassment, discrimination, people not finding jobs and housing, which he knew existed, and which happened every day but which he had wiped out from his interest and consciousness, these things which magazines like *Chatelaine* always wrote about, and could think only of writing about, worried him. But as he flipped the pages, he promised to write a letter to the editor of the magazine. He had wiped practically all of the words he had read out of his mind, but this portion refused to leave him: *Olivia was crying softly almost inaudibly the tears rolling down her face only an uncomfortable silence until Olivia spoke, "It's my son . . . I'm not a happy woman when I am here and he is there, he is lonely and I am afraid they don't care for him properly back home, I miss him terribly but I don't know what to do . . ."* It was strange that this piece should stick in his mind! He was approaching his bank, and he wanted to have a talk with the bank manager. "Who the hell is this Olivia? I wonder if she is a Trinidadian, a *Trickidadian,* or a Jamaikian, or a Sin Lucian, 'cause she sure as hell is not talking like a Wessindian"; his thoughts were framing themselves in his own idiom, and he saw for the first time the power in being able to talk as he liked: because there was no one in the truck with him, just his goddamn lonesome; and he could talk for so! lick his mouth, and refuse to speak the King's English which he felt he had to do, and did in fact do, when he was talking with the young Canadian fellow or with Mr. MacIntosh. He had done this same thing, talking in a formal and forced way when he had to confront Dr. Hunter, his wife's ex-employer. "You know something? This is damn interesting! This Olivia. Now she obviously is a black woman like Dots or like Bernice, but the way she talking in that magazine ain' the same blasted way a Wessindian would use words!" He was parking his truck in a public park lot, and Olivia was still in his mind: "Wonder how old she child is? But I going tell yuh something else! I bet it don't take much for any Wessindian reading this blasted foolishness that that white woman write 'bout we women to know that the name Olivia is ninety-nine per cent a Jamaikian name, and that reading between the lines, he would know that Olivia's child can't find his blasted father, neither, hah-hah-hah!"

The manager was coming towards him. He had learned from Mr. MacIntosh that he should always be smiling when he faced a person like a bank manager. He had seldom had occasion to smile before. "Smile, boy! Smile, Boysie, boy, whenever you facing one o' these white people and you want to get something outta them. They *like* to see we smiling. They love to see we happy, so smile, boy, like you ain' got no blasted sense." Strange how all these unconnected thoughts were coming at once into his head. Like Olivia. He should be thinking about the loan he wanted to get from the bank manager right now, and instead he is thinking about a woman named Olivia, who talked to some damn woman in an empty room at the YWCA on McGill Street. The manager was showing Boysie to his office, while Boysie promised to get a copy of *Chatelaine* and find out the name of the editor and the name of the woman who wrote the piece on Olivia so that he could curse both of them. "What the hell do they know about we, 'bout us?"

"Well, well-well-well!" the manager said. Boysie could not distinguish exactly what all these "wells" meant. The manager was a smart Scotsman; he told Boysie which county he was born in, but Boysie couldn't remember. "You certainly look like a very prosperous businessman and very happy this afternoon, Mr. Cumberbatch." ("You know something, Dots? That son of a bitch at the bank, the manager, is the only man in this place who calls me Mr. Cumberbatch!" But Dots was not impressed. "You know why? Because," Dots said, "he feel you got money, thats' why." Boysie wasn't impressed. "Not because," Dots added, "you don't look like the rest to him!")

"I came to talk about what I asked you about on the telephone."

"No problem at all." The manager was searching through some files on his desk. He lit a cigarette and offered one to Boysie, who took it. The manager smoked Gauloises. They smelled awful the first time Boysie took one, but he was impressed because it was the first time he had smoked a French cigarette, and he felt there was class in smoking French cigarettes in Canada; so he bought a package himself to try them out; and between driving all over Toronto and inhaling the first one, as he would have inhaled his own Rothmans (which he began to smoke after Henry died and in spite of South Africa), and trying to pronounce the name "Gauloises," not knowing it was a French word, calling it "Galoshes," and having the salesgirl look funny at him . . . "Would there be any problem about the loan?"

"None at all, Mr. Cumberbatch . . ."

Well then, why should I worry my blasted self concerning Olivia, whoever the hell she is . . . "Six thousand dollars we are prepared to lend you, Mr. Cumberbatch . . ." she probably come into this country illegal anyway, and now trying to mash-up things for people who come in legal, like me. Be-Christ, I could walk into the biggest bank in Toronto and walk-back-out with a cheque for six thousand dollars . . . "I would like to spend piece o' this 'pon the same Olivia if she would give me a little piece o' " . . . The important thing, Boysie surmised, was not to let Olivia submerge him into a feeling of depression . . . He was thinking of the letter to the editor which he had outlined in his head while he was driving to the bank. He tried to think of the name of the editor and the name of the writer of the article. He had memorized them while sitting in Alfredo's barbershop, but "goddamn, this head o' mine only have in water, not brains, yuh! Why I finding it so hard these days to remember things?" He drove his truck slowly along the street, and his face was relaxed and was at peace with himself. "Wonder how badly-off Olivia's little boy back home is?" He had been thinking of children so much recently because the stillness of the apartment in the morning was driving him crazy; and if it wasn't for the strange woman and writing letters to the editor, he didn't know what he would do.

"Dots, have you ever thought of children?" They had just eaten supper, as Dots called dinner.

"Thrildren, boy? I see too much o' them when the days come not to be thinking 'bout them, boy!"

"I don't mean so."

"Well, how you mean, then?"

"Like having . . . well, for instance." He had picked up this deliberative, halting way of speaking from the Canadians on the CBC television and radio. "To put the point to you" (at which Dots raised her eyebrows), "you know I am here all morning by myself, while you are at work . . ."

"Boysie!" Dots slapped her heavy hand on the tabletop.

78

She beamed. "Only today! This very afternoon whilst I was turning-over a patient in her bed, the same thought run through my mind! Imagine that, eh. Ain't that what that man on the television call ESP?"

"Well, as a matter of fact, Dots . . ."

"At last! Lord look down! At last, me and my husband thinking alike!" She was happy now; she was a woman of great resiliency, and of substantial stubbornness; and it was not her nature to allow anything to defeat her. She had looked at the relationship in her own marriage in this way; and although she would chide him, and at times abuse him, for the strange ways in which he was acting lately, still deep down, in the pit of her guts, in her deepest in-guts, as she liked to say to prove her conviction about a matter, she knew she had Boysie still within her control. "I got that bastard by his balls!" she told Bernice only yesterday. "He freaking-out 'pon me? 'Pon Dots? An old whore like me? And you telling me 'bout seeing a marriage counsellor or a head-shrinker? Me? Dots Cumberbatch? Me, soul?" She poured herself more wine. Boysie had discovered Mommessin. "Yuh know something? It ain't right, and it ain't healthy as far as I concerned, for a man in your position to be here by your lonesome, with not even something with you that breathes . . ."

"I was thinking the same thing!" Boysie too was hope-ful. "That is why I asked you if you ever considered children . . ."

"Yes, boy! Yesss! I even talked to Bernice 'bout that, and asked her to bring over one o' them cats that her missy want to throw away!"

Boysie was listening to "Both Sides Now." Was the song really a dead song, did it really denote death, as Dots had said? *When every fairy tale comes real so many things I would have done but clouds got in my way;* and he could write about the things he wanted to do in his life. This tune was the only one in the whole album to which he listened; it was, simply, the one he liked, and he never worried about not playing the other tunes and he never wondered what they had to say.

He is listening to it now, not very attentively, because he knows all the words by heart, and also because the woman in the winter coat is late coming out of the subway. She had been late often, recently. He made a note to himself that she had been late two mornings already this week, and it is only Wednesday. The song peoples the lonely apartment, and prevents him from becoming even lonelier; and it helps him to do things in his mind and promise to carry them out, in action, later on. One of these things is to decide which colour and which styling he wants on the new Buick which he picked out yesterday, and on which he had to pay down only two hundred dollars. His credit was so good. The salesman didn't even bother to ask him if he wanted to make his panel truck a trade-in. Boysie could not believe the treatment he was getting; and the fact that he got it helped to buoy his spirits higher, made him more secure, and therefore more unbearable to live with. He was successful. "How many other West Indians living in this city could get this kind o' treatment?" he asked himself, as he left the luxurious show-rooms of Hogan Pontiac downtown? How many other West Indians could talk, man-to-man, with a salesman of this rich-looking place, and not have to fill out a lot of forms, answer a million questions and put up collateral before they could be taken seriously by a salesman? He was successful. He was a businessman talking to another businessman.

The moment the deal was signed, waiting only for

him to make up his mind about the colour of the car, and whether he wanted a telephone installed in the car, the moment he had finished walking slowly around the car in the showroom, Boysie felt depressed. Perhaps he should have bought a cheaper car. "You know what they say about black people driving big cars? Pimps!" But hell, nobody, nofuckingbody in this whole town could look at a man like him and mistake him for a pimp! He didn't even know what a pimp did. He didn't even look like a pimp. Or did he? But what did a pimp look like? He knew one man who used to be a pimp, years ago out in a western part of Canada; and this man had come east and was now settled and living comfortably, after serving his time as a pimp in jail for being a pimp, and still people said good morning to him and called him Mister, and some even called him Brother. So, what is this thing about being a pimp? "Isn't you suppose to be living as a man, and not as a black man? Eh?" He should have repaid the money he got from the bank the next week, to establish his credit even further than it had been already established. Mr. MacIntosh had told him that; and he had in fact done precisely that the first time he borrowed money from the bank. So his credit was already established.

But he should not have bought a car at all. What was he going to do with a new car? Drive it out on Sundays, polished like a dog's stones, with Dots dressed off and sitting in the front seat, like a black queen? He did not even think of giving Dots a lift in his new car. This car was going to be his. He would keep it in the underground garage, and she won't even know it belonged to him. He knew what he would do with it! He would drive it out every morning just when the strange woman was coming out of the subway, that's what he would do! But he should have put the money down on a house, Dots would have liked that. Or he should have taken a vacation in Barbados. He hadn't been back to Barbados in all the time he was in Canada, and sometimes he yearned to go back; but at times like this, when he could go into a dealer's and bring out a new car, knowing that in Barbados there was no possibility of his ever doing that — he had never known anybody in his village who was able to do that in the thirty-seven years he lived there — well, Boysie was not ready to see Barbados so soon. "Perhaps, when I ready to dead, I would go back and get buried in Westbury Cemetery!"

He made up his mind he would tell the salesman he wanted a black Buick. It looked more conservative; and he was not going to paint tongues of flame and fire on it, as some West Indians did, and he would not put cushions and blinds in the rear window, and he would not paint his initials on the bumper, and he would not, "Jesus Christ, not for hell! I ain't sticking no blasted Black Power flag on my new automobile!" The car would remain, like its owner, very conservative. And it would remain most of the week in the underground garage. Satisfied that he had made the correct decisions about this matter, a matter which had taken him three days to deal with, he was less tortured now, and he could listen more closely to his favourite song and at the same time watch out for the woman.

"Meooooooooowww!"

"Jesus Christ!"

"Meow!"

It was the cat.

Dots had got the cat. Dots had brought home a cat. The cat was to be Boysie's companion. And Boysie had to feed the cat, and empty its box, because when these things needed doing, Dots was not at home.

The cat was not trained. It was not a very big cat, else

Boysie would have kicked it many times when it crawled into bed with him, when he was relaxing in the last troughs of his morning sleep. And the cat had a habit of messing under the bed, for which at the beginning Boysie was grateful, until he began to smell this strange odour, and thought it was Dots's and then grew ashamed of himself for thinking this about his wife, and then realized whose smell it was, and then dared once to throw the cat from the living room into the bedroom, but the cat liked it, and landed on all fours, because "godblummuh, this blasted cat like it have nine fucking lives, yes!" But Boysie intended killing one of these lives soon. The cat. The cat would climb on the table, and smell the food and Boysie's stomach would be turned, and he would pretend he wanted to vomit, and Dots would be disgusted too, but since it was her cat, she would pretend that it did not matter, because "cats is the cleanest things living!" and would hold the cat in her hands and say, "Cat, catty-catty, cat?" and try to laugh.

Boysie was glad because of the cat: for one reason. He had become sensitive to the size of his stomach, and secretly, in the morning, when he was alone, he would try to do some calisthenics and read articles about diet, and try hard to cut down on the starches in his food. But the first time he refused to eat, Dots lost her temper and accused him of eating at another woman's place.

"Wait, at your blasted age, you are eating at some woman?" This was another thing he disliked about her. She was not delicate with her words nor with her accusations. She could have worded it more delicately.

"I don't have any appetite, Dots. It must be the work."

"You don't like my food?" And before he could say any more, she had taken his food and had scraped it into the garbage pail. Part of it she put on the kitchen floor for the cat. "Be-Christ, as I standing up here this Sundee afternoon," she said, lifting her eyes and her hands to the kitchen ceiling, "I wish that that whore will *poison* you!"

She went on and on, cursing him, swearing at him, threatening to leave him, and accusing him of being too good for her. And right there in the midst of her talk, her words as fierce as a warrior's, Boysie understood why all of a sudden he had begun to hate the noise of the West Indian clubs and the noise of West Indians. It was his wife. This raucous way she had, which injured his ears. And he understood it and still it frightened him, because it brought home to him the extent to which he was himself changing: he was a man who could quarrel about a small insignificant point most of Sunday, which in the past two years seemed to be the day he and his wife had set aside for quarrelling. But now, in his new peace of understanding, of a broader vision of things to do with his life and with his work, he was insulted. He was never insulted in the past. Why was he insulted now? He could not answer that question. The song was coming to an end, and he must get up, cross in front of the window, perhaps glance subconsciously out the window to check on the woman, even have to put down his newspaper, and put the needle back to the beginning of the record. *Floes and floes of angel's hair* . . . Dots had brought the cat to keep him company, but he was still lonely, and he had not abandoned his own thoughts about children. Not that he felt he could have children from her; and not that he was thinking of adopting any. But he was thinking of a living being in the apartment with him. Not all the time, like this cat. "This fucking cat! One o' these mornings, I am going to strangle your arse, cat!" Dots called the cat, "Cat-come-catty-catty-cat!" and he called it "you-goddamn-cat!" and he did not even smile nor see the irony

84

in his christening of the cat, even although he always remembered it, the thing that should have made him laugh, each time he called the cat "you goddamn cat!"; for if the cat was not on his nerves so relentlessly, he would have been able to laugh at what came into his mind each time the cat crossed his path like a curse. It was what a Canadian girl had told him one night when he was out drinking with Henry; she had said to him, to fend off his drunken advances, "Buster, I live with two cats, one white, the other black. And I'm sure I won't like to see the black one kick in your ass, so git! Git lost!" He could not laugh now when he called the cat "you goddamn cat!" because those were the exact words which Henry had used when the Canadian woman warned him about her cats. "You shouldda been one o' them goddamn cats, you goddamn cat!" Boysie was still thinking of having a living person in the apartment with him.

He took up the telephone and dialed a number. After many rings he put it down. He looked into his address book, and dialed another number, and when this one rang a few times, a recorded message came on: *The number you have dialed is . . ."* He dropped the telephone. He would spend some mornings, sometimes the entire morning, ringing old numbers of persons he had met many years before. And they were all changed, or else moved away, disconnected, or the numbers of different persons. There was no one he knew. No one he knew whom he wanted to talk to. He remembered a man named Freeness, from years back, and he tried to track him down through about six telephone numbers which he had taken down over the years, and when he reached the last one, Freeness was said to have moved to Montreal. And then one morning he thought of a Jamaican man he knew, with whom he and Henry and Freeness used to play poker and crap, and he called this man's number, and there was no answer at the other end. He promised to call him in the evening, but he never remembered. The woman should be coming out of the subway any minute now. The cat was curling around his ankles and he did not stir, he did not move, so that the cat would continue to make his acquaintance, to make its acquaintance with him: he was as lonely as that. So, he must have a living person in this apartment with him. When he came in after working ten hours, Dots was in bed; and before he awoke, she would have left for work. He had been thinking for some time now of a young boy, the son of a friend of his, whose father had disappeared to America. He knew it would be a delicate situation, but after all he did not want to adopt the boy. He just wanted to take him places, like to the races: every boy liked going to the races, or to listen to jazz on Saturday afternoon at the matinees at the Colonial Tavern. But he would have to be careful. There were a lot of grown men taking out little boys nowadays in Toronto; and he did not want to be suspected as a homosexual. He was nervous about this. The boy's mother might think it strange of him, all of a sudden, his coming round to take out her son. And he could see her feeling that he was after her. Either way, he had to be careful. It would be so much easier to have Dots make the arrangements; but there were many things he wanted to discuss with his wife, and could not, because of her attitude to discussion, his new language and conversation, or rather because when he really felt the need to talk she was at work, and he never wanted to call her at the hospital. There were many brilliant plans he had had: like the one about hiring a helper for his cleaning jobs, and he had worked it out to the last detail, and when it came time to discuss it with Dots, she was at work. He did call Dots once, about the new car he had bought (for his guilt had had the better of him), and when he reached her after many switches to different extensions and floors in the hospital, Dots came on the telephone and her rage was so loud that he felt the whole building had heard. "Look, man, I am at work. What happened? You sick?" and when Boysie said he was not sick, she said, "Is the cat sick, then?" and when he said the cat was not sick, she said in a bitter voice, "Well, wait till I come home."

When she came home, he made sure he was out of the apartment. In all the other ways he was successful: at the bank with the bank manager; at the barber's chatting and joking with Alfredo; at his job, entering into conversations with Mr. MacIntosh and with the Canadian young fellow, and exchanging ideas with them, on life; with the car salesman who didn't worry to check his credit rating, simply because the salesman knew the bank manager — in all these things, Boysie was successful and had respect and some name; but with his wife, and trying to impress her, he was a very ordinary man, a man with great failure. And he wanted to change this too, for it took away from his success. As a matter of fact, he did not consider himself as successful as he really was.

These things were the gnawing thoughts in his head this morning, waiting for the woman, and feeling the futility of wasting so much energy on a prospect which he did not really believe could be developed into more than a prospect. The tune had come to an end. He got up to put the needle back at the beginning of "Both Sides Now" when the thought hit him that he should look at the other two records he had decided to keep out of the large collection he had had. At times, in his weakest moments, when he doubted that he was wise to have thrown away all those records into the incinerator — all that "noise" as he called them — he would yearn to hear the happy beat of the West Indian calypso, or the funky rhythms of the black music of America; but he held steadfast in his determination not to listen again to that kind of music. He was beginning to regard the music he listened to as being part of the quality of the life he wanted to live. But he had to remind himself of the titles of the other two record albums. One was a jazz album by Miles Davis, named *Milestones*. He used to play all the tunes in this album years ago, but he grew tired of jazz and started listening to rhythm-and-blues; and after a while *Milestones* was the only one that he liked. He liked this album very much, but he had not played it lately. It had been given to him by his friend Brigitte, who had heard the Miles Davis Quartet in Germany, and when she met Boysie, seven years later, she was still raving about this album. She bought it for his Christmas present at the end of their affair's first year. The other record, also a gift, was Mendelssohn's *Incidental Music to A Midsummer Night's Dream,* and this became his favourite record of the two until he discovered that part of the album which contained the Wedding March. He was surprised to find the Wedding March on a record. For he had felt all the time that it was just a special tune which somehow came about and which was chosen years ago to be played at weddings. He did not know that it was composed for an entirely different reason. Mr. MacIntosh gave him this record. He had heard Boysie whistling the Wedding March one night, to a calypso beat, and he thought he would surprise him. But it had taken about six months before Boysie realized the real significance of the gift. And when he found out, he felt that Mr. MacIntosh had tricked him.

One Sunday — and it was only on Sundays that he

played Mendelssohn, even when he had his full record collection — he played this record. He had not played it before. He was in a good mood. He was listening as he lay on the bed, deciding whether to get up and clean out the truck and the mops and the cleaners and detergents; or whether to remain in bed, and wait for Dots to bring him breakfast in bed. And between these two minds, all of a sudden, out came the Wedding March.

"What the hell is that, Boysie?"

"Heh-heh-heh!," and he thought of Mr. MacIntosh. "That man is as smart as . . ."

"You mean to tell me that you still listening to that damn nonsense?"

But every Sunday after that, it was Dots who not only requested to hear Mendelssohn, but who actually put the record on herself. Adversity and her own depression were swept away by the full, heavy and powerful music which sent her back many years — "About how much, now?" — time passed in this country was beginning to wipe out the milestones of time passed back in Barbados, and she had found herself recently counting time in vague areas of time: "a few years ago," or she might have been speaking about her marriage, or about her emigration from the West Indies. But this powerful music whose discovery was such a shock — "Never, never, never, Boysie, would I have expect to find this nice music in a ordinary grammaphone record! You know what I mean? This is something I had expect to find, originally when it was made, inside of a vault, or some stone inside that church where we got married, St. Matthias Church on St. Matthias Road, in St. Matthias Parish . . ."

"St. Michael's, Dots."

"Is a long time ago, Boysie! This music bringing it back now, fresh fresh as anything, as the Mayflower flowers and the lignum vitae and the red roses and the white roses, and flowers of all kinds and denominations, the day when you married me, that was the day when first I really understand what this piece o' music mean . . ."

"We got married in Canada, Dots!" And then they got into an argument, because they could not remember whether they were married in Barbados before they came up to Canada, or whether the wedding had taken place in Canada. "That is what I mean when I tell you that time does do some funny things to a person's mind. Imagine that!"

Boysie would remember whole passages of conversations like this one, spoken many years ago, in different circumstances, and if the circumstances then had not held his interest, when the conversations came back he would be able to focus on the interest and the significance as they should have been comprehended at the first context. Conversations were like people. He encouraged them, and he exchanged words with them, and he twisted them to fit his moods, because he could not talk to a cat. He had never had a cat. The only cat he had ever had any relations with was one strayed cat which he found dead under his mother's cellar: not that he had found it dead the moment it was dead, but he found it dead through its smell, on a hot day, in a far corner of the limestone cellar through cracks of which he first saw columns and battalions and mounds of dark brown stinging ants moving in some form of their own battle array: and the smell. The cats he knew used to kill mice and keep mongooses from eating the chickens, and sometimes if the cat was frightened before the chicken and the fowl-cock thief, its cat's eyes might frighten the thief and scare him; but this cat which Dots had brought into the house, "this goddamn cat" was being fed on food from a tin, Pampers, and Dots had even bought medicine for it.

"It is a very important cat, Boysie, boy. This cat have pettigree and breeding and class that neither you nor me could come close to having! This is a first class cat you see here, Boysie!"

"And who I is?" Boysie shouted, in his most belligerent Barbadian accent. "I's a second class cat?"

"Boysie, boy, the truth does hurt sometimes, but when all is said and done, the truth is the truth. And neither you nor this cat here, eating outta this can, nor me, could put a hand 'gainst that truth . . ."

"Fuck the truth!"

But he was no easier in his mind about this cat. He would wait until Bernice came over later in the week. She had promised to bring over her young man to introduce him to Boysie (she did not say she was going to introduce him to Dots, and Boysie noticed this suspiciously, and wondered whether Dots knew him, whether Dots had chosen him from among the hospital orderlies at the Doctor's Hospital, for it had come out in conversation that he worked there part-time), and Boysie was going to ask her about this goddamn cat. In the meantime, these were not really so important as the woman: he was thinking of confronting the woman this morning; but she had taken such a long time to appear, and he was not sure whether it was better to go down and wait for her in the truck, or whether he should first get his new car and try to impress her into accepting a drive . . . it was now four hours that he had been waiting for her, and she hadn't come, and he didn't know he had lived through all this time while waiting for her. And he had to find an envelope for the letter to the editor of *Chatelaine* which he had written to answer the misleading account of a black woman's loneliness in Canada. What made him angry about the article was that the woman who wrote it didn't know anything about black women. He could tell that from the way she wrote the article; for she had spent so much time on this woman Olivia, and Boysie knew many Olivias, Olivias who would cry on your shoulders morning, noon and night, and when they had you sympathetic in their grasps, they would rip out your balls; Olivias who always had a sob story, and when you counted their earnings, they could pay down five thousand dollars on a townhouse on Belmont Street or any other exclusive street in the city; Olivias who told you they were single, never had a man, and when you arrived five minutes too early, or too late, there was, standing before you, the biggest Jamaican man you had ever seen, and did not wish to see in those circumstances; Olivias who said one thing and lived the next thing: he wanted to meet this Olivia and beat the living shit out of her for giving all West Indian and black Canadian women a bad name, talking a lot of shite about *"I'm not a happy woman when I am here and he is there. He is lonely and I am afraid they don't care for him properly back home,"* to a reporter named Linda Diebel. Boysie wanted to meet Olivia and he wanted to meet this Linda Diebel — if she was a real person.

He unfolded the letter he had writen to the editor Mrs. Doris McGibbon Anderson: *Dear Mrs. Doris McGibbon Anderson, the Editor of Chatelaine. Have you ever thought of writing a story on the poor black women who get raped every day in Toronto? Have you ever thought of writing an article on black women who work in the hospitals of this city? Have you ever thought of writing an article on one of them, who if they were not working so hard in the hospitals of this city, there would be an epidemic of grave proportions* (he remembered this phrase being spoken on the CBC radio during the earthquake in Latin America, someplace) *in this city? Have you ever thought of writing an article on the thousands of black university students, professors and administrators at universities in this province?* (Boysie had never met a black university professor or a black university administrator, but he figured that if they had some in American universities, there had to be some, perhaps even more, here in Canadian universities, what with all the West Indians and Barbadians especially going to university for so many years. He knew there were hundreds of black university students all over the place.) *Why have you not thought before, of writing an article on the black woman who got elected into the Legislature out in British Columbia? Or the black woman who is a doctor at one of the biggest hospitals here in Toronto? Why do you always think you know more about black women and black men and black youths than anybody else, including black people? And who the fuck is Linda Diebel? And who is Olivia? Yours respectfully, Bertram Cumberbatch. Power to the People!"* He did not know why he had put "Power to the People" after his name; for he was a man who had long stood outside the paling of that kind of verbal militancy. And he did not know why he had taken such a long time to write his real name, "Bertram," instead of "Boysie." He was beginning to be embarrassed when he was addressed as Boysie by persons who did not know him intimately. Bertram sounded good, he felt. And he was sorry that he did not have some kind of office, some kind of rank to put after his name. He thought about it, and hoped that by putting "Power to the People" behind his name, Mrs. Doris Mc-Gibbon Anderson would think he was a powerful man in the black community who had written the letter. Perhaps it might even scare her into doing something about the article, if not now, then in the future. But most of all he worried about not having some office or rank or organization to put after his name. He should try to join some organization for the purpose of giving his letters to the editor more weight, not because he really had his heart in organizations. Power was what he was after now — not political power, for he was smart enough to know, even before this new awareness, that he could not have political power in a place like Canada unless some Canadian had given him that power, and even then, it would not be true power. But he needed some organization to put behind his name. He had been asked to join the Toronto Elks, and the Bathurst Lions, and some church organizations had asked him to join them; but he knew they were only interested in him because he was a successful businessman. He wanted an organization he could use when the time became fruitful, not an organization which could use him.

He liked this letter better than any other he had written. And he would read it over and over searching for mistakes (he had actually written it four times, before it was in this present form); and when he liked it in its present form, he had shown it to Dots. Dots read it and folded it back into its creases, put it into its envelope (she was cooking at the time) and said, "Why all of you black men always being so abusive to white women? Fuck white woman, fuck the white man, fuck this, fuck that, and still always ready to jump into bed with the first one? You didn't have to tell the woman 'Fuck' in this letter!"

Boysie noticed that the envelope was smudged by tomato ketchup. He put it into another envelope and wondered what he could say to Dot's comments. He was so angry, he regarded her as so ignorant for making that comment, "What the fuck does that have to do with it?" but he could not get the strength to talk with her about his own reaction to her comment; it was irrelevant, but it bothered him. Dots, he found out at last, was a fool. Her comment made him even more keen to send the letter to Mrs. Doris McGibbon Anderson. "Fuck her!" And he was not even running behind white woman when she made her generalization! Out of the corner of his eye, he saw the brown winter coat emerging from the subway station, just near the eave of a house which was his benchmark of her arrival. He ran to the picture window and saw her. This woman, I am sure, won't make such a foolish comment on my letter, he said to himself, watching her walk upright, sure and secure of her gait, along the short street of his vision.

She was about five feet seven inches tall. She was wearing a brown winter coat which was cut like a man's coat. She wore a white scarf around her neck. She carried a white plastic shopping bag, like the ones you got in expensive stores, in her right hand. She wore a slightly sloppy hat on her head, on the right side of her head mostly, and it gave her a touch of smartness. Her boots this morning were white and shining. And she wore large glasses that made her look a little like an owl. He saw her for exactly three minutes, and then she disappeared. And he knew he would not see her again until the following morning.

He remained at the window looking out. Toronto was white this morning. The snow was coming down, and when he followed it, he could see the swimming pool and the tennis court and the badminton court, and the play area with the dead trees planted in white cement snow, and they all looked like slightly oversized games for children. There were children skating down below. No one was in the area where the swimming pool was. Boysie remained looking down, and the thought of jumping out of a window occurred to him, and when he saw the games of the apartment grounds, and the people walking through the games, he thought of other things. He had never really thought of suicide. He just wondered what people who thought seriously of it thought of just before they contemplated doing it seriously. He thought some more of the people down below in the transformed playing area of the apartment building and then he left the window. He was ready to go out now.

"Meeeeoowwwwwwwwwww!"

"You goddamn cat!"

"Meeow!"

"What the fuck do you want, cat?"

He opened a new can of cat food, left it in the jagged-edged can, and dropped it on the newspaper on the kitchen floor, just beside the cupboard in which Dots kept the vacuum cleaner. "When I come back, I hope you are dead, you goddamn cat!"

Just then the telephone rang. Who could it be? Perhaps the car dealer calling about his new car, or the landlord. Had he paid his rent? He was paid up three months in advance.

"Hello?"

"You feed my cat, yet?"

It was Dots. It was the first time she had ever called him from her work.

Boysie was sitting in his new 1973 black Buick that had everything in it, power brakes, power window winders, tape player, FM and AM radio, and he did not feel elated. He had been sitting in the car for ten minutes, in the parking lot of the car dealer's; the keys were his, possession was his, all the papers were signed and in order, and he could not bring himself to feel the power of ownership. He tried to feel elated, something of the pride he had felt when he and Dots drove the panel truck along the street where Henry lived the day they first got it: that day marked his change in fortune in this country. A secondhand panel truck with nothing inside it but two old ripped and soiled seats and a lot of metal space behind him. And he was so happy then. Now, still owning the truck which took him to work, with all his cleaning materials, with his name printed on its sides, BOYSIE CUMBERBATCH, CLEANERS, INC. ("I must remember to change that to BERTRAM CUMBERBATCH, JANITORIAL SERVICES, INCORPORATED"), and sitting in this new car, it was as if nothing had happened to him. "I must remember to get my new batch of cheques changed to Bertram Cumberbatch, Janitorial Services, Incorporated, too! And I should have put that as my office and title after the letter to the editor of *Chatelaine!*" But he decided it was wiser not to have done that: just another case of a black person who was a cleaner; and to own a cleaning company was the same thing as being a chief cleaner.

Where should he drive his new car? He thought of the persons he knew, and like the telephone calls he would make to check on them, or see whether he wanted to talk to them, and finding them all disappeared, Boysie again felt the helplessness of being without friends. There were lots of friends to be got, but these were West Indians, men he had met as he visited the Colonial Tavern during his coffee breaks from cleaning the downtown offices of his contracts, and would see leaning against the bar, talking to Canadian women, men dressed in the latest flashy clothes, like pimps, as he found out when browsing through a magazine, *OUI*, which the young Canadian fellow had brought into Mr. McIntosh's office one night. These West Indians he would see at the Colonial Tavern all wore dark glasses, shades, as if they were standing outside in the West Indian sun; and the way they walked! with their fists clenched and dropped at their sides while they moved their feet, as if they were merely sliding, and being so important and so silent inside the Tavern, but laughing so loudly when they were standing up outside on the sidewalk just in front of the place. Goddamn pimps! They disgusted him. And he would drink his Scotch fast and get away. He could not talk to any of them. To be seen talking with them on the street would be to mark himself as one of them: and he couldn't have that! for he was moving up.

And he thought of going for a drive. But to go for your first drive in a new car, by yourself, without even a woman beside you, that was no fun. He thought of going up at the Doctor's Hospital and showing Dots the car, but that was against his plans. This car was going to be his car. His. Not his and hers, nothing like that. His. And hers? No, he wasn't such a Northamerican as that! If he was in Barbados, the first place he would drive a new car would be up at the airport, to see all the people who were leaving the island, and those who were coming in as tourists, and he would see many people he knew who were sure to walk round his new car and ask him, "How much horses under the fucking hood, Boys, old bean?" and kick the tires, and look inside, and ask, "Air-condition in this blasted thing?" although none of them had ever sat inside a car with air-conditioning; but they would have heard of these from the tourists and in magazines. But he was not in Barbados now, and that kind of literacy about things never owned and observed was not common here. He started the engine, and drove out of the dealer's parking lot. He peered through the windshield, wondering why the people were a different colour from when he drove his truck. And then he turned

98

the windows down, and realized how cold it was, and that the glass was tinted. "Good!" It meant he could not be seen easily from the outside.

He drove along College Street going west, and he relaxed inside the luxurious upholstery, fiddled with the press-buttons on the dashboard, changed the stations in the FM radio, searching for the CBC, and all the time the Buick, moving like water on glass, carried him aimlessly through the lightly falling snow. He got annoyed with the snow for falling on a day like this. It was only two in the afternoon, and he had still lots of time before he had to get home, change, and drive to work in his panel truck. For the time being, he would try hard 'to enjoy this latest possession, which was so difficult for him to enjoy by himself.

The light at the corner was long in changing. He looked through his tinted windows at the West Indians and Italians and other immigrants bundled up, most of them in cheap winter coats because they had little money for such luxuries, most of them walking fast but not moving fast because the ice under the snow was tricky, all of them serious with expressions of caution on their faces. A woman the size of Dots was coming out of the West Indian shop owned by a Portuguese just where he was stopped, on his left hand, waiting for the light to change. He should stop a little further along this street, right in front of the other West Indian shop which sold Jamaican meat patties, and make them see who was getting out of this big black goddamn Buick. Yeah, do that, Boysie.

There was a time when he would wrap the steering wheel of a car, of his truck, round and round as if it was a piece of elastic rubber band, and park in the smallest possible space, wrapping and wrapping, tires screeching, and he laughing as he looked out and saw people marvelling at his dexterity with a car. But now he drove slowly along the line of parked cars on the north side, looking for a space big enough to park his new automobile. And when he found one, the size of his car and almost half as much again, he pulled alongside the car in front of the space, and turned his steering wheel until the body of the car was exactly forty-five degrees from the angle of the parked car (although he could not have worked this out mathematically in his mind: it was practice and having the car at that angle from the sidewalk); he moved in, and stopped, exactly equidistant from the car in front and the one behind. He peered through the windshield and saw the greyish snow coming down lightly, and he saw a few aimless West Indians walking in the street, their colours now darker and looking purplish. He revved up the motor and then turned it off. He locked all his doors, and he remembered to press the button which lowered his car aerial. "Can't have nobody damage that!" A man came out of the shop while he was still adjusting his clothes to get out of the car. The man stopped. He looked at the car, stared through the tinted windshield at the driver of the car, and without changing the expression on his face he walked on. "You blasted . . . these doors locked, though!" The man was eating what looked like a meat patty.

Boysie got out of the car, and locked the door. He straightened himself, adjusted the fit of his cashmere winter coat on his shoulders, pulled his felt hat down at a firmer level, not too cockily, and went into the shop.

Noise hit his ears the moment he opened the door. The place was filled with West Indians and it seemed that all of them were talking at the same time. It took him a while to understand what they were talking about. They were not talking about anything in particular, just talking and making noise.

"Wappning, man!" one man screamed.

"Oh-God-oh-God-oh-God!" another shouted, as if he was intending to make his words into a song, with a beat like a calypso. And he spoke so rapidly that all the "Oh-Gods" seemed to be one word.

"Wappneeeeen! wapppneeeeen! wapppneeeeen!"

"Oh-God-oh-God, why all-you didn' come to Dresser par-tee, last night? Dresser had par-tee for soooooo . . ."

The place was cluttered with pictures of soccer stars and cricket stars from the West Indies. "Two more patties here!" There were old photographs of the Honourable Marcus Garvey. All the photographs were taken in the same shot. Garvey was wearing a derby hat, and his cheeks were fat as they say of a man who eats too many pork chops, and his lips were thick and his whole face like the face of a prosperous West Indian small merchant, who was dressed in tweeds and standing in the hot sun. There were flags of red black and green. The music was loud. Nobody was listening, but they all seemed to be moving to the rhythm of the song. *". . . give the donkey first second and third . . ."* and Boysie wondered what Sparrow was singing about: he had never heard this calypso before. It might have been the latest tune from the last Carnival in Trinidad. "Bring more pep-puh, bring more pep-puh, oh-God-oh-God, all-you turn Canadian fast, yes!" *. . . if you was the king of beasts, you would be toting that . . .* Boysie wasn't sure whether one of the customers had spoken this, or whether it was part of the calypso; and the place was dark, and he couldn't get his eyes adjusted to the gloominess, although he used to be at home in the Paramount Tavern just down the street from here. ". . . oh Christ, man, this blasted country *hard* like rass! I know two-three fellows who walking 'bout for six months still looking for their first work, and people telling me this country, Canada, more better than the States . . . give me the States any time!"

"What can I do for you, sir?"

A man was shaking most of a bottle of pepper sauce on his patties, and the waitress, a young woman from one of the islands who hadn't talked yet, was standing like his judge over him and over the bottle, waiting perhaps to see that he didn't use too much of the pepper sauce, for this was a West Indian eating place, and a lotta Wessindians going come in here and first thing they going axe for is for peppuh, and if there ain' no rass pep-peh in the patty shop, what the rass, man, "What the rass!" Some of the pepper had been spilled on the waitress's dress. She was not wearing an apron. "Looka this man, though!" she said, and moved away holding on to her dress which was very short for this type of weather. "What can I do for you, sir?"

The man behind the counter had been talking to Boysie almost the moment he came into the shop. And he had moved away to serve other customers, but had come back to stand in front of Boysie, behind the counter, where Boysie was now watching a fly. A goddamn fly in winter?

"Can I help you?" The man had seen the fly too. He swiped at it, knowing he would miss it, but would chase it away for the time being. "Hey!" Boysie did not know what he wanted. He did not remember why he had come into this shop.

"You want something?"

He was watching the man, very young and very strong-looking, dressed like black Americans with long hair, and floppy hats pulled threateningly close to one eye, and looking so very strong and masculine and like criminals . . . criminals? "Criminals?"

"What you want, my man?"

And there were some women too, and some of them were dressed in white as if they were nurses, could be nurses, and carrying on with the young men, and laughing and talking while they were eating.

"Gimme, ahhh, please give me a pack of chewing gum, sugarless!"

"Ha-ha-ha-hah!" The man behind the counter started laughing. He had overheard something said down in the dark back of the eating shop, and he was giving his approval to the joke. His eyes were closed during his laugh. When he opened them, Boysie had placed a ten-dollar bill on the counter. He looked at it, he looked up at Boysie, and he exploded again, and he made change. "Hak-hak-hak-yak-yak . . ."

Sitting back in the car, Boysie was nervous. The doors were locked, and he was glad the windows were tinted. He could hear the laughing and the shouting and the noise and *he give the donkey first second and third! . . . he gie the donkey fuss secunt and tird . . . he gave the donkey first, second and third . . .*

It became peaceful again inside the car. It was warm like a bath. He would take a very hot bath very often when he didn't need to bathe; but he would take the hot bath, as hot as he just could bear it, and he would sit in the water, and try to think of nothing. He was thinking of nothing now. Just sitting in the warm womb of the new car, protected from discovery and disclosure and recognition behind the tinted glass. He wished he didn't have to go to work tonight. If he didn't have to, he could remain sitting here, just a few more minutes, and when he was rested drive all the way up to the Toronto International Airport, watch a few planes take off as he sat in the bar on the roof of the terminal building, drink a few slow Scotches, and then return home via the Don Valley Parkway, and he would try out the power of the engine on that highway. There was nothing wrong with the world at this moment. Olivia was a bore, and the woman who wore the brown winter coat, well, she could arrive in the morning or not: nothing was wrong with the world now. Those letters to the editor of the newspaper, and to *Chatelaine* magazine, if he had them in his pocket now, he would tear them up, for nothing was wrong with the world as he sat in this new, black, shining Buick.

And then he saw the woman. He saw her first. The moment he saw her he was still thinking of how comfortable it was sitting there in the car. He did not expect to see her, certainly not in that frame of picture and reality and surprise; so that when his eyes first picked her out from the rest of the people, in his eyes and in his mind, who she was, was farthest from his mind. But he saw her. And after his eyes got accustomed to this reality, which was not in the first place reality, but just a dream, perhaps a desire or even a suspicion, he became alert. The woman was coming out of the Jamaican patty shop, and close behind her was a young man. And he would have looked off, just at that moment, had he not noticed that the man held the woman's elbow helping her, like any gentleman would, through the door. And they came out into the bright winter sun, and they stood up for a while, and the man turned the woman in the direction he wanted her to go, and the woman succumbed to his directing, and they moved together along the sidewalk as if they had been accustomed to travelling over this same portion of cement many times in the past, in the heart, at all hours, and at all feelings of emotion. And when they drew near the part of the street where they crossed, day after day it seemed, the man held his hand near the woman's waist, to protect her from the traffic coming along the street. Boysie saw the hand, and he saw the hand wander lower than the waist, and he imagined the hand being placed on other parts of the woman's body: in the dark, in bed, in a movie, in the elevator when only the two of them were travelling up and down; and he wondered how long this had been going on. But most of all he felt very angry that he was there, that he should be there to see it, for it was something which appeared to him to be unfortunate for him to have seen: it was not meant for him to see. The woman crossing the road, with the young man, was his wife, Dots.

Part Two:

"Donkey first,
second and
third!"

H E WAS FULLY DRESSED. And he was listening to "Both Sides Now." The weather was turning warmer, and he could not see the clouds in the snow falling, but he could see real clouds in the sky. The song no longer held the meaning of peace and comfort which he had got from it all throughout the winter; and his dispirited feeling, plus the regularity of the woman arriving every morning at the same time and disappearing out of his view a few seconds afterwards, nothing new taking place in his life, nothing strange in the apartment — all this made him feel hollow inside. He had spent a long time thinking of what to do with the discovery of his wife being handled by the young man. He would have been happier had he permitted his imagination to take its course to the natural conclusion of the man's handling his wife, but he blocked his imagination from going along to that extremity. He had come to assume too much about his wife: that she was there when he wanted her; and he did not want her above the ordinary performances of her duties. She would cook. She would wash. She would iron. And she would occasionally lie close to him in bed at night, usually on weekends. And if the magnet of need got the better of her body, she would roll over and lie on him, and he would breathe slowly and then fast, and then he would breathe more heavily and that would be the end of that. He had grown accustomed to her, as he was becoming accustomed to the cat. The cat "meeooowed," he called the cat "You goddamn cat!" kicked it out of his way, and then fed it. The cat understood what relation it was living in with regard to Boysie, and it left Boysie alone. But he was so used to Dots, to her sound in the apartment, and to have to let his mind follow the picture of the young man holding her round the waist, and travel down the concluding road, with the man's hands touching the naked body, was too frightening for him to face. And he had nobody with whom he could even lie a little, and give half the facts to, and from the person's replies try to chart the correct action he should take; think the correct and manly thoughts he should harbour, or inflict manly violence on her.

The afternoon it had happened, when he did eventually get the car started, and had almost smashed the car behind him (he tried to move off in reverse gear), he moved out of the parked spot like a man moving out of a movie house, after an entire generation of life and death had come before him: moving out into the street as it had been before he went into the cinema, and returning to the street like a lifeless tableau, with all that action and vitality and life and death in the back of his mind. He had moved the car, more cautiously after his near collision, up College Street, up, up, going West, into the Italian district, through a stretch of road filled with West Indians and black Canadians, through the High Park area where there was a park and large beautiful houses one of which he wished he had owned, or was living in, until he found himself approaching the airport. It was only then that he realized how far he had driven. He had come far in this car, and this car was not to him like the vehicle which people called life: and he had come far in life too. He parked the car, and he walked through the terminal, and he found himself standing at a ticket counter. "I wonder what the temperature would be like in Barbados?" He did not know. He had remembered very little about Barbados, and things like the names of streets and the shapes of things he had forgotten long ago. But he would not think of leaving right now. The man's hands might be free to travel over further expanses of his wife's body. And although the sight of the hands had not welled up inside him any feeling of vengeance, or even a feeling that Dots had betrayed him, he did not want to leave now. So he went up in the elevator, and got off at the level where the bar was, and he chose a seat near the large picture window where he could see the planes taking off and coming in.

After his first Scotch, he felt a little better. But then a large plane landed, and out of it came many West Indians. At the distance he was from the plane, and protected from the full blast of the engines, he thought he heard them laughing and talking as they went into the building and out of sight. He had seen hundreds of them down below, with their faces flattened even more than their noses were, stuck against the glass, peering into the Arrivals section, waiting for their friends and brothers and sisters and delayed husbands and wives. They were wearing clothes which seemed to shout at him; and whereas the Canadians were just as many, they seemed to be in the minority, due to the noise of the West Indians. He searched among them for the men in their midst, looking perhaps to see whether the young man with his hand round his wife's body had followed him here to the airport, perhaps to see whether he could see a duplicate of that man's body among these merry West Indians. But even to think about that had hurt him a little, and it was then that he went up into the elevator.

He thought of what he would do in Barbados, had he boarded a plane and left. Barbados had done very little to him, even less for him. What job would he get should he decide to go back? Not only now, in the rush of this blood and feeling. But next year, or even in five years. To be a cleaner? He was a cleaner there, too, and a gardener, for many years; and he did not know it until Henry had told him so. "We is all cleaner-crabs, Boysie! Me, you, Bernice, Dots, all o' we. Old Man Jonesy himself is a cleaner-crab!" Boysie remembered it: it was around the time when Old Man Jonesy had given him his first job, his first "ipso facto" job as he had called it, jokingly, at the Baptist Church House. Such a long time ago! But what could he do in Barbados should he go back? If he had to go back?

Floes and floes of angel's hair, ice cream castles in the air . . . and the clouds in Barbados would be blue, they were so white against the brilliance of the sun; and in all that sun there was bound to be a faster rotting of life. The fish on the beach, left there by the fishermen, rotted before Boysie could steal one. And life there had the habit of getting out of hand in quick time, too.

He put the other record on the player and listened to Mendelssohn. Music was the only thing which made him relax these days. He wondered what was really a midsummer night, and what was so peculiar about a midsummer night's dream. Clouds were dreams, he knew, the song on the other record said that; but was a midsummer's dream the same? He had dreamed quite a lot recently, and in his dreams he would be doing things which he felt he should be doing in real life. But the dreams were fulfilling, and after that kind of orgasm, he had no strength for the action, apart from the thought of the actions in his dreams. He had come home that first night, after he had seen his wife crossing the street hand in hand with the man, and had planned his words and his actions. Before he could say anything, he had, he thought, to create an atmosphere of war. And he dropped his vacuum cleaner on the hard floor and prepared for her approach. He always brought this vacuum cleaner into the apartment, for it was very expensive, and it did the job well. He was ready to face her, at the disadvantage of being disturbed out of her sleep. He slammed the door, and stood like a boxer in the middle of the pugnacious living room, waiting on her to come blearily and sleepily out of the bedroom, in her woolen pyjamas (when she wore these, he knew instinctively, after many trials and errors, to keep away from her body), like an opponent not sure of her adversary. But there was no answer to his challenge of noise. He sat at the table and drank a Scotch, and dreamed of all the things he should have done to raise her from her sleep; of all the things he should have done, even before he went to work that afternoon; he thought that he should have called her on the telephone, from work, and throw the evidence into her face.

And as he thought of these alternatives, before he even realized it, she was standing behind him, in the woolen pyjamas. He could smell the breath of sleep on her, and he could feel the sound of her body ruffled in her tossing bed ("Be-Christ, I know you can't sleep with a thing like that on your conscience!"). She was standing behind him, still breathing as if she was deep in sleep, and her body was bulging out of the legs of the pyjamas, and her breasts like two large bags of water were almost hidden in the bulge of the pyjama top.

"You making a lotta racket this time o' night, boy!" she had said, in a sweet loving voice. "You not too tired even to make that kind o' noise? Eh? And she moved straight into the kitchen, into the routine of custom in which he always saw her: she was the accustomed sound in the apartment, she was the provider of things to eat and drink.

And she said to him, "Lemme make you some hot chocolate, and bring up some of the gas in your stomach. Man, you working so damn hard these days, sometimes I feel sorry for you."

She moved from behind him, and he glanced at her, terrified by his own thoughts, that here she was, a secure woman in the sense of not knowing the thoughts he held for her and against her, a woman past that mark in life when she is prey to an avaricious man's lust, a woman almost at the peak of her desire for men and love and loving, a woman well seasoned in the years of her having all these sensual satisfactions, a woman about to merge into the woodwork of assumed middle-aged menopause, and here he was, sitting at his own table in his own apartment, looking at his own wife, and not knowing before this moment, as he looked at her body, that other men, and younger men too, would have eaten up that body and eaten it without preparation, would have swallowed it whole and attempted to digest it after the devouring. He remembered how he lay beside her, not daring to go to sleep, although his body ached with the work he had done in order to forget what he had seen, how he lay there, not sleeping, and heard her breathe, and heard the different rhythms of her breathing, and how she put her heavy woolen leg on his thighs, as if it was a natural gesture of closeness to him, and how eventually he drifted off to sleep, with the evil taste of her action and of his own inaction in response to that action, in his mouth.

"I should have put my hand in her arse, the moment I came through that door!" But it was too late now, for he had been overcome by the youth and the vigour in her body, and he had been conquered by his own lust, made more hectic now through the thought, and the fear, that somebody else had used her body. For it was using, he decided. It could not be love. And that was what really cooled his anger. He did not see it as fornication, he did not see it as infidelity, he did not see it as immorality. He saw it as a using of the body. She had permitted this young man to use her body, because she was not capable of having the young man as her lover. It would have destroyed him: not the fact that she had, or might have had, a lover. But the fact that she had gone into the act, with love for the act. She had not made love to him with love, or with the instinct of the lover, since the time, long ago on a beach in Barbados.

Then sleep came to him, and rescued him from his inaction, and from the violence in the planned actions which gave him a severe headache. The dream that night. The first of two recurring dreams which he had been trying to understand for a long time. *He was parking his new black Buick in the underground garage of his apartment building, and he was a younger man, and Dots was the same age as she is now. And he had just locked his car door, and all of a sudden he heard a noise somewhere in the darkness of the grey cement pillars and parked cars. He had been alone. But the dream had altered that and for no reason that the dream could explain, Dots got out of the car just after he got out, and after he had locked the doors. And Dots was wearing her quilted pink housecoat, and underneath it she was wearing just panties. He walked in the direction of the elevator, ignoring the noise, since the noise was not suspicious to him, and out of the darkness, and like an apparition, so close to him and so unreal, that he was almost*

115

about to walk over them, was Dots sitting on a stool with the young man he had seen her with that afternoon on College Street. The young man was sitting in a blue upholstered chair with a high back and comfortable cushions. The stool on which Dots was sitting was a bright patterned one. And they were looking at a large book that had pictures in it. They were photographs, Boysie could see that as he drew closer to them. And the man was turning the pages in the picture book, and at the same time he was turning the coat hem of Dots's housecoat, and Boysie could see right up her legs. One of the pictures on the page which Dots held with her hand with her wedding ring was a picture of a man making love to a man. And the picture of the man was the picture of the young man with whom she was sitting so close. He was wearing a very tight-fitting trousers of greyish blue, and a reddish-brown round-necked sweater, with long sleeves, so that his shirt collar, which was really a sweater, was shown just above the neck of the long-sleeved sweater. And all of a sudden, Boysie was no longer a spectator in the dream, but had been sitting with them in a room somewhere, all the time. But he had fallen asleep. They had been drinking, all three of them, and Boysie had drunk too much and had fallen off into a doze in the room with them, and it was when he opened his eyes that Dots had moved the stool from beside the wall of the living room where it always stood under a wall hanging of an African print, and had moved it closer to the young man's blue upholstered chair, and their knees were touching and he could see inside their hearts and their hearts were beating fast. And he noticed that the young man's grey trousers had a bulge where his . . . And then he woke up. He had cursed himself for waking up at that moment. But he was glad he had seen no more. And it was this same double-minded feeling about the waking up so soon from the dream that haunted him whenever he thought of Dots and the young man: he wanted to know more; he wanted to follow them further along the street back to the hospital where she worked, and he wanted to follow them further along the paths of their relationship, but he did not want to see what was at the end of that path.

The music is peaceful. It is putting him to sleep. He does not want to fall asleep again, and certainly not in the morning before he has seen the strange woman emerge from the subway station. Many times, since this thing happened, he would dress in his three-piece suit and sit and wait for her to appear and then arrive and then disappear, and he would be listening to his music and he would fall asleep and live in that sleep for years, and travel places, sometimes back to Barbados, and when he awoke, miserable and dislocated from the moment of what he knew to be fact and reality just before sleep came, he would find that he had been sleeping for three minutes, or five minutes, and that it was not yet time for the woman to appear.

He got up from the chair (after the dream, the first dream, he never sat in the blue upholstered chair in the living room, and he never sat on the reddish-brown stool: for they were the same as in the dream) and tidied his clothes. This morning he was wearing a dark grey suit with a pin stripe, black shoes, black socks, a dark grey shirt and a deep blue tie. He went into the bathroom to wash the rheum from his face and eyes, and he brushed his teeth. Dots brushed her teeth once a day at the same time: just before going to bed. He ran the comb through his hair, and cleaned out his ears. He looked at himself in the mirror for a long time, not really seeing his reflection but seeing somebody who represented him. "I look like a blasted undertaker, you know!" But his suit, which was custom-tailored, fitted him well. He searched in his drawer and chose another tie. This tie was striped, with red and navy blue against a red background. He put it on, and his spirits lighted up. But he did not think that his shirt was the correct one, so he changed that for a blue and white striped shirt. He did not like his appearance any better now, but he was too tired to change again. Back outside he went, feeling more blood pouring through his body, feeling as if the morning and the afternoon held something lively for him. But it was only eleven o'clock, and the woman could still be on her way.

"Meeeoooooooooooooowwwwwwwwwww!"

"The goddamn cat!" he said, and he went into the kitchen, and opened a can of something and dropped the can ("I wish that one of these days, cat, you will cut off your goddamn tongue on this goddamn can!"), and went through the door of the apartment. He locked the door. He looked down one side and then the other side of the long, quiet, scented broadloomed corridor, listened to hear if anybody was alive in the building along with himself ("What is so goddamn strange about this country is that you could be living in a goddamn apartment and not know if anybody else besides you is living too! You know what I mean?"); and then opened the apartment door again and went in. He left the door ajar.

He went into the kitchen and stood over the cat. He thought of killing the cat. What explanation would he give his wife? Dots had been sleeping with the cat. Dots had been sleeping lately with the cat. Heh-heh-heh! my wife sleeps with a cat, a goddamn cat, a cat, a real four-legged cat, not a *cat,* not that kind of a cat! He thought of the misrepresentation: *my wife is sleeping with a cat.* He could not use this kind of language in the Paramount Tavern to ex-

118

press Dots's peculiarity, or to Henry. "Man, you mean your old lady's horning you?" He would have to use his language carefully. "Man, is you a man or what? Your old lady turning tricks on you, and shit like that? And you didn't beat her ass?" Dots had been sleeping with the cat in the bed with her lately. He had to put some order into the thoughts of his language. The morning was running away from him. The cat was eating, like a cat. He should kill this cat. That would give some order and logic to the quarrel he wanted to have with Dots. He had tried dropping the vacuum cleaner and that didn't work. He had to find something to ease him quietly but deliberately into the quarrel. And he had thought of waking her up one night, and slapping her. But she might be too deep in a sleep, and she would only quarrel and curse him for waking her up. He wanted her, not to quarrel about being waken up, but rather about something else, so he could get into the quarrel he had in mind to make with her.

Boysie opened the refrigerator next, and took out all the pork chops and pork roasts and spare ribs from the freezing compartment. He searched some more for the bacon and the ham, and he dropped them into a large paper bag with a handle. The bag had DOMINION'S printed on it. He took the bag, went through the door, and locked the door. Outside the apartment door he thought he heard classical music. The Wedding March was being played. But he was not sure he was hearing The Wedding March; he was not feeling as if he had ever been married. He never counted wedding anniversaries, and he did not remember birthdays. And Dots never told him, nor held his forgetfulness against him.

Going down in the elevator, he tried to remember what his life in Barbados had been, but he was having a difficult time these days remembering things from that part of his past. He would remember pieces of conversation he had had with Dots, or with Bernice and Estelle, or with Henry, with all of them in one room, and he would gasp almost to see how that snippet of conversation, spoken in that context, suddenly came back to make such sense in this time of perusal. He was perusing everything these days. He could even remember what Dots wore to work last week, on Monday. And he knew what she wore every day of the past two weeks. And she did not know that he was paying this attention to her because he was doing it with a third eye, so it seemed. It was like a kind of inner light from somewhere inside him which showed him these things. So that to remember these pieces of conversation, which in themselves meant nothing, and to tell someone about them, to bring them up again to Dots, would make him look to her, or to anyone else, like a fool, like a person going slowly but surely mad, like a shingle in a pond drifting somewhere. He was perusing things these days. He had gone back into her drawer and he had seen the "pop-gun" thing, and he had seen it when it was recently used, and he tried to remember which night it was that she had used it, with him, but he could not remember. And he could not remember because he really did not want to remember, since he was sure that it was not used with him, in mind or in body, for him. He went through the underwear in her drawer ("Heh-heh-heh! In her drawer, in her drawers"; this Canadian sense of humour and twists in language! Would he ever master them? "Oh Lord, what a funny thing, *in her drawers*' . . . it always makes me laugh when I even think of this!"), through the unworn nightgowns, through the underclothes, searching for something close to her body which he knew he would know to be the thing he was searching for when he hit upon it.

And he was surprised that Dots had nothing more personal than clothes in her drawer . . . "in her drawers! haiiiiiiii!" Not even a bunch of old letters which he would have been glad to have come upon, and read, of course. Not even a faded photograph, not a letter from him. But he did not write letters. The only thing Dots had in her drawer, "apart of course from what you would expect, naturally, a woman to have in her a-hem!" was a book of matches, on which was printed the name Mary Jane Restaurant, and the address of the restaurant, somewhere on Elm Street. He had made a note to look into this book of matches, but he soon forgot, through the pressure of reminders he was carrying around in his mind.

He was standing now at the door of Apartment 101. He had walked past this apartment door many times before, almost once a day, on his way up from the underground garage, when he did not take the elevator from the basement. He had heard children's voices bursting through this apartment. "Eating all this damn pork and pork products isn't doing me any good. I really have to agree with that Canadian young fellow." He knew the woman inside the shoe of the apartment lived with her five children who had no father living with them, or with her; and he knew she was not a rich woman. Her clothes did not tell him that. And her unkempt hair and her badly kept light-complexioned skin did not tell him that. And the snot running from some of her children's noses, and the noise they made when, normally, children ought to be chewing food noisily, told him that they were hungry. Perhaps not often. Perhaps not hungry in a starving sense, but without the milk and cookies, the candy, the chewing gum which all children liked to eat, and steal from the refrigerator. "I wonder what it would be like living with a woman like this?" But

121

the number of children scared him, and the woman's appearance bothered him, and the chance that her body smelled bothered him, and not knowing how often she brushed her teeth, and cleaned between her toes, and in her other various creases — all this bothered him. And it pained him deeply because he knew he didn't have to live with her, would never live with her, but could not even imagine living with her because she was so obviously repulsive. But perhaps, he thought ("Somebody is coming!") she was clean on the inside.

"Look, ma'am," he began, "I don't really know why I am doing this . . ." The woman was unkempt. Her dress was open around the waist, and he could see smudges of food or work or toil showing on her petticoat. Her slippers were torn and her hair was uncombed. "I just thought that you wouldn't mind if I gave you these few things. I know . . . look, what can I say? I scarcely know you, well . . . I know, man, this country could be a hard place to live, and for years I didn't have a job myself, and well . . ."

"Come in, come in." She opened the door wider and he went in. The room had a strange smell. It was a smell of food, of air freshener from a bottle, of clothes sweated in and slept in, of life that was bare in its luxuries. He looked around and was surprised that the room was as tidy as his own living room. Everything was in place. There were doilies on each table, and one on top of the television. It was a colour television, and it was turned on, but playing low. The radio was also playing. The station was CHUM. Boysie knew this station. Everybody, almost everybody, in Toronto listened to CHUM. CHUM always had gimmicks for making people listen to CHUM. He had laughed, only yesterday, when he called a number by error, and the voice of a child blared out to him, *"I listen to CHUM!"* hoping to win a thousand dollars cash if the caller had in fact been CHUM. There was a colour print of a man painted by Rubens hanging on the largest wall space, over the television. And on the television itself was a picture of a family group. He could not make out from where he was standing whether the family in the picture was the woman's family in life. He was standing all this time, and he did not hear the woman offer him a seat. But then he heard ". . . you are a strange man, Mr. Cumberbatch. A very strange man." She had been seeing him, and watching him for months now, as he came and went.

"Can I make you some coffee?"

"No, it doesn't matter."

"Won't be any trouble, at all."

"No, I don't want you to go to that trouble. I'm all right."

"I been seeing you coming and going, Mr. Cumberbatch. You own the panel truck, don't you?"

"Yeah."

"You better give me those things outta your hand, before the blood spoil your clothes. And where're my manners, eh?" She took the bag from him; but he was not sure if she had accepted it. "You sure you won't stay and have a cup of tea, then? Something? What about a beer?"

"No, I was just on my way out, and I said to myself, why don't I give . . ."

"Don't feel bad about it. I know how you could feel. Mr. Cumberbatch, you must never feel bad about giving. Enough people don't give. People shouldn't feel bad about giving. Anything. To feel bad about giving is very bad. Won't you say?" And then the woman sneezed. It was a loud sneeze, which he did not expect from her. But what made him pay attention to the sneeze was that it was a sneeze similar to Dots's. Dots sneezed in a loud, vulgar, sensual way, like the passing of gas loudly, or like an orgasm, if an orgasm, and not the voice of the woman having the orgasm . . . if an orgasm could talk . . . this woman's and Dots's sneeze was like an orgasm. And straightaway, Boysie knew something more about his wife, that nothing before, word nor deed nor even observation of her personality, could have provided him with: it was possible for his wife to have been fooling around with him all these years. It was the message in the sneeze. Everything she could control, except that sneeze. "Mr. Cumberbatch? Mr. Cumberbatch?" the woman was saying.

"It's all right, ma'am."

"You seem to be so far away, as if you are not really here. Anyway, we should introduce ourselves, properly." She smiled. When she smiled she lighted up the entire room, and if he was not in that depressed mood, his heart would have been brightened too. But she smiled sweetly. And her teeth were strong and youthful and were her own, and as bright as he had seen once in a television commercial. And indeed, he joked in his mind, and said to himself, "Ultrabright, Ultra-bright, or brite?" and she held out her hand for him to take, and he took her hand by the palm, and touched it in a handshake, and before he let it drop out of his grasp, he remembered, he saw in his mind, the picture of his own wife with the young man turning the pages of the picture book and her housecoat hem, and he could not determine whether he had seen that in his dream or on the street when they were crossing over together. And in his heart he was sorry he had not accepted the coffee, or the tea, or the beer, so that he could just remain here, not to intrude upon the woman, for he was conscious of that, and of her situation; but he just wanted to be invited to sit down,

124

to rest, to flop down and breathe with ease until he fell asleep and never woke up again.

"Millie. Millicent James. What's yours? I know you are Mr. Cumberbatch, but you were Mr. Cumberbatch before you were so kind to me."

"Boys . . . Bertram. Bertram."

"You're not sure?"

"No, just that I never asked anybody before . . . but I prefer Bertram now."

"To what?"

"Boysie."

"Boysie?"

"Yes, Boysie."

"You know something, Bertram?" She said "Bertram" in two distinct syllables. And he liked that. At last he had got somebody to call him by his correct name, somebody to see the value in calling him by his real name. "You know something, Bertram? A man like you, the way you dress, the way you go and come in this building, a man like you, you shouldn't allow *anybody* to call you Boysie. It is not manly. You should always watch out for your manhood." And she laughed (those strong teeth!) and he laughed, and in his heart he wished it would never end. And then, it did end: it ended but just for a second, for into his mind came the passage from the newspaper: *a 37-year-old mother of five who was beaten by a suspected purse snatcher in the underground garage . . . died of her injuries;* and he painted in more details, some of rape, some of brutalization, some of loving. And he wiped them out of his mind and continued laughing with her.

"You know, Bertram, life is so funny! I was just here listening to that show on the television where they give away cars and things like that, and I say to myself, I said to myself, I wish somebody would bring a five-dollar bill and lend me right now! As you know, it is harder for a woman in this city to go out on the street and be a beggar. She could be something else on the streets. And then, out of the blue, here you are!" She smiled again. "You see what I mean, Mr. Cumberbatch?"

"Bertram."

"Yes, Berr-tramm."

She shifted her position in her seat. She pulled her dress down well over her knees. She held her legs, from the knees down, close together.

"I must thank you for the gift, and I'm not going to open it until after you leave. No, no, no! I'm not hinting for you to leave now. No, please." He sat back down. But he knew he had to leave soon. And she knew it. The relationship, the breathing, the sounds they were making when they were not speaking, the vibrations were telling them both that they should part, right now, because if not, they would have to do something. And they both knew what it was, what it would be. But they were more interested at this moment in what had prompted them to meet like this. "Have you ever met my children? They are all at school now. My eldest is fourteen. I wish he would learn." Boysie began to dream, and to hardly listen; for he had stumbled upon what he had been waiting for. He had thought of this, and he had planned in his way of planning — refusing to face the consequences of the first exertion of thought; but now he knew, now he was strong enough to do it.

They were standing, he at the door, outside, she just inside the door. He wanted to be able to tell her "I am going to call on you again," but he knew he could not, and he knew he did not have to say it. For she was smiling. She held the dress together now (not like Dots had allowed her housecoat to remain unbuttoned in the eyes of the young

126

man, even in a dream: even if it was a dream!) and so he knew his distance and also that he did not have to take that distance . . . Boysie saw it now: what was disturbing him about the incident on the street with the young man and Dots was not jealousy, not that; but that Dots had made the invitation with so little style, and had invited the manliness in the young man, and as a man, he had nothing to do but . . . it was a cheap way to behave. Was this on the street, or in the dream? In the dream. In the dream, she had invited the man's hands. Boysie saw this now, clearly. The woman was smiling, and he was smiling as he walked away. She left the door open until he walked away from her, until he reached the lobby, until he went down the front walk; and in all this time he wanted to look back and wave and smile, because he knew, he *knew* she was there, but he knew also, that he did not have to look back.

Why had he not thought of taking a walk at this time of day before? It was such a simple thing to do. Walk out of your apartment and walk into the street. His apartment had held him captive, and the strange woman from the subway had been his guard; so that he had to remain indoors in order to feel some life from the outside. But the street is easy now. There are people all around. And now that he is outside and seeing West Indians, he likes them, he even feels something close to them, with them, for them. Them. He feels more like a West Indian now than a Barbadian, in all these smiling numbers of people from the Caribbean. He began to understand now why he had held so much contempt and resentment for them. He had despised their youth because he was made to feel that he had not much left himself; and that he was already laden with a bulging stomach. "Look at your blasted belly, eh? What more use is you to me?" Dots was saying this almost every day. And the fact that he was on a diet, which is to say, that he was eating less, and finding it embarrassing to refuse her food at dinner, was making it more unsatisfactory for him. He had not really hated these young men, he told himself. He had rather resented . . . what the hell was he trying to argue? The day was fresh and alive with people. And he had forgotten to wear his topcoat, but he did not realize this until he was walking along Church Street heading towards the Lake, going south. "Why the hell you don't jump in the lake, eh, Boysie?" Dots had told him that, once, and they had laughed about it then. The woman in Apartment 101 is younger than he: and yet she seemed to be much older; and older women have always had this reputation, this history, Boysie, women with reputations are not fit for you to talk to, or about ("You are a decent man, and what the hell you're doing thinking of going with a prostitute? A woman of ill repute, heh-heh-heh!"); women who are older have had a long history of teaching younger men the meaning of life.

In Barbados there was a woman who lived next door to his mother's place, and she must have been, let's see, about fifteen years older than he was at the time. Oh yes! She is the woman who gave him a coconut bread one Saturday night. Now, let's see what year that was . . . ahhmmm! Nineteen forty-two. *Forty-two!* Because in forty-two you was wearing your first long pants! Oh hell! I remember that as if it was yesterday . . . yes, old man, women who are older have this frigging gift to show a man the ways of the world, and this woman didn't even talk about rudeness, what a word! We uses to call it rudeness back in them days. In this country they call it *screwing*. And what a terrible word. Ducks do screwing. Human beings make love . . .

March is such a beautful month to walk out in! Men and women tired of wearing winter coats, and of wearing the haggard look of winter in their faces, are now walking with more life, with more meaning in their limbs, and two clumps of young people are sitting on the steps of stores and shops and houses, sitting there where you won't normally expect them to be sitting.

Boysie walks slowly, breathing in rhythm with his strides, which are slow, his hands folded behind his back, and he looks left and right like a movie camera panning and taking in surroundings as if to place the context of his walk in some new lively meaning. He tips his hat at an old lady who fumbles into his path, and she looks back, a bit astonished at his courteousness, smiles a second time in complete feeling, and says, "What a nice day!" They walk side by side for a moment of mutual respect for each other, and he says to her, "A nice day!" He says that more than four times, and she answers in the same feeling.

"What a nice day!"

He understands now how loaded a sentiment it is to say "a nice day." He understands now, for the first time in all his years in Canada, that when a person says it is a nice day, it is a nice day, and it has a meaning that could be the motivation for great deeds, or the motivation for some ironical misconception about oneself. It is a language he must learn more carefully. The crowded bus lumbers down the street, jerky from running on the now-unused tramcar tracks, and the giggle in the movement of the bus capsizes onto the faces of some of the passengers. The bus stops, somebody gets out, and he could swear that he knows the person. But he does not. Beyond him, about two blocks, he sees the pawnshops. A long time now since he has walked on these streets. He used to. With Henry. Days back. Laughing and drinking and calling out after women, and some of them must have been whores. But it was Henry who always did the calling: he did the wishing, because those were days of a horny time, rimmed by desire, a desire born of mere looking. "Look, look, be-Jesus Christ, but don't touch! Don't *tech* as the Bajans say." Oh Henry, good old Henry, sweet Henry!

Boysie is walking with his hands in his waistcoat pockets. Something is missing from his waistcoat pockets. A man in his position. What did the lady back in the apartment say? "A man in your position." Boysie smiles. He likes that woman. He likes the way she speaks. And when she said, "A man in your position," it filled him with joy and pride, and a bit of power. She had said something to him which his wife had never said to him. But wives do not have to say that, do they? Do they? They do, as they should, sometimes. A man in my goddamn position . . . should be wearing a pocket watch, goddamn! . . . "I'm beginning to talk a little like that bastard, Henry." A man in your position is a man in a position to buy a solid gold watch right now, from one of these secondhand pawnshops.

He was quick to remember the feelings he had when he entered this same pawnshop about six years ago with Henry. Then he felt like a man on the way down, like a man who had failed, a man who was vulnerable to the slightest tug which would have pulled him down to the same level of the first step of any one of these houses or stores where he had seen other witnesses of that failure, drinking wine from the mouth of a brown paper bag, twirled around the top to fit the concealed bottle mouth. Now he was a man in a certain position, going into a pawnshop for the sake of going, slumming even. "Slumming? Heh-heh-heh! that's what they call it, isn't it? A man in my position coming down to this position!," a man with a certain sophistication and style used in this case, when whatever he touches in a dark alley, with his foot or with his fingers, is being protected from touching his body, or his social status, or his personality. He was buying a gold pocket watch with cash.

Boysie selected the most expensive one he found in the glass showcase; and before the man asked him whether he wanted to buy it, he was fitting it into his waistcoat. He paid the man in twenty-dollar bills; the watch cost fifty dollars, which was pure robbery, but at least he could boast that he had bought an overpriced pocket watch from a pawnbroker's; and he gave the man the receipt to keep, and went out into the fresh afternoon.

For it was afternoon now, the bells on the cathedral tower were ringing, or tolling (it didn't make much difference to Boysie now), and there was a scampering along the streets of men and women coming out for lunch from the businesses along the street.

He stood up. He could not move. He stood up where he was, and he was in the middle of the crosswalk, and cars were waiting for him. "Let them fucking wait! I am a pedestrian!" He was standing looking at six black women who were coming out of a building that looked as if it was some kind of government offices. He did not even know that there were black women working in this part of the city. He did not know they looked so good. He had forgotten all that. And he had not very often walked along the streets as he was walking today. A new life was opening up itself to him, and he was enjoying it. He just looked at the women and thought how nice they looked, and how sure of themselves and how they were not noisy. But he could have endured them, even liked them, had they been as noisy as the men and women in the Mercury Club.

Three of these women crossed the street (they did not have to) and walked purposely slow and soft and full of perfume as they came towards him, and he was sure that the most beautiful of them smiled with him. It was an emotion he did not wish to have proved, as he once would have done, and looked back and challenged the woman. But now, merely to think that she could have smiled was enough for him.

He turned the corner and came in front of the cathedral. In Barbados, there was one cathedral. There was another one, but it was a Catholic cathedral, and he did not consider it to be as important because he was not a Catholic. He did not know any Catholics back in Barbados, and in Canada he hadn't met anybody who had to say he was a Catholic. There was one cathedral in Barbados. And because in those days he did not wear shoes (there were shoes in his house, but they were left back from his father when he died, and Boysie's feet never grew to that size, so he never could step into his father's shoes), he was not allowed to enter the cathedral by the sexton. Only the rich people went to the cathedral, even when church services were not being held. But he had always liked the cathedral and he would stand outside in the shade of the spreading tree, with the men who gambled with dice every other day of the week in the shadow of the cathedral, because they too did not wear shoes and to gamble in the sun would be punishment for their soles, and perhaps their souls, too; along with the women who sold "comforts" and "lollipops" and "sweeties" and "cocks," red "cocks," and white "cocks" ("Man, don't laugh, man! I don't mean *penises*. Cocks! A cock is a thing made outta sugar and things like that, and when it is cooled off, it is shaped like a fowl cock. That is what a cock is." And the Canadian young fellow had laughed, and had afterwards laughed at his own ignorance, pickled in presumptuous sensuality. Boysie was satisfied now), and other things like roasted peanuts. Even whores used to congregate under that tree, under that shadow, from the broiling, relentless and rotting hot sun, near the cathedral, waiting to pick off the winnings of the winning gamblers.

The steps of this cathedral in Toronto are easy to climb. He can climb them without raising his shoes too high. And he can enter this one. And he knows he can enter this one without shoes on his feet, for he had seen hippies doing that during the summer months. "A man who ain' accustom to shoes don't walk-'bout without shoes, like how these young Northamericans does do, yuh! That is a different story altogether, yuh!" He was at the main portico, and he could hear people inside. There were actually people inside this cathedral talking! Now, back home in Barbados, you couldn't talk in a church. Not *talk,* you had was to whisper in the white man church back there, boy! *Whisper,* so you won't wake up the holy spirits and the deads that was buried inside the walls of the cathedral-church, man. You couldn't do *that.* Talk? In the white man church, godblindyou, and let a police come and throw a couple o' bull-pistle lashes in your arse, and then lock-up your arse for talking in the presence o' God? Man, there wasn't nobody, nobody at all, you hear me? nofuckingbody ignorant enough to talk even in a church, a ordinary church then, not to mention in that big cathedral that we have back there on Roebuck Street, or Crumpton Street, or is it in Bush Hall . . . anyhow, no man would be such a gorilliphant to have *talk'* even on the doorstep o' that big powerful cathedral, with the choirs dressed so pretty in their crimpson robes with them ruffs looking so pretty just like a fresh white sugarcake, or like goat-milk from Mammy sheeps, and with the organiss parading 'pon that blasted organ like if he is king self, and the Lord Bishship that man with the fat red face and the big belly, rolling-off them words offa his tongue in the prettiest Kings and Queens English and Latin from the Classicks, so blasted sweet that everybody who ever heard him, and those who didn't have the privilege to have hear' him, but only hear' 'bout him through hearing and talking, man, that Lord Bishship from up in England could talk more prettier than the six o'clock news 'pon the BBC radio! That was a Lord Bishship! And that was a cathedral!

But inside this cathedral there are people moving about, and just as Boysie took off his hat, to acknowledge his lesser mortality in the powerful hanging walls of banners and church regalia, before he could get accustomed to this heavenly gloom, this majesty, this strange-smelling presence, the organ was roaring from a cavern below him, deep down into the church basement and belly, and then climbing the walls with the banners and other things hanging on them like ivy, rising, rising until his head started to spin.

So he sat down. This was too powerful to take while standing. Besides, he had always been ordered to sit in a cathedral. Only God was powerful enough, he was told, or his representative the vicar or the Lord Bishop, to stand up in a cathedral. "Boy, always remember, if it is the last thing outta all the decencies that I drive in your damn hard head, always remember to humble yourself in the presence o' God, the Lord Jesus Christ." He smiled. He could see the face of the lady in Apartment 101, and the face, from a distance, of the strange woman from the subway; and he could see his mother's face, in that one smile. They all smiled alike. His mother: what is she doing now? He caught himself. His mind was straying again. His mother had died even before he left Barbados.

134

"Mendelsunn!"

He had to remember he was in a church, more than in a church, a cathedral. The organ was playing Mendelssohn. His eyes were opened by the music and the power inside it, by the surroundings, and he could see clearly that there was a wedding. The organ was playing the Wedding March. And he knew it, and it became very clear to him, the meaning of things in this context. He also remembered that he had not turned off his record player. But he was happy here. He even made a promise to himself, to come to church here one of these Sundays. But he was not too serious about this. He knew he would never come. He liked the music. The young couple of Canadian bride and Italian bridegroom came cautiously down the aisle towards him, carefully not treading upon the dress hem nor veil nor marching out of time to this very slow waltz whose time might or might not capsize their lives the moment they got outside the door, into the car, covered with artificial flowers, the loud horn blowing, the homemade wine and the liquor flowing like Niagara Falls, and then eventually with the bridegroom too drunk to drive for better and the worse of his promises and oaths to the same Niagara Falls, to find out with this ironical legitimacy whether she was in fact intact, a virgin, as her parents said she was . . . and he was left alone, for hours afterwards, in the cathedral to ponder on these things, with the organist giving him a recital of various kinds of organ music, as if it was a command performance. And when it was all finished, when he was washed by the blood of the music, with the lamb, from one of the hanging church banners now within his heart, his body cleaned-out and rinsed by the music, like Sunday castor oil, before he could decide to rise and put (as he had promised to do, in the fulfilled acknowledgement of the concert) a dollar into the Poor Box, the organist emerged from the darkness that is so common in temples, and when he got close to him, he said, himself bathed in the perspiration of the music, "Good afternoon!"

Bernice came to visit, and she brought along her young man. She had promised to do so. Boysie did not know they were coming, probably had not remembered, but Dots did. So when she went to answer, and let them in, Boysie took the opportunity to go to the bathroom. He had diarrhoea. After work last night, he had found himself in a bar on the main street in the city, where they had a rhythm and blues band from America; and he had gone in for his drink after work, to help take the taste of work out of his system, and had remained long past the time he would normally have spent. He was comfortable in all the noise and the laughter; and the West Indian men and the black Canadians, and some few men from America, judging from their antics when they walked and from their speech, had not troubled him at all. He was at peace within all this noise. He could not give the reasons for this new inner security, but his happiness held him there drinking until the place closed. And he had had to breathe in deeply, and actually tell himself he was not drunk. The diarrhoea this morning had addled that enjoyment. The buzzer was pressed again. He was rushing into the bathroom again and closing the door. And when he got his trousers down, and had seated himself in the most comfortable position on the toilet bowl which Dots had covered with some imitation fur material that was white; and when he had taken a deep breath to control the thunder and the brown geyser ("Shit! I hate to have these runnings! And with strangers around!"), Dots was answering the door. Boysie closed the bathroom door more firmly.

136

He reached over and grabbed the can of air freshener. Just then, he had forgotten to hold his breath, and the explosion occurred, and in his panic, he heard his wife outside shouting, "Come in, come in, come in, man. Come in!" She was covering up the evidence.

Boysie could not even relax in the bathroom. "I have to shit with a can o' air freshener in my blasted hand!"

"How you?" Bernice's voice came through the bathroom. If he could hear them out there, could they also hear him in here? So he tried to keep quiet, and pass the time and the Scotches and the chili con carne which he had eaten from an all-night stand on Yonge Street, and the gas that was in his system, hoping that Dots outside with the guests would anticipate each explosion and each eruption of the brown geysers inside his system, and raise her voice again to cover the evidence of sound. And then he broke out laughing. "Imagine me, in my own blasted apartment, and I can't shit as I like for fear that people out there hear me! Jesus Christ!" But he held on more firmly to the air freshener and to his self-control. Sound was one thing, he knew, but smell was another. ". . . and I thought you would like to meet . . ." He hadn't quite heard the young man's name, because the toilet bowl held the echo.

"You forget that I met . . ." That was Dot's voice. He couldn't mistake that voice anywhere. Dots's voice was a trained voice.

"Oh, that's right! I forget that you meet him already . . ." Boysie became alert. Where had she met him, this young man, before? But he had to concentrate on his business, and get outside to greet his guests, and he had to be careful that he had wiped properly, because "this kind of thing always bothers me to do clean . . ."

Bernice looked good. She was wearing another new dress.

137

It was new to Dots. And to the young man, who had hinted to Bernice that she should wear her styles a few years younger. This one was too young. It was a short black dress, fitting almost too close about the waist, and bringing out the uneven bulges and form of her hips. If you looked closely, you could see the outline of her panties beneath the material. The sleeves were long, and the neckline was cut low, low enough for the eyes to wonder and the hand to wander, mentally, about what was contained deeper down. Her shoes were in the latest style, with thick soles; and Dots saw that her pantihose were charcoal grey, and when she reached down to pick up Bernice's scarf which had fallen as she took off her spring coat (although spring was not yet here, but the day was pleasant in its temperature and disposition), that Bernice's calves were still firm, and that the blue veins were hardly visible.

This bitch looking more younger than me! This young man must be good for her. "Come in, come in, come in, and have a seat," Dots said, with both their coats in her hands, showing the man to a seat. "So, how Lew is, today?"

"Fine, thank you," the young man said, not quite at ease. He had watched Dots closely as he came in, and he had stolen a glance at Bernice, and in the comparison, he was a bit uneasy that he was going with a woman so old. For even although Bernice was taking great care to look younger, and was wearing her hair in the natural style, which though it was almost completely grey, still gave her a youthful look, he still was not unaware that he was taking his grandmother to bed. His own grandmother had been fifty when he left Jamaica ten years ago. Age meant something to him. But Dots, as he saw her, must be somewhere in her thirties . . . his mind was wandering.

"This boy always studying," Dots said.

"Oh," he said, and tried not to look as if his attention was straying. He glanced around the room, took in the furniture, and liked the standard of living of his woman's friends. He could be comfortable in this home.

"We are going to a concert later on," Bernice was saying. Dots felt she was behaving like a girl in love. "We are going to hear the Toronto Symphony play. Lew says that they are playing a very good symphony this evening, and he wants me to hear it."

"You living good, girl! You living!"

"I don't know if you are versed in classical music," the young man began; and Dots said to herself, Looka this young bastard! "But the concert is pure Haydn."

"Hiding?" Dots said, ready to burst out laughing. Boysie inside the bathroom had heard the young man, and he liked him for his preference in music: he and this young man could have something to talk about. Boysie, too, was on the verge of another explosion. *"Hiding?"* Dots asked again, waiting for the correct moment to pull off this joke which was an old one among them. All except this young man. "Hiding?" she said; and when the moment never came, she added lamely, *"Hiding from who?"*

And they all three of them burst out into a laughter that shattered their souls and their bodies of any pretence. The young man, who was now at ease, uttered a curse just below his breath, the joke was so good. And inside the bathroom, Boysie, who was laughing, felt the time was opportune for his own explosion into the toilet bowl. And he did just that, and felt relieved, and certain now that he had come to the end of his panic. They were laughing outside. He regained dominion over his kingdom.

"Where Boysie?" Bernice asked.

He did not hear Dots's answer. He was pulling up his trousers.

"Estelle says she sorry she couldn' come. But as soon as she gets Mbelolo off, she coming, she says."

They had changed their minds about christening Estelle's son "Boy," which was Boysie's choice (but not a serious one); and instead they had spent weeks searching through a book on African names, until they came up with, and decided upon, "Mbelolo." Mr. Burrmann, the child's father, was with them during the search for names, and it was he who actually chose this one. Nobody could remember what "Mbelolo" meant, but they liked the name nevertheless.

"Today is visiting day, isn't it?"

"Yes. Mr. Burrmann comes as regular as the postman. The way how that man looks after his son! And after Estelle! And the things he does for Mbelolo. Sometimes, I have to ask for forgiveness for all the things I said in the past against Mr. Burrmann."

"Well, that happened a long time ago. Still, I can't stomach his wife, Mistress Burrmann." Boysie was listening. It was the first time he had heard such compassion from his wife. He was alarmed to witness it. For Estelle had got pregnant from Mr. Burrmann, and Mr. Burrmann had treated Estelle a little roughly before he had been able to face the responsibility of his action. Boysie was the only one in their group who had tried to understand Mr. Burrmann's reservations; and the others gave him hell for it. Dots was outspoken in her condemnation. Mr. Burrmann, she said, was nothing more than a blasted criminal. Boysie listened now to hear what more she would say about Bernice's former employer. She surprised him so much lately about her views on things which, although they never dis-

140

cussed them, were yet matters of great importance to her. "Estelle loves Mr. Burrmann, he takes care of her and looks after his son, and I don't see nothing, *anything,* wrong with that." She appealed to the young man for support. The young man nodded. "How old Mbelolo is now?"

"Four, going 'pon five," Bernice reminded her. "And suppose you see him! Bright? Child, that boy is so bright? Bright isn't the word, then. His father have him going to the Toronto French School, and already he tell me, the boy's name is down on some private school's list. I think the name he mention' was Upper Canada College."

"Well well well, if it isn't Bernice!" Boysie was standing in the middle of the room. His face was washed, his shirt pushed too tidily and tightly into his trousers, he was feeling relieved and very expansive in his greeting. "And who is this young gentleman who likes classical music so good?"

"Where was you? Listening to people's conversation?" Bernice teased him.

"Emptying his guts, that's what," Dots said from the kitchen. Boysie waited to see whether she was saying it in a teasing manner, or whether she had already begun her practice of "bad-talking" him in front of strangers. He was not sure which way she had said it. But he made a point to be watchful. "Gal, all this man been doing all morning is running from the kitchen to the toilet!"

"Pleased to meet you," the young man said.

"You too!" Boysie said, sizing him up. "The name is Boysie."

"This is my young man, Boysie." The young man winced in his heart. "Boysie, this is Llewellyn Prescott that I was telling . . ."

"I know, I know. Llewellyn, pleased to meet you. My

name is Bertram. But around here, they call me Boysie."

"Don't let that man fool you!" Dots said, bringing the drinks. "From the time I know this man, he was Boysie. What is so bad about the name, Boysie?"

"Well, you know, Missis Cumberbatch . . ."

"Call me Dots! I not ashamed o' Dots!"

"Well, all right, Dots, but I still have to call you Missis Cumberbatch, as a sign of respect, seeing you are older. . ."

"Old?" Dots was screaming now. Months before, she was able to make a joke about this too; but with Bernice sporting this young man all over Toronto, and with her own private grief over getting old before she had accomplished what she wanted in life, and with Boysie now outstripping her . . . "Old? Looka, boy, who the hell are you calling old?" And very wickedly, she patted herself on her backside, and came very close to him as she did it, patting herself again and again, the sound of her hand on her fat body, making a noise which was like whiplashes on Boysie's sensibilities. "You call *that* old?"

"Oh my God," Boysie said in his heart. "Something is happening to this woman."

"You were telling me something very important, Llewellyn."

"Yes, I was going to say that, that . . . I was going to say that in my own opinion, it is extremely important that a person determines what name he wants himself to be called by, by which he wants himself to be called. There are great psychological reasons for that." Bernice was looking very proud at her man. Dots, who felt she had got the worse in the exchange, merely handed the young man the drink, and chose a seat opposite him. Boysie was paying attention. "Thanks, for the drink. The whole question about names is that it is the first stage of self-determination. For you see, if you could be called by any name which anybody wants to call you by, by which anybody wants to call you, then you see that you are not free, in a very delicate sense of the term."

"Oh God," Boysie said in his heart, "he is a gorilliphant." This is the kind of talk he wanted to hear a long time ago. Could this young man also explain the new language he was seeking to understand and master? Could he also explain, in those same psychological terms, exactly the meaning of the strange woman with the brown winter coat?

"Yuh know something, the way you just put that tells me you are a damn bright man."

"Didn't I tell you so, Dots?" Bernice said. Dots was left out of the conversation.

"Yeah, yeah," she said.

"I am sorry, Missis Cumberbatch, if you feel that I have slighted you," the young man began, speaking in the way Boysie himself wished he himself could use language, with that amount of ease, as if the words were completely in his command. His wife's efforts to speak properly in strange company were actually not very successful, he realized, since her words did not come out as naturally as this young man's. Perhaps you had to have a lot of education to put your words, and the thoughts those words had to convey, in the way this young man was doing.

"So, what are you studying, man?"

"Law."

"I going tell you something. The day you hang up that shingle, call me. Call Boysie Cumberbatch. I am going to give you your first job."

"Brief," the young man said.

"Brief?"

"Brief is the word for it."

The atmosphere was less tense now. The young man saw a friend in Boysie, perhaps his only friend in the room. He also felt some pity for Dots. He understood what she was doing to Boysie through her vulgarity. And he tried to put all this in perspective, taking Bernice into the picture too. Bernice was proud of him, he knew that. He very often had to restrain her from spending her money on him. He knew the function he performed in her life and to her body. But in a way, which he could not help thinking would take away from the lustre and the freedom of his relationship with her, he felt it was an obscene relationship: he, a young law student, completely broke, and only twenty-six, as the boyfriend, the lover, the man of this woman in her early fifties, or late forties, with a body of a twenty-five-year-old woman, but with the frustrations and the depressions of a woman who had gone beyond that stage of life, when her body itself was cautioning some pause in sensual and sexual activities. Deep down, he loved Bernice. He would continue to love her, for the duration of his penury, and even after he had graduated; even after he had married another woman, which he knew he would do: there was no question about it. Sometimes, however, he hated her because she was old. And she loved him. He looked at Dots, and could not make up his mind whether he loved her, too. But he knew he would readily take her to bed.

"Aren't you drinking, Mr. Cumberbatch?"

"Oh yeah, man!" Boysie did not realize before this that his wife had not made him a drink. Dots did not apologise for the oversight: perhaps it wasn't an oversight at all. So Boysie got up: "What's that you have there?"

"Rum and Coke, I think." Dots liked rum and Coke.

And so did Bernice, sometimes.

"What about Scotch?"

"If you don't mind."

"Come, man, let's do some serious drinking." He got up and went to fix their drinks.

"Bernice told me that you have very good records and a good record player, with a nice tone, so if you don't mind, I've brought along some sides . . ."

"Sides?"

"Records."

"Christ!"

". . . you don't mind, eh?"

"What kind o' records you bring?" Dots asked him. The situation was getting completely out of her control, and she wanted to do something about regaining her position in her house. "Boysie don't listen to *every* kind o' music these days, yuh know." She was talking now as she used to talk. Free, easy, and in her Barbadian language. She knew she could gain the upper hand among them. "Boysie only plays one record. *One* record. You would think that something was wrong with his head. Bernice, gal, my husband plays *one*, one record these days. And it isn't no calypso, neither!"

"Now, that's strange! Very strange!" The young man sipped his Scotch, liked its strength, and continued. "Very often, I find myself listening to only one record out of all that I might have been listening to before. And I find, personally, that it depends upon a certain mood. I even gave away a box of classical records once, when I was in third-year economics at the University of Toronto, and a week later, as I was crossing the campus, I heard a piece of music that I used to listen to every Sunday morning, instead of going to chapel . . . ahhmmm, it was the *New*

World Symphony, I heard the *New World Symphony* being played on a record player in the women's residence as I was passing it, and you know, Mr. Cumberbatch, I stood up for a while listening, and the thing hit me in a certain way, and I could then understand what that piece of music meant." He paused to take another sip of his drink. He held the napkin which Boysie had given him with the drink in the same hand as the drink, at the bottom of the glass. Bernice was listening very attentively and with more pride than she had shown earlier; and Dots was bending over to catch each word. But the impression on her face seemed to suggest that she was waiting to catch him on something. "I mention the name of the music because I had been going through a period. You know, depressions and things like that. No money, no possibility of any, either, and my finals just around the corner. And I had been listening to classical music all the time. Nothing but this kind of heavy music. The other fellows used to laugh at me, and call me white man. And in my state, that got to me. And I woke up one morning and said, You know something? They must be right. And I must be wrong. What is a West Indian, a Jamaican whose father didn't even reach Fourth Standard in the elementary system back home, whose father didn't know how to spell *university,* what am I doing up here listening to classical music, and so on and so on. You see, and I ought to mention it, it was during the period when the blacks in the States first started talking about Black Pride, when even in Jamaica we were beginning to understand the meaning of our local music, you remember? The *Ska.* Well, I gave away all my classical albums. But I was saying. I stood up that afternoon and listened for a while to the *New World Symphony,* and then at the window that the music was coming out of,

146

through which the music was coming, there appeared this West Indian girl. Shhhiit!" He immediately apologised for using the word, and added, "Shoot! A West Indian girl. Well, when I got to know who she was, I found out that she was studying classical music at the Royal Conservatory here. You see what I mean?"

"Go on, talk."

"Talk, boy," Bernice said, somewhat unnecessarily, enraptured by the cleverness of her young man. He had every intention of talking more. "Take yuh time and talk." And with pride, she turned to Dots, who was still holding over, and she said, "You see the brains that this boy have? This boy is going to make the most smartest lawyer in this country."

"What did I begin telling you about?"

"You was talking 'bout playing only one record," Dots said.

"Oh yes! So you see, Mr. Cumberbatch, it is nothing strange that a man plays one record all the time. I remember playing a song by Sarah Vaughan day after day until I had to buy three more albums just so I won't wear out . . ."

"What song? What classical song did you play when you played only that one piece o' music?"

"Something from Wagner." Boysie was disappointed that it was not one of his favourites. The young man seemed so capable of calling all these strange names without making them seem strange. He was capable of talking in a powerful way, so it occurred to Boysie, without making much effort. This, Boysie surmised, must then be the meaning of language. And education. The kind of education they give you in universities, he concluded, must be a rather strange thing, because it made you able to choose tit from tat, just as this young man was doing, with no effort at all. "And what is the piece you listen to, to which you listen, Mr. Cumberbatch?"

"Floes and floes and floes," Dots said. "Boysie does only listen to floes and floes."

"Better than that," Boysie said. "I going put it on for you now." Before he reached the record player, the cat which had been hiding all afternoon emerged from the bedroom and came to Dots and rubbed its body against her legs. You goddamn cat, Boysie said to himself.

"He still living, eh?"

"Yes, Bernice, girl. This is *all* I have to keep me company when the nights come."

"You feeding it good? Giving it the Pampers cat food that I brought you from the place I works?"

"Meeeeooooooooowwwwwww!"

"Wha' kind o' breed o' cat you say this cat is?"

"Sia-sia-something or other," Bernice said.

"Meeeeeeese!" her young man told her "Sia-mese."

"It is a Siamese cat, Dots. You didn't know that?"

"Child, without this Siamese cat, my nights would be lonely."

Floes and floes of angel's hair, and ice cream castles in the air, feathered canyons everywhere, I look at clouds that way . . . The young man was engrossed in the song. When it was over, he took a sip of his drink and beamed.

"I know now what you mean, Mr. Cumberbatch. This song is by a white singer, right? Now, I never heard it before, but I know by her voice, I don't mean the way her voice is, but by the timbre in her voice that she is white, and there is a sadness in the song . . ."

"That's what I tell Boysie!"

". . . so that if you were listening to songs by Aretha

Franklin or Nina Simone, well . . . you know what I mean?"

"Is that what it is, boy? Be-Christ, gimme the black singers, any day!" Dots continued.

"I do not mean that she is a bad singer because she is white, she is a very good singer, and her rendition is brilliant, but you are talking about the aspect of culture and background and social context, which are all mixed up in the song, and it is a different perspective from that of a man who lives in a ghetto, if you see what I mean?"

"Man, don't say no more!" Boysie felt he had an ally. He did not understand exactly what the young man had said, but he understood enough of the language and its sound to give him confidence in playing the song again, alone. "Man, look, don't talk no blasted more, man! Man, you don't have to tell me no more. You hit the nail on the fucking head!" He felt he could afford to be expansive in his own house, and with his new friend.

"Good!" said the young man, as Boysie selected now a calypso by the Mighty Sparrow. This was one of the records the young man had brought with him. This changed the atmosphere in the room to one of ease and a little joy. Dots eventually got up and went into the kitchen. Bernice followed her.

"Let me treat you this time."

"Treat me? To what?"

"Don't worry yourself to cook."

"Well, what we going eat, then? I know my duty is to cook and to wash and to clean. You don't want me to look after my duty? Tha's all I am worth. You don't know that? And I don't have no young man to make me feel young and as if I am somebody." Bernice wondered whether she could be heard in the other room. "You all right, girl. I's

149

a married woman," Dots continued; and it sounded very bitter to Bernice. "I past the young-men's stage!" She passed her hand to her cheek, and when she took it away, Bernice saw the tears. Her eyes were red, too. "I have every convenience. The rent gets paid every month on time. Food, as you see," she said, opening the refrigerator, "is always in this house. Drinks. A job. Everything. But what the fuck do I have, after all?"

"Dots, you don't mean to tell me, you don't mean to tell me that you are really unhappy, or jealous . . ."

"Who, me? Of *you*? Looka, don't make me laugh!"

"Let we send out for something to eat. Let the men go out and bring in something to eat." Dots nodded, as she wiped her eyes. "Lew, darling, here's twenty dollars. Go and buy some chicken or Chinese food, or."

"Chicken?"

"What about Chinese food?" Boysie suggested.

"Chinese *or* chicken!"

. . . he gi'e the donkey first, second and third, and then tell Lion flat, if you was the king o' the beasts, you'd be toting that!"

The young man got up a bit groggily, put down his glass after he had drained it, and prepared to go with Boysie. Boysie went into the bedroom, made sure he had the small leather case with the keys for the new car, and came out to leave. The moment they were through the door, Dots began to talk to Bernice . . . *Who tell them to let Monkey judge? Monkey have an old personal grudge, since the days they make him bring water* . . . "Sometimes, Bernice, I wish I was right back in the domestic system."

"What would make you wish such a judgement on yourself?"

Dots turned on the tap, and as the water filled the sink

150

with the breakfast dishes, she held her hand in the water, testing its heat and the amount of detergent in it. She held her hands in the sink for a long time, as she was talking, and she did not look at Bernice. "When I was in the domestic scheme, you know, things were a lot better. I had Boysie under control then. I uses to worry about him running after the Canadian girls, and spending my money on gambling with Henry . . . may he rest in peace!" She made the sign of the cross on her chest, all the while the suds dropping down on her dress front. She allowed them to remain there, and eventually they burst. "I uses to be so jealous. And so *vexed*. You know what I talking 'bout? Me, making the little money which I thought was the end of the world. And Boysie spending it on women. I was jealous, but I was in control. And in a strange way, I had some love for him." She began to wash the dishes. "But now, with Boysie making all this money. And feeling free . . . you want to know something? Boysie doesn't even ask me now for a dollar for cigarettes! Not even for that. I mean, Bernice, a man could be working for the most money in the world, and his wife could be working too, and there must come a time when one or the other o' them must be broke and don't have a dime to save their soul. And one would have to ask the next one for a loan. You see what I mean? You must. You uses to ask me for streetcar fare, when you worked for the Burrmanns and I for the Hunters. Or I would ask you for taxi fare. It seems we was always broke. But there was money. And we thought that money could buy everything under this sun. Including happiness. And a man! Now Boysie is so independent! So independent, Bernice. I do not even have the power over him to tell him that the rent ain' paid, that there ain' no groceries in the house. And he has never ask me for a dollar since he start that cleaning business. I don't even have that chance to get vex as hell with Boysie, and refuse to lend him that dollar bill, so that maybe he might be forced to treat me different, or behave different from the way he might be behaving, or . . ." The cat was rubbing itself against her leg. "This cat. Did I feed this cat since you come? Cat-catty-catty-cat!" Bernice nodded. "Child, I am getting so absent-minded and forgetful! And at my age?"

"Well, yuh know, Dots, women our age have to make the most outta life. You see Llewellyn there? He is my present insurance 'gainst going stark raving mad in this place. The older you get, the more lonely you get."

"He's a good boy."

"I think so. You really think so?"

"Gal, I just say so. I watched him as he come in here this afternoon, and at first he did look a bit nervous and cocky, as if he think we wasn't going to approve o' him and you. And all that talking 'bout listening to only one record, and calling me Mistress Cumberbatch. I hope he don't think that I am out to get him in bed with me?"

"God, Dots!"

" 'Cause they is thousands o' orderlies and intern-doctors at the hospital where I works! I only have to turn round to see how they does be looking at my backside when I pass. The lust in their eyes! And horny as hell. It seems that they only have to see my backside shaking before they don't have a hard-on, Christ, child, heh-heh-heh." She took her hands out of the detergent water. And she shook them into the sink. "There's one. A orderly. From Trinidad. I think he say he come from there. He is after me, a woman my age. Like if he is in heat. *Half my age*, you hear! Every blasted day I go to work, he have something to give me. A chocolate. A flower. A bouquet that he thief from some patient's bedside. Some damn thing. He *must* greet me every morning with some gift. And the first two or three times that this bastard pushed that flower-bouquet in my face, and started grinning, I nearly spit in his blasted upstart face! *I am a married woman.* But after all a flower is a flower. And when a man gives a woman a flower, it takes a very hard-hearted woman not to notice. So, talking 'bout this thing 'bout being a woman of my age, I decide one afternoon to test this little force-ripe bastard. Child, he would have spend *all* his wages on me that afternoon. Good thing that the place he took me to, to have lunch, was only a half-dirty place where they sell patties."

"What happened, what happened? Dots, what happened?"

"Nothing! Not one damn thing!" But she could feel that she did not fool Bernice. And so she had to add, "Nothing at all."

"Something happened, *some*thing happened."

"Meeeoooooowwwwwwww!"

"Cat-catty-catty-cat!" She took up the cat, and patted it, and put it down almost immediately. "I wish that this cat was a child. Bernice, I wish this blasted cat was a child. I need something to tie-down Boysie with. Having another man isn' going to do it. And it isn't going to prove nothing. I would just lose him by doing that. He might even kill me first! He just might!"

"What is this you talking?" They were now like the two close friends of years ago: Bernice comforting Dots, and Dots comforting Bernice. In their earlier years of friendship, they had come together in such moments of confusion, and they had tried to talk the problem right into the open of greater understanding and humility. And now they were again close. "*Some*thing happened that afternoon when you went for lunch with orderly."

"How you know that?"

"Because I am a woman."

"While crossing-over the street back to the hospital, and we was only in that dingy place for fifteen minutes at the most! . . . and the flies in that place, and in the middle o' winter, too! . . . I don't know. But I had to come straight home and look into Boysie's clothes cupboard to make sure that the person I see wearing . . ."

"Oh my God!"

". . . a grey three-piece suit . . ."

"Boysie saw you?"

"That is what I don't know. I am not sure. Bernice, this isn' a thing you could come right out and ask a man about. If he saw me in a place where I wasn't suppose to be . . . I am not talking about unfaithfulness, in me, or in any other woman. I talking 'bout the disappointment. Well, even if it was a decent place, like the Park Plaza where my husband takes me, or the, the . . ."

"Was it he? Or wasn't it? Was it Boysie that you see? Did he see you?"

"I don't know. All this could be in my mind. And do you know how I happened to see him? A man had just dropped something, a plate or a bottle or a cup, and I wasn't paying much attention, 'cause I wasn't feeling too comfortable with this orderly-fellow. A woman in my place . . . but the moment I looked up, the person was gone!"

"My God!"

"What had me really nervous, more nervous than when I went in that place, was that, Bernice . . . I couldn't get

154

that man's hands from all over me . . . whilst crossing the back-over, that man's hand was all over my behind. And this car. A new car. Black and with windows that you could barely see a person through. In this damn car, and I swear . . . no, it couldn't be! We only have the panel truck. And unless I am a blind woman, a panel truck isn't no motto-car, but I would swear that . . ."

"Don't worry yourself. It's only your conscience. And conscience could ride a person like hell, like if that person was a racehorse. It's probably only your conscience, Dots. and your conscience is clear."

"I could have sworn *blind* that . . ."

. . . *animal beauty competition, listen 'bout confusion!*

"And the moment Boysie stepped in this house that night after work, he put on that blasted record 'bout floes and floes and angel's hair, and straightaway I was frightened, 'cause I thought he had seen me."

"Conscience, child. You know you couldn't do a thing like that unless he had driven you to do it."

"Lemme look in here again, Bernice, and check to see if Boysie really have a suit like the one I think I see that man was wearing. Because, I could swear . . ."

"This is a nice car, man, a damn nice car," the young man was saying, as he shifted his seat. "New too, eh?" Boysie was watching him closely. He wasn't sure whether he should tell this man not to mention the car, or whether he should tell him and then bind him to silence. But he knew that he could not yet bind him to this moral silence, since he did not have anything on him. Perhaps, if he could get him to talk about Bernice, and about his intentions, perhaps if he could get him to admit to something. But this bastard is so bright, Boysie thought, it would take a great deal of cleverness and language to outwit him. However, Boysie's common sense told him that he could have something over this young man. This man was bright. But he was hungry. He was hungry for money. And it looked as if he was hungry for woman, in the wrong way. And the way he was dressed, so extravagantly for a student, told Boysie that Bernice must be spending quite a lot of money on him. "You are real cool, Boysie!"

"How you mean? This car? Oh Christ, man. What you expect from a old hard-stones man like me? I have been working like a slave in this country. Hard labour. Now I am reaping the rewards."

"You are self-employed, man. You are a capitalist. And to be self-employed in a civilization like this is the first step to liberation and self-realization."

"I don't know what the arse you're talking about, Junior, but I worked hard as shite for everything I got today! Now if you mean that I could go and come as I like, buy a bottle of Scotch and things like that, without feeling the pinch, and if that means liberation, well then . . . But in a way, I see eye to eye with you. One hundred per cent."

"Goddamn!" Boysie heard something of Henry in this exclamation. He thought the man was commenting on what he had just said. It was only after a while, when the man had actually turned his head to follow the couple, did Boysie find out what had caused the exclamation. Boysie knew then that he had him within his grasp.

"You don't object to that?"

"What?"

"The man and the woman."

"Hell, no!"

"You think he's a West Indian?"

"No, man. That man is a' *African*. The way he is walking with his head high in the fucking air? I could talk straight to to you, but around Bernice, well you know, I have to watch my language. After all, she's paying my fucking bills." He said it so crudely that Boysie knew he was learning a lot about this young man. "I am going to call you Boysie. All right?"

"Yuh coming down to my level, now!"

"We is men!" And the thing the young man felt he had to tell Boysie about was that he was already bored, and ashamed, to be with Bernice.

"You believe in dreams?"

"Dreams? What kinds?"

"Just dreams."

"I thought you was thinking of *wet* dreams!"

Boysie laughed, but this man's crudeness was upsetting him. "Just dreams." He wondered whether he should tell this young man about the dreams he had.

"Man, I believe in *life*, not fantasy. And after life, *money*. A pity Bernice doesn't have enough. Although she thinks she's the richest black bitch in Toronto!" He laughed a very sneering laugh, and Boysie felt suddenly very sorry for Bernice. "Boysie, man, I believe in *life*, money and pussy!"

"You're something else!"

"I shocked you, didn't I?"

"Shocked *me*?"

"I know you. From somewhere. Like I've seen you somewhere before. The moment I met you, the minute you came in the room, I knew I knew you."

"I know you, too."

"That is a philosophical point."

"A point, though."

"Yeah, granted. You scored on that. But I was talking,

philosophically. I know you, by which I mean, I know you as a type, and . . . "

"That's what I mean."

"I was looking at a book in your place with pictures in it, before you came out of the bathroom. You had the shittings, didn't ya?"

"You know that too, boy?"

"It was written on your face." Boysie passed his hand over his face, looked curiously at his hand, saw nothing, and then smelled his hand. He looked at the young man. "That's it! The smell. Speaking philosophically, of course, you understand . . ."

"You want to know something, Lew? If I didn't like you. If I didn't feel that I could learn from you, and I don't know if there is anything you could ever learn from *me*. But if I didn't understand you, I would tell you right now, *Get to-arse outta this car!* — philosophically speaking, you understand."

"Of course!"

Bernice and Dots were in the bedroom, sitting on the bed. Bernice liked the way Dots kept her bedroom. It was so bare: there were never any "women-things" in Dots's bedroom, she felt. And it was always so tidy. A man, Bernice surmised, liked to see "women-things" in a bedroom. Bottles and curlers and lipstick and perfume and lots and lots of bottles; and there must be a smell to the bedroom, too. Why else would a man want to come into a woman's bedroom? Bernice now looked around the bedroom. She saw the large bed, tidily made up (Dots had learned this craft during the crash training period for domestics back in Barbados; and later at the hospital, and had kept the knowledge) with a pink bedspread ("You really have something young in your soul, girl!"); a mahogany dresser with a doily on it, and on the doily was a Bible, which she knew Dots very seldom opened; another chest of drawers which she surmised was Boysie's since it had a tie on it ("No man would dare to be untidy or even comfortable in a room like this! and he won't dare being a man, neither!"); a large ugly television in a cream cabinet; and two pictures on the walls: one was above the head of the bed, and it said GOD BLESS OUR HOME; and the other was a picture of a palm tree on a sandy beach with very blue water. The floors were immaculately clean.

"Well, we didn't find that suit." Bernice was becoming tired and bored.

"What you think 'bout adoption?"

"What you mean, adoption?"

"A child."

"Are you adopting a child?"

Dots got up and went to her dresser. She straightened the doily and then lifted the Bible. She flipped the pages and took out a piece of paper. It was a clipping, an advertisement for adoption. Bernice took the clipping and read: *'Jane was lying flat on her back with both legs in traction when this picture was taken.'* What 'traction' means?"

"Read on, you would get it."

" *'The position didn't affect her cheerful disposition and certainly didn't dim her sweet warm smile. But then Jane is used to splints and casts and bandages because she's had a lot of them. The darling was born with a long-name condition called os-os-osteo . . .'* "

"Osteogenesis imperfecta!" Dots had memorized the pronunciation. "I had a hell of a time learning this word. But a intern-doctor helped me pronounce it. It means 'brittle bones.' "

It was a fairly long story about Jane. Bernice was too tired to read all of it. She wanted instead to find out what was happening to Dots.

"But why are you doing this? There's lots of children up for adoption. The newspapers are full o' them. Every day, every week. Children and more children. And healthy ones at that. So why you had to pick this one?"

"I love her eyes."

"You love her eyes. What about the rest of her body? You didn't know that this child is a *invaleed*, a cripple? Are you thinking of bringing a invaleed child into Boysie's home?"

"Her eyes haunt me at night, Bernice. The fact that she's suffering from osteogenesis, well, I see all kinds o' diseases every day in the hospital."

"Okay, okay, Dots. But number one, a invaleed. Number two, the child is adopted. Number three, the child's background. Did you consider these things?"

"Bernice, you don't understand. I am a nurse! Not really a registered nurse, but enough of a nurse to know what to do and how to take care o' Jane. And you can never know how much concern, how much pain, how much love you have inside your heart until you face such pain in children." Dots was wiping her eyes again, with the back of her hand. Her eyes were beginning to get red. "I already called about Jane."

"Boysie know about this?"

Without Dots's answering, Bernice knew she hadn't told her husband. "First the cat. And now a blasted invaleed? Dots, are you going out of your mind?"

"It's sad, eh? You have your young man. And he fulfills some o' the sadness in your heart. And in your body.

I have only Jane. A invaleed as you call her, but to me she is a human being, a person. And even the fact that Jane is a invaleed — we can't get away from that fact — but that brings her more closer to me . . . I know she would be expecting love from me . . . But I don't want to talk about it anymore." She got up from the bed, and took the clipping from Bernice, and put it back carefully between the pages of her Bible. "I says a prayer for my child, every night. For Jane." She came back, sat beside Bernice, and sighed. "At night. In this bed. I am so lonely. And Boysie my husband could be laying down right here beside me. Imagine that. When he was out cattawoulling at night, I used to worry. But I knew he would come home sometime. I still knew that I had something hard, something alive beside me. Now? Child? The cat there on the floor keeps my company in bed. Before I found Jane. And I would put my leg out to touch Boysie. And the bad feeling I would get from touching him! Not that he gives me this bad feeling. But at nights I am so tired from working all day in that Doctor's Hospital that nothing hard like a man could bring comfort to me. That's where the cat comes in." She sighed and called out, "Cat-catty-catty-cat!" The cat came obediently. She seemed relieved. She was the only one who showed the cat any love. And the cat had got accustomed to her voice. "Read this."

Bernice was hesitant. She thought it would be another clipping about an adopted child. It was not. She gave it back to Dots and said, "*Boysie* write that? You kidding!"

"My husband is a writer, nowadays!"

"What he know 'bout writing letters to the editor? Llewellyn is a writer. He says he is writing a book o' poems about liberation and freedom. But I didn't know that

Boysie was doing writing too? Just like Henry, eh? I almost said I wonder what became o' Henry, forgetting that he dead."

"Dead and gone!"

"The Lord rest his soul."

"Life!"

"Death, too, Dots. Don't forget death. Lemme read this letter that Boysie write. *Dear Sir, If the TTC* — that's the Toronto Transport thing, isn't it? Thought so! — *If the TTC is going to issue one dollar family fun passes, why not lower the fare for the people who have to work on Sundays and holidays, especially nurses? Hospitals can't close down on Sundays and holidays, you know. Bertram Cumberbatch, Toronto* . . . Hurrah, for Boysie! I like that piece where he say, 'You know,' right at the end. That's talking to them like a real Bajan, eh? And the 'nurses'-part, too."

"Boysie isn't as hard sometimes as even I make out. You know, he is a strange man. And I suppose he must be going through a lot. Many times I would want to go up to Boysie, and hug him and bring him close to me and give him a good screwing in bed, like I was once able to do years back, or even just to talk to him. Bernice, you don't know that I can't even talk to my husband! Something's always holding me back. I can't talk to him, Bernice. I can't utter one sentiment to my husband. I feel as if he feels I did something to him. And the minute I am too close to him, if I go close to him, standing up, or when we are in bed here, something goes off in me. And I suppose that something goes off in him, too. And I can't talk to him at these times. Bernice, I can't even talk to my own husband."

162

"Now-now-now-now, now!" Bernice was shaken. "Now, dear-dear-dear-dear, *there!*"

Dots's tears were dropping on Bernice's new dress. Bernice eased her off a little, not to save the dress, for this was friendship too deep for such a material blemish, but rather to help her wipe her face. The cat, probably attracted by the changed voice, probably mistaking the sobbing for its call, jumped into the bed and then into Dots's lap. "Look, go to hell, you damn cat!" she said, and tossed the cat back on to the floor.

"Meeeoooowwwwwwww!"

"Dots!" Boysie screamed, "why don't you feed that goddamn cat, before I drown the bastard!" He was back home.

Boysie had been visiting the lady in Apartment 101 for some time now. He did not know he was capable of visiting a woman who had no husband and no man without wanting to seduce her, or at least to bring the question of sex into her mind. And it was this absence of the sensual which first got him worried about his virility and then about the relationship with the lady. She had called him one morning as he was going out, to tell him, confidentially, "You understand that is between yourself and me, eh, Mr. Cumberbatch," that her son was in some trouble at school. This was the eldest son. He was fourteen, and was only in grade seven. And his teachers were treating him as if he were retarded, she said. But there was another problem which made her very sad, as she told Boysie about it. This was a remark made by the principal of the school, who said that her son was bound to be that way, "that way," because there was no "father-figure" in the boy's home. Mrs. James did not cry when she told this to Boysie, she just became very bitter, and with a sadness which she felt could have coloured all her future dealings with the school, if she had not tried to get over it.

Boysie was faced with the problem of going to the boy's school to see the principal. He had never entered a school in Toronto before; and he did not know what to expect. As a matter of fact, he felt that Mrs. James had trapped him into going with her, and had seduced him into going, by some implied feeling that he was now the "father-figure" in her home. She did not mean this, of course; but Boysie, being very sensitive about these things, felt this was the interpretation of his accompanying her to the boy's teacher and principal.

The meeting with the principal went surprisingly well. Boysie had entered the office with the feeling that the school was wrong and that Mrs. James was right. He made sure he wore his best three-piece suit; perhaps his appearance might make him look like a lawyer. The least he could appear, and be mistaken to be, was a very important person, *a man in his position*. It turned out that the principal was very understanding: "Mr. Cumberbatch, as an immigrant myself, I know what these children under my care go through. I couldn't speak English until I was nine years old, and I suffered taunts from the kids in my class. All I am trying to have Mrs. James do, Mr. Cumberbatch, is to make sure that the boy does his homework. I did not even tell her before meeting you here with her that the boy has been absent from school without an excuse from his parent." Mrs. James did not like the principal's attitude, but she did not say so to his face. She said so afterwards, as they were walking through the snow. But she could say no more than this. The boy's record did not bear out her words, because Boysie helped him do his homework one night, and the boy was very backward, indeed. But Boysie did not like having to be depended upon to be the boy's "uncle," and he would refuse, later on, to allow himself to be sucked into this manless home. But all the time he saw himself being sucked in, nevertheless.

That was how he found himself taking the boy on Saturday afternoon to the Colonial Tavern to listen to a jazz group. When he picked the boy up he was excited. He pretended that the boy was his own son, and he felt the boy did look like his son; but the nearer they got to the Colonial, the more nervous Boysie became: he was taking on a responsibility he was not sure he could cope with. They reached the place, and he chose a seat upstairs for them, overlooking the bandstand. Boysie ordered a Scotch for himself and a glass of orange juice for the boy. He was more confused about ordering for the boy than he had imagined. This was the first time he had taken a boy out. And he had almost told the waitress, "Two Scotches with water." But as the jazz began, the more relaxed he saw the boy becoming, and he wished that this boy was really his son. If he had a son, if this boy was his son, he would be taking him to this jazz place every Saturday to hear the matinee concerts; he would take him to the O'Keefe Centre where the big international stars came to perform; he would take him to the Ontario Science Centre where they had all kinds of scientific things, for boys and girls and grown-ups, too; he would take him on a bus tour of Toronto, and show him Casa Loma, where "some madman build a castle, man, and put in a million bedrooms and one toilet, or something like that." Boysie started to dream about the son he was going to make out of this boy. But his son would be bright, he would be beautiful, and he would be a killer with the girls, all those pretty Canadian girls; well, *his* son would be the *Casanova* of Ontario Street. And the jazz became even better, and the dreams more fulfilling, and the boy sitting beside him, his eyes focussed on the black musicians below, dressed in their ritual and their music, their eyes a bit red from the lack of sleep or from too much playing, held his lips apart and sucked in the music with the orange drink. "But my son would know how to drink in a more proper way from a straw, though," Boysie said to himself. He waited to see if the boy would continue to slurp through his straw; and when he didn't, when he put the glass down at the right time, and wiped his lips with the napkin, and made a comment on the music, and how pleased he was to be to be taken out, Boysie felt sorry that he had judged the boy so harshly and then rejoiced that he was with the boy. He was treating the boy harshly because the boy had been accustomed to being treated harshly: by his teacher, by his principal, and by his mother. His teacher had told him, "You will never learn." And the principal had told him, "Anybody like you, who lives in a low-rental project like that one on Ontario Street, well, what can I expect from you?" And his mother had told him, many more times, "You are just like your damn father." But when she was told what the teacher and the principal had said, she had screamed and had called the teacher and the principal racists. Soon after that, she herself had occasion to tell the boy, "Boy, you will never be *nothing!* You are going to turn-out the same as your bloody father! That's what you will be!" It was the boy who told Boysie this; "My own old lady, Mr. Cumbatch, eh, Mr. Cumbatch?" And Boysie had tried to cheer him up, and had told him of things his own mother had said to him when he was a

166

child; "it isn't anything, man. Your mother loves you. She only said those things because she was vexed with you."

When they left the Colonial Tavern that afternoon, Boysie took him to a bookstore, The Third World, and bought him three books which he thought the boy should have read years ago. The boy thanked him, and five weeks later, which was the next time Boysie dropped in on Mrs. James, who was cleaning the apartment when he arrived, she said the boy really liked the books. "I can't tell you what effect you have on that boy. He walks around the house with those books in his hands, all day. He takes one to school every day, and he tells all his school friends that a "big important businessman" took him to hear jazz and bought him three books. He called me from school yesterday to say that the book is so interesting, would I allow him to miss gym, so he could read some more. Mr. Cumberbatch, what have you done to my boy?" Boysie felt proud. What greater things would he do for his own son! He had misjudged this young man, in the same way as he had misjudged those thousands of other young West Indians around the city. Soon after, he saw the boy.

"How's it going, man?"

"Good, Mr. Cumbatch."

"How's school?"

"Good, Mr. Cumbatch."

"Any problems?"

"No, Mr. Cumbatch."

"What did you think of the jazz concert? You liked that kind of music? Perhaps, next Saturday, you and I will go back down to the Colonial, eh, or to the Science Centre, or to the O'Keefe, or even take a trip to Buffalo in my new car, and I could show you some Amer'can history, and even watch the falls at Niagara Falls, what do you say?"

"Yes, Mr. Cumbatch."

Boysie was thinking of what the principal had said: that the boy showed no interest. Jesus Christ, Boysie thought, can't this boy talk?

"How do you like the books I gave you?"

"They're good."

"Which one did you decide to read first?"

"The one you said."

"And how far have you got?"

"Page fourteen."

Boysie quickly told him goodbye, and went on his business. The boy was a problem. Perhaps he should tell his mother about this. But before he left, he asked the boy, "Hey, man. When was it that we checked out that scene at the Colonial?"

"Five weeks, Mr. Cumbatch."

"Oh, well . . . take it light, man." Boysie was never good at mental arithmetic; but he knew he had to puzzle over the average number of pages a day this young man had read: "Ahhmmm! lemme see now; five weeks, seven days make a week, seven days . . . seven times five is . . . ahhmmm, seven twos are, seven . . . seven fours, twenty-eight . . . ahh, *thirty-five*. Seven fives are thirty-five, and thirty-five into fourteen . . . nooo! fourteen into thirty-five is, ahhmmm . . . *shit*, this boy can't read at all!"

Boysie became very critical of Mrs. James's methods of dealing with the boy; he thought she made him do things which she should have got one of her daughters to do, that she was turning him into a sissy, that "shit, why am I getting involved? This woman isn't my wife." Mrs. James continued to be very kind to him. When he visited her on

168

his way out, she would always have a glass of beer for him, and one morning, he was so tired from the previous night's work, he sat and was so comfortable that after a second beer, something happened, and he was still there sitting in the same chair when the children came home from school. The children liked him, loved him, even; and he grew frightened that Mrs. James was putting them up to it, coaxing them, telling them things about him in his absence, to bring down this avalanche of feeling for him. Before he left their apartment to go straight to work, he had cooked them one of his specials, a Barbadian dish, and they were all calling him "Uncle."

"Come on now, you kids, say goodbye to Uncle Bertram, now."

Sometimes he would be sitting down with Mrs. James, just sitting and watching one of the many television daytime shows she watched, as if she felt that one day it would be her turn to get rich, to get the first prize, an outdoor barbecue set or a new American car; and he would become sad, and try to compare his life with Dots to his life with this woman. And the answer would be the same. Terror. He was becoming terrified of women. They were becoming such problems to him! He imagined himself coming home to this house, with all its noise (noise was beginning to bother him again: it must have been the television set and the radio and the record player which Mrs. James played all at the same time), to all these children; and wanting to go out, perhaps to play poker with his friends, just to escape; and being carried away with a good-looking hand and betting, *"Two hundred on these pair o' aces, here! I come to gamble tonight . . . shit, money is only money anyway, and I making it!"* and what then would happen, if he had lost, and had had to come back to face all these mouths? *"Uncle Bertram, can you take me to that place to hear jazz again?"*

"Unca Bertram, you take me, too?"

"Unca, takee me, too?"

"Berr-tramm, I need some money from you. You ain't been uncling these kids o' mine proper!"

"Look, Boysie, haul your arse outta this woman's house, eh!"

Boysie was no longer sure of himself now. He had tried to encourage a friendship with Mrs. James, which he knew he was using as a buffet against what he considered as the lack of consideration he got from his wife. But Mrs. James had proved to be too clawing, all fingernails, always clawing; someone to whom he could not think of lending ten dollars (which she borrowed often), because with ten dollars she was laid bare and exposed with all the countless other ten dollars needed to make her solvent. She became dull, too. This was the biggest disappointment, because he had liked her friendship in order to get out of the cramped boredom which he had been experiencing in his own home. Dots was dull. He saw her awake very often; he saw her asleep most often. He had hoped that Mrs. James would keep him alive, and put a mild and sympathetic hand against the tide of age which he thought was the cause of his inertia. But Mrs. James proved to be clawing. From her, he learned every social problem in the city, particularly those problems that affected poor people. Mrs. James's husband left her when their last child was not yet born; Mrs. James's husband was out of work for most of the time the last child was being conceived; Mrs. James's

170

husband was a bouncer at a downtown bar; Mrs. James had had to work at two jobs when she was early in her last pregnancy, or when she wasn't sick; Mrs. James took him to the Family Court; and Mrs. James took her children and herself to the Family Practice Clinic at the New Mount Sinai Hospital, once a week, in order to get medicine and medical attention, free; and Mrs. James told Boysie once of a middle-aged, grey-haired black lady who worked in that clinic, and who everybody liked because she was "such a nice person." And Boysie had listened and had become very depressed and very saddened. He had continued taking her son to the Colonial Tavern to hear the Saturday afternoon jazz concerts, and they had eaten steaks and had drunk Scotch and orange juice, as they did each time and at each place they went together. But the responsibility of being a "father-figure" to this boy, which was the moral obligation Boysie assumed, and of being "Uncle" to the entire impoverished family, was more than Boysie could tolerate.

He wished he could talk to somebody about this. To the Canadian young fellow. Or to Llewellyn, Bernice's young man. Because there were things in the relationship between himself and Mrs. James (who progressively became less tidy in her appearance, and once said something to him which he felt only his wife should have said) and in his attentiveness to her children, and he needed someone to discuss these things with: he started to fear that one morning, as he went to knock on her door, that he would be transformed into a man married to her. He needed a son. He wanted a son. But he did not want so many children around him. He began to dream: about her, and about being married to her, and about being unable to drive in his new car, and do things he liked doing, which were not many.

Once he took the entire family for a drive to Niagara Falls, because Mr. James had forgotten he had promised to do so, ten years ago, and of course had never taken them; and when he wheeled his car into the underground garage that night, tired and edgy and angry, the footprints of Mrs. James's children were all over his luxurious upholstery, and the floor mats were painted by the potato chips and the crumbs of the hot dog rolls they had eaten going and coming. When they had got out at Niagara Falls, Boysie was so angry that he refused to watch the falls. His new car, in which he could escape from the noise around him, in which he felt safe and like a man, like a "man in his position," in which he hardly heard the engines of other cars passing beside him, in his new car of which he had made a point of not letting Dots touch it, not even see it, Mrs. James had sat all through that distance, all through the noise of her children, and all she had said was, "Never mind the few spots, Uncle Berrtramm! A little soap and water and you would never know the difference. And anyhow, you are a cleaner!" Michael, his friend, his only friend now in the James screaming household of dirty paws and teeth filled with bits of potato chips and bread from the hot dogs and ketchup, he had sat, prim and proper, silent and inwardly annoyed that Uncle Bertram had allowed the others to drive in the car. Now he was no longer the only person in his family who had experienced the car.

"So how far you reach in the book, now, young man?" Boysie had asked him, as he helped him brush out the potato chips and bread crumbs. Boysie was now talking more loosely than he had ever talked before he met the

172

James family. He was becoming lax with his language. Once, when he had first met Mrs. James, he was talking in a proper Canadian-English manner, and she said to him. "But you don't have to be so straight with me, Mr. Cumberbatch." He had liked her informality then. As time went on, he found himself becoming more and more relaxed, and eventually he was talking as he used to talk when Henry was alive. Dots was reacting to his lack of formal speech, too. But she did nothing about it: she just made a mental note about his "humanness." Boysie did not like this influence of the Jameses upon him. "So, as I was saying to you, Mister Michael, how far have you reached in the book now? You should be very far in the book by this time."

"Oh, the book!" The boy was absent-minded. He seemed always to be very far away from the present. "It is a very interesting book, Mr. Cumbatch."

"So, you must be well into it by now."

"Yes, Mr. Cumbatch. I am at page thirty."

Boysie saw the total hopelessness in his relation with the Jameses. But he was still not prone to drop the friendship. It had served him well against his earlier boredom, and he thought that he was perhaps overreacting. He had spent some happy times with Mrs. James, sitting in her cluttered but tidy living room, when the children were away. And she had given him confidence in himself, although she did not know that she had in fact done so. He always thought of the meal he had cooked them, and how the children begged him to come back the next day and cook for them. It was a simple meal. He was a simple man. It was peas and rice cooked in the juice of the chicken which he had parboiled first before cooking in grapefruit juice for five minutes, and then putting it into the oven.

He had made a dish of souce as an appetizer, and he had put hard-boiled eggs into the salad, and had thrown a generous portion of brandy and Scotch into the cooking. Everybody was happy and full and drunk with food.

"This is happiness," Mrs. James told him, when the last child was somewhere behind the whispering partition from the living room. "This is the happiness that every woman asks for. Not that she expect every day to be a happy day. God know that most o' my life I have been unhappy. But at times like this, Berr-tramm, I am happy. I watched you cooking that meal for my family, and I have to confess that I wished you were my husband. I actually wished that you were my husband. And that I was Mistress Cumberbatch. I don't mean that I am taking you away from your wife. I don't even mean that I want you and me to be . . . well, you know what I mean. But standing there handing you all that pepper and hot things, which we never eat in our meals, I said to myself, This man could be my husband any day! And still, as happens in life, I know that the minute you are my husband and I am your wife, things will take on a different meaning, a different picture. That is life. And that is what I mean by telling you thanks, thanks very much for bringing this little happiness into my home, what little it is. You see what I mean, now?"

She had looked very beautiful when she said that. She was the woman he had seen that first day when he brought her the pork chops, about which she never said one word afterwards (not even if she had eaten them, had thrown them out, or had liked the idea of his first gifts), and her hair was tidy and she was wearing a new dress, and without making it obvious, without making him feel uncomfortable, she had mixed five Scotches for him, while he was cooking, and the children were dressed for the occasion. That is all he knew, the children were wearing different clothes; he could not pinpoint the difference in their appearance, but they looked quite smart and clean, and he wished that he was in his home and that she was his wife, and that they were his children, so that when she said all that about the exchange of fortune and place and husband and wife, it took him quite by surprise, as if she had been reading his thoughts. For he had just said the same thing to himself, that it would have been a good thing if he could have exchanged her, in the presence of time and circumstance, for Dots, and miraculously replaced the goddamn cat by all these happy children, and live in a ready-made bliss. "But Dots so rass-hole miserable these days she must be experiencing her mini-pause!" And with Mrs. James's explanation of the sentiment and the rush of feeling in which she had clothed her feelings, and the beauty in her face, in addition to the closeness of his legs against hers, and not one thought of seducing her in his mind or in the groins of his desire (he had not made love to his wife now for more than five nights, because she was either sleeping when he came in, or pretending to be, or she had left by the time he awoke), he wondered whether it was not he who was going through this pause in his anatomy which had caused this forbidding of hand and muscle from asking Mrs. James the question. It was bigger things he was involved with in their relationship, and he had always hoped that these bigger things would show him the light he had been searching for all these years. This bigger light.

It had come when he least expected it. For instance, he had driven one morning, alone in the purring automobile, secure and feeling the rewards of his position of material comfort, right up to the International Airport, and had parked in the upstairs parking area, got out, taken the elevator, and going down had helped an older person with her bags, and had stood up for more than thirty minutes near the cigar counter, watching the redcaps and the throngs of West Indians pressing their faces against the expectant glass that cut them off, for a while longer, from their friends and relations coming into the country, some as bona fide immigrants, others as scamps and criminals and pimps and "unwanted persons," as the government had begun to regard them. And Boysie had watched them, these young men and young women, in their loud dress, their colours out of all kilter, out of all perspective even if there were militant blacks among them, and he had watched them as people coming into *his* country. For he was here first. He was settled, he was a taxpayer, which he was quick to point out, in any matter of civic importance, and in some of no great importance; and he was a man who had written letters to the editors of all the newspapers and of the leading women's journal in the country; had had them published, with his name under them. He was a man in a certain position, and he could therefore behave like any other Canadian citizen. "That's the next thing I am going to do. Send for my Canadian citizenship. Not even Dots will know."

He had watched them and had felt secure with them in the country. They were not making any less noise as they waited for their friends and relations. They were not dressed any more suitably for the harsh Canadian winter. They were still talking loudly, and gesticulating and prancing up and down, and saying things to each other in loud voices which should have been secrets, or half-secrets, but which they said without regard for the ears of the neighbouring Canadians also waiting for friends and relations; but they suspected that the Canadians could not understand their language. And some of the Canadians, in their faces and in their attitudes, moving a little farther away to allow an energetic West Indian to jump up above the heads of the others to see if "oh God, I see him, I see heem! He here! Oh God, Dresser arrive, boys! Dresser in Canada!" or to toss a cigarette to a friend nearby. They were the same as ever, and he loved them. He understood also why he should not like them, for they were really too noisy and unnecessarily loud and prone to display. "Jesus Christ, you see that young fellow there! the way he walking in them brown and red shoes, as if he is the only son of a bitch who ever wore shoes, and I know back where he come from, he never seen shoes!" And he understood why he should like them, because they were the same as he was: "I just making a damn lotta money in this country, but basically them and me is the same thing. I could pretend that I am a different man, whiching I am, but deep-down, if ever I should need a glass of water, in an emergency, who is the first person to come?" He thought about this for a while, and the facts of his history stuck in his conscience, and he had to admit that on all those occasions when he needed that glass of water, the first person who came running was *not* a West Indian. He should control his new emotions and sentiments about West Indians and remember that he was a *Barbadian*. He had said this before; he should stick to it always. He thought of those "friends-in-need," and among them were the Canadian young fellow, his friend Mr. MacIntosh, and, and . . . "But still, our people have less money than the others," he rationalized.

This new awareness about "our people" had first been

177

mentioned to him by Mrs. James. But Boysie was not disposed to giving her too much credence for her ideas, and he was not the person who had known the arguments and the language with which to contradict her; still he knew, through common sense, that people like Mrs. James, poor people, tended to want to stick together and scream and cry for help together more than people in his position.

"I really think that a man in your position, and with the kind heart you have, and which you have shown me and my family, ought to join some organization, Mr. Cumberbatch."

What organization? He had lived happily just cleaning offices on a contract. He had enough to eat and drink. And the only problem he had was Dots. But he could fix Dots. He could either get drunk one of these nights and come home and kick in her arse; or he could throw her out of the house ("I paying the blasted rent for this apartment now, woman! You done supporting me. I am a man!"); or he could continue to ignore her, and hope that she eventually would become crazy and stop persecuting him in her silent warfare of the mind.

"There are a lot of people, our people ("And who the fuck is *our people,* tell me? You mean Barbadians? You are a Canadian-born, but I am a Barbadian?") who could benefit from a man in your position. Even an old magazine. Lots of youngsters do not even have as much as a magazine to read, or a man to take them to a movie. I am lucky, but I always think of the more unluckier than me. A man in your position should think very serious about contributing your free time to a social organization."

Boysie had kept very far from organizations. His life had been patterned on demand and supply, but more on demand. He always wanted things. For years, during his

178

struggle in this country, he had heard nothing from an organization, and no organization ever heard about him. He had never thought that there were organizations existing for the purpose of helping people like he was, years ago. And because of this experience, he had said years ago to Henry that he was strictly a man who needed nothing but one break, "Just give me *one* kiss-me-arse break" (this he had said exactly five years ago to Henry) "and leave the fucking rest to me." But nowadays he would tell people like the Canadian young fellow, and Dots, and he had occasion to tell the same thing to Mrs. James, "I am a laissez-faire type o' man. I don't believe in begging. I do not believe in asking nobody for nothing. I don't even believe in credit cards and crediting. Cash. Cash on the line. And I do not believe in organizations, particularly black organizations."

Mrs. James had not stopped there: she begged him and she bugged him to go with her, some night, to a place named the Home Service Association, to attend a meeting.

"What kind of meeting?"

"A meeting."

"You have to tell me what kind. I am frightened for black people, yuh know."

"Just a meeting. You will come."

"We will see."

It terrified Boysie very much that he was falling into the wrong company. Never in his life in this country had he thought about organizations. He knew, actually, only a small part of the city: from home to work, with stops along the way to visit some of the bars. But beyond that he knew very little of the physical outline of a country in which he had been living for so long. The idea of visiting the organization and attending a meeting fascinated him never-

179

theless, but at the same time it scared him, for he was letting himself in for all kinds of strange goings-on. Nobody was going to brand him as a Black Power advocate, or a Black Militant. He was a businessman. And he had to make a living, buy a house, and move away from this slum, to the suburbs, from this blasted place on Ontario Street which seemed to be the final resting place on earth for the aged, the prostitute and the wino. He had broadened his light of living by reading and by observing and by talking with such persons as Mr. MacIntosh and the Canadian young fellow and with Llewellyn. He had substantiated all this knowledge by writing letters to the editors of newspapers, and by watching television, particularly one American station from Buffalo and primarily the Canadian Broadcasting Corporation.

Actually, he knew very little about the country of his adoption. The walk along Church Street had shown him that. But he knew that Church Street was there, in the same way that he knew that Dots was there, in bed after eleven o'clock every night during the week, and out of bed, like a grasshopper ("Dots, sometimes, you know what you remind me of? A goddamn grasshopper!"), each morning after seven o'clock, except on Saturdays and Sundays, when she got up from lying beside his snoring, aching and very sexually hungry body by nine ("As if she is going to work even on the fucking weekend!"); and even if she was not there, one of these nights, or mornings, even if she did not cook the meals and leave them in the oven or in the refrigerator, he knew she was there, in the spirit. For she was not a revolutionary. And she did not believe in women's liberation. But suppose she was! Suppose every night when he was at work, Dots was out working on a different job, doing other work, doing other things? Suppose she had decided that he would no longer find her lying in the bed, on her right side! Suppose . . .

He is sitting in the living room, thinking of going downstairs to Apartment 101. But Mrs. James has gone for the welfare cheque which will feed her and her children for two good, stomach-filled days, or below the poverty-line for the week which the government says it will have to feed her.

He has just listened to the song about floes and floes and he gets tired of this, so he turns to Mendelssohn, and as he listens, he remembers what Llewellyn said about classical music. He thinks too of the day he sat in the cathedral and listened to the organist playing this same piece, and he tells himself that he understands it now. It means peace and tranquillity to him, and he listens to it as loudly as the machine will allow without vibrating.

The strange woman has not yet passed. And he is waiting for her head to appear, clothed in its usual white beret, and then see her body (he had forgotten that the first time he saw her, he had noticed that her chest was flat, as if she was not a woman), and then her entire brown coat, and the white boots or the brown boots, and always the white shopping bag from the exclusive shops along Bloor Street West. He was fully dressed: in his light brown double-breasted suit with the faintest of stripes; a suit that had a slight sheen to its conservative material; and he was wearing a silk tie of a matching brown. His feet felt comfortable and soft, and the bunions he had accumulated, and which had embarrassed him in years past because of the way they hurt when he walked, were now painless, and were relaxed in a pair of dark brown shoes, so brown that sometimes they looked red. And in his silk stockings. He was standing by the window which looked out on the other buildings, and which afforded him enough space and perspective through which to see her.

Mendelssohn was coming to his Wedding March; and he thought fleetingly of Mrs. James and of his boyish daydreams of being her husband; and just as quickly, Dots came through his mind, and as she paused in it, he recollected the nights and the days of making love to her, how her body was so soft and her behind was so firm for a woman her age; and Mrs. James came back, and with her, her image and the fat the fat the fat slobby tumbling of her behind, and he stopped thinking about her. The woman from the subway, not yet in sight, was in his mind. He felt himself falling asleep while standing. He was always tired; it was not really exhaustion from the expenditure of strength, if he could put words to it, not that, but a weakness of the body and the mind to go further towards seeing the light he yearned to see. And he knew, he could just feel that he was falling asleep, through the lack of activity. He sometimes wished that for some reason, perhaps a lingering flirtatiousness in his wife (he was always ready), that Dots would come home from the hospital at eleven o'clock in the morning, which hour was the most unhappiest of his days alone, and which contained the most impossible dreams, impossible to believe and to interpret, and would surprise him, and grab him and throw him in bed, and would say, if she would only talk to him, "Come let me screw you! You look as if you need some loving" (for he was now powerless to talk to her, except to criticize her, or to call her a bitch, in his mind, they had grown so far apart, through his being by himself: "That's what it is! being by myself. I spend too much time by myself"), and would make love and then go back to work. But Dots's mind was always on her work, and she was becoming very ambitious about being a registered nurse. She was grumbling recently about being not educated enough to become a registered nurse, for "if I was only a RN, Lord, what wonders I would perform! I would work miracles," by which she meant that she would put more money into her bank account. He changed the record. He put on his other favourite tune, *Milestones* by Miles Davis. This was a tune, this *Milestones,* which had so much in it that he promised himself many times to have Llewellyn explain it to him. By chance, in his recent confused mental state, he had found himself once, making love to his wife while the tune was on the radio; and he had wished that he was the man to have been able to say, "Wait a minute, Dots, we have to screw to music. I know just the piece for you!" Not for him, too? He was leaving himself out of everything here of late; and leaving himself out of every criticism: this was the way he was seeing things; for he was the only inhabitant of the world he chose to live in. He could not find the real explanation for this attitude either; he knew it was not selfishness, he knew he was not just "miserable as shite!" which was Dots's diagnosis; and he was sure it was not what Henry would have called "your fucking mini-pause, 'cause don't forget, Boysie, and you's my goddamn friend, but a man does go through a mini-pause, too!" No, it was not that, it was not either of them; he told himself so.

Milestones; he promised himself to have Bernice's young man, who knew everything about classical music and other kinds of music, explain it to him; the things about his moods, well, he could get that explained by the Canadian young fellow, in a "strictly philosophical way." He could feel the music ("Man, I really have to get this piece explained. This is a serious piece of music, in truth") doing something to his body, he could see how it quickened, and how his own pulse and heartbeat responded to it; he could see that Miles Davis was making the beat go faster, and although he could not understand that in terms of music ("Lew going have to explain that part to me, next time we talk"), yet he knew something was happening. He found himself being weakened by the music, as he had had a feeling of being soothed while in bed, and then falling off to sleep, and waking up with a start to find the radio still playing, and Dots snoring, and to discover that he had slept for only *ten minutes* and not for a lifetime. He had discovered this strange trick that time and his body were playing on him; if it was not always time by itself, then it was his body: he would be sitting reading the newspapers, and he would fall off into a doze, and from that moment when one reality ended he would be capsized into another reality, and this new world would take him and carry him miles all over the place, sometimes to Barbados, sometimes right into the subway steps seven flights down below from the very chair in which he had been sitting, and he would romp and play, look and see, talk (for only his dreams were the loci of conversations), and then when he re-emerged back into the chair, still dressed as he had been before that first death, when the dream became death and his loneliness, life, he would be out of sorts, like a drunken man, amazed that he lived two lives, and such long ones (one longer than the other, of course, but still two lives) in such a short time. It would be about the space of three or five minutes.

He is drifting off now, because the music is like a horse cantering, and he can feel himself being carried on the rollicking flesh through the up and down canefields back in Barbados, and then it is soft, as if the horse has fallen

184

down, but he does not experience the fall of the horse, the horse just falls and he is still lying on the horse . . . in his mind, he is riding Dots ("Boy, you riding me like a bloody horse," she said when he was bothering her about something, or when he was in the same difficult mood, as he seemed to be always in, these days), and Dots, though not a horse, though not his horse, or anybody's horse, was underneath him ("Boysie, why don't you drop your blasted horse-stylish manners when you are talking to me!" is what she would say when he was gruff); he thinks of when she is unpalatable, when he would prefer to be riding the strange, unknown woman, who herself walks like some kind of horse; and to satisfy himself with Dots, he imagines that it is the woman in the music of his cantering thighs; and he doesn't tell this to anyone, because it would be like murder; just as he had not told anyone of having seen his wife with the man crossing the road, his wife crossing the road with the man holding her hand . . . and he sees her now, from his shielded car, from his car with the tinted windshield, and he sees her coming out of the same junky West Indian restaurant, with the orderly (he is dressed like an orderly, in white trousers and white shirt), and the man is more daring this time, because he has his arms round Dots's waist, and there is not a car, nor a pedestrian, nor a streetcar in the road, so he could not be shielding her from any of them; Dots becomes tense, and he wants to drive the car over them, but he sits and waits and plans in his mind the attack he shall make on her as she comes through the door.

Tonight, as is his custom, he will not leave at five o'clock, because she comes home punctually at five o'clock, and because he wants to see her; tonight, this afternoon, he will be waiting for her to come through the door, and

185

"I'm going to go up to her, and drop my fist in her blasted face, so hard that she won't know what hit her, the bitch; a woman her age should be ashamed even to mention the name 'man' in front of anybody. I am going to sit down here, in the bedroom, with the lights turned off, that way she would think that I have left as usual, and when she walks into the bedroom, bram! my hand will be in her arse, in the dark, and then I am going to turn on the light and let her know what hit her, the bitch; a old woman like her, out with a man so young, horning me, a man like me! I am going to sit here peaceably, and when she comes in, we are going to talk, she will say, 'Boysie'; and I will say, 'Dots,' and after this conversation, I am going to wait until she has food in her mouth and then I will say, 'Look woman, you playing the arse! What the hell do you mean walking all over Toronto with a man?' Or I will pretend I am sick and sleeping, and when she comes in, I will open my eyes and make her see the light . . ."

Boysie is in the bathroom, and it is night, very late at night, and there is no one at home but himself, and he feels lonely again, but with the same kind of tragic alienation from everything, and he is standing in front of Dots's dresser, and he fumbles inside the drawer where she keeps her underwear, and he counts the number of pairs of panties (there were ten dirty pairs in the washbasin in the bathroom), and he sees there are six. The book of matches is still there, and the bar of soap with something written on it. He searches, expecting to find something: it is not anything about the young man who is the orderly, but it is about Dots. He does not know anything about Dots. She comes. She goes. She cooks. She cleans. He lies in bed, alive sometimes, dead most of the time. He comes out of the bedroom and pauses just before he enters the living room, for Dots has flashed through his mind, he sees her crossing a street and she is alone . . . and he sits back in his chair and listens to the music. The music is still *Milestones*; but before he makes himself comfortable in his brown double-breasted suit, he goes into the bedroom, for he can feel the sound that Dots makes, in the bedroom which he has just left. He goes in expecting to see her, in her aging pink quilted housecoat with the quilted appearance, in which she dresses and in which she lies, not more than five minutes after she has come home, even with her clothes under it; and in her bed, he sees the cat, barely to be seen, under the housecoat which it has somehow managed to wrap itself into.

Boysie opens his eyes and looks at his watch, and tries to understand where he is and in what state, for the music that is playing on the record player is *Milestones*, and the time is three minutes past that time at which he had first put the record on, for there are four or five other cuts on that same side; and he has gone so far in life, and yet it is only three minutes past whatever it was. He looks at his watch; the woman has not come in spite of all the time it has taken him through his travels sitting in that chair, nodding and cantering with the music, and so he brushes his suit, makes it tidy, takes the record off, and decides to take a drive somewhere; perhaps he would see the woman coming up the steps of the subway, if he got around by that street in time . . .

Boysie went into a discount store nearby to buy a package of cigarettes. He saw some magazines with SEX written on their covers; he pondered on the wisdom of buying one of them, but then changed his mind. He had tried before to get a better picture, to see the bigger light about

Dots and about women in general (when he used to run about with Henry, he and Henry felt they knew everything about women). But that was when neither of them was very close to a woman. Now Dots is close, so close to Boysie in the physical sense, that sometimes he wonders whether she doesn't have a friend, another nurse's aide, with whom she could talk, or even gossip. He feels this lack of friends in her, because more than once, when rifling through her chest of drawers, and expecting to find something, he had set his mind on finding some letter written to her by somebody. But never has Dots written anybody, and nobody so far as he could discover has ever written to Dots. But he wants to know her, inside out, and he stands now in front of the revolving rack of books, that has so many books about sex and getting to know a woman . . . *Everything Anybody Ever Asked About Sex!* . . . was that the name? or was it *What You Always Wanted to Know About Sex and Was Afraid to Ask?* He took this book out of the rack, and as he turned the pages he noticed the manager of the store looking at him. There was a smile on the man's face. Boysie put the book back down, and paid for the cigarettes. The man kept smiling even as Boysie went through the door.

The envelope was stamped SPECIAL DELIVERY. It was an official envelope, and the address was typed tidily in a block. Her name was on it, but she could not think of anyone in the world who would be writing her. All the letters she ever received, in fact, all the envelopes she ever received, had a small rectangular window in them, which showed her name, and a part of the name of the company which had sent it to collect her unpaid balance. They were all bills: for the payments on the furniture, for the payments on the clothes which she bought from Eaton's and for the colour television set she had just bought. The only real envelopes without windows came around Easter, and Christmas, and occasionally one would come from a European nurse's aide who was getting married, or from a family member thanking Dots for looking after some patient, or for sending flowers. She picked up the envelope as she entered the door, and she closed the door and went straight to the window where the light was strongest to see whether she could see through the envelope and therefore have some idea of the news inside. But the light was not strong enough: it was late March, or was it April? . . . Dots knew only the days on which paydays fell . . . and it was a dull afternoon, and she had to turn on one of the table lamps. The cat emerged from the bedroom, dragging her nightgown behind it, and after bending itself into an arc, it rubbed itself against her ankles.

She got on the telephone and dialed a number. As she waited for the telephone to be answered, she wondered whether in fact the letter hadn't been addressed to her husband; and so she looked at the name again, and saw that it said Mrs. Boysie Cumberbatch. But still, the typewriter could have made a mistake. Boysie himself never got any letters, either; most of the envelopes in their letter box were addressed to her — except those at Easter and Christmas, and she knew that Boysie paid all his bills in cash.

"It's me!" She had called Bernice. "Not too bad. And you? And Estelle? And the boy?" She took the telephone to a chair and sat down. She threw her shoes off her feet and the cat ran to them. The shoes were too heavy for the cat to lift or carry, but it tried nevertheless, and this made Dots laugh. "Looka, you blasted cat . . . I talking to this cat, here . . . that's true, because sometimes I think that I myself am going mad as hell, always talking to a bloody cat! Looka, cat, looka you!" She gave the cat a slight kick. "What I called you for is, do you know anybody who would be writing me a letter in a big official envelope?"

"Wait," Bernice said. Her voice was clear. "Let me go into the bedroom and talk to you."

Llewellyn was visiting her. He had taken his books with him, to study, but he had not got around to doing that yet. Estelle was at the hairdresser's, and Mbelolo was with his father.

"I could now talk," Bernice said. "Lew was too near to me for me to hear you good enough."

"I axe you if you could think of anybody who would write me this letter."

"Noooo . . ."

"It typed, too."

"Really?"

"Let me read you the address it have on the top. The Clark Institute . . . you know where there is?"

"That is the mad people's place where they does examine you to find out if you have a mental breakdown. Did you say you get a letter from there? Perhaps Boysie getting you committed, girl!" And Bernice laughed, just as Dots would have laughed had she made the joke. And when she sensed the silence at the other end, she said, "Why don't you open the letter and read it?"

It was such an ordinary suggestion to make, but Dots had not thought of it.

"I know," Bernice consoled her. "You been looking at it through the light!" She had done the same thing, many times. "Open it, man, and read it to me, then. I will keep you company as you read it, if it is bad news."

190

"But before I open it, I want to tell you something, though."

Bernice thought she was stalling for time, and she said, "Lew here. And I can't spend too much . . ."

"All right, all right. I opening it, I open it!" Her hands trembled a bit, and she snatched the letter out of the envelope and shook it open (it was difficult doing it with the receiver in her hand), and with some surprise she looked at the one-line letter before she read it to Bernice. "Oh Christ, I thought this was a letter, in truth! Lissen to this. *My dear Dots, It's been so long since we have seen each other that I wonder how you are. Yours truly, Agatha.*"

"Is that all she could think of writing to you?"

"And in a big letter this size!"

"You think she wanted to write something more?"

"Now that you mention it, I think so. We haven't been exactly friendly to Agatha. Not since Henry, her husband, died. He and Boysie were so close! I can feel sometimes how deep Boysie must miss Henry. He don't tell, but I know. Feelings."

"We should really answer-back the letter, though. Even if the two o' we sign it. I always wonder where Agaffa is, whatever happen to her! The address . . ."

"Clark Institute is all."

"Poor child, you know."

"I blamed her for killing Henry. And that is a thing that I can never understand. Whether it is she who really kill Henry, or if Henry commit suicide, as the newspapers claim."

"That is a part of our lives that we can't talk too much about, Dots. All we know for sure is that Henry dead. He dead a long time now. Only yesterday, Estelle and me was talking 'bout Henry. I dreams about him sometimes."

191

"I never tell you that before, but I dream about Henry sometimes, too. And in some of my dreams, me and Henry are in bed together. But I won't tell Boysie about them dreams!"

"That is wishing, you old bitch!"

"Is that what it is, gal?"

Bernice was now less depressed about hearing about Agatha. Dots was, lately, not the type of person she wanted to spend much time with, not even on the telephone. So strange a relationship did they have these days: before, she and Dots would have talked an entire afternoon; they would have knitted their lives closer in the common torment and problems of women who had left their homes for this big new land of Canada. They would have shared secrets which Bernice did not entrust to Estelle, and Dots to Boysie her husband.

"How our friend?"

"Who?"

"The orderly-man who . . ."

"That bastard?" And Dots exploded in her sensual gurgling laughter. Bernice knew that the conversation could take any bounds now, perhaps no bounds at all. "We went to lunch as usual. And last night he got me to go to his room. Christ, child, I almost didn't get back in time for work." There was a pause, during which only the crackling of the telephone made a comment. Bernice knew. She knew all the time that it would happen. "He still think I have money to give him. One or two remarks he dropped to me last night warn me that that bastard isn't really interested in me. Is my money on his blasted brain. Somehow, I hope that Boysie won't find out. I think he would kill me. But . . ."

"Put your ears closer! Can you hear when I whisper?

This person, a certain person I know that you know, is the same thing. Axed me yesterday if I could lend him two hundred dollars to buy books!"

"No, not Lew!" The pause again.

"Took me by surprise."

"It's a sad thing. A thing you can't even discuss with him, eh?"

"I lost faith in him." Dots could hear the change in her friend's voice. "A woman my age still have to have some hope. Hoping against hope. But hoping is hoping. The happiness he gives me. Never mind. I can't tell you what is going through his mind. In bed, and I can say this to you, as one woman to a next, in bed, well . . . I don't have to say more."

"Let me axe you something. Very personal. This thing is bothering me all day." Dots was not sure that what she had to ask Bernice could be asked in such a way that Bernice would not be critical. And being a woman of great suspicions, not wanting to remember all of the past, but wary of the present, she tried to cloak the question in such a way that Bernice would have at least to see the question as a theoretical one. "When a person is making love. Let us say a person, a woman. A woman, then. When a woman is making love with her man or her husband, and that woman is unfaithful to that man or to that husband, in a way that she was never unfaithful before, is there some way that the man or the husband could find out the truth?" The pause again. "Also, do you think there is anything wrong when a woman dreams or wishes that the man doing it with her is another person?" She could hear the sudden intake of breath. She had, in spite of her caution, shocked Bernice. But Bernice started to laugh. And so Dots laughed too. "Could it be that a woman, whilst she

is having one man, and dreaming about a next, could it be
that she is . . ."

"Jesus Christ, girl!" Bernice said. She was laughing and
Dots was laughing.

"Could it?"

"You asking me?"

"Could it?"

Again, Bernice laughed. "When a certain person isn't
here, I am going to tell you about all the fantasies I hear
the lady I works for say a woman can be guilty of. And
she is a expert at that. At fantasies!"

Dots would come home from work, and before she did
anything else, she would put on her pink quilted housecoat, sit down and glance at the newspaper, from cover to
cover, and spend the rest of her time with the paper, reading very carefully the column Today's Child. Even after
she had decided to adopt the child with the osteogenesis
she would look at these columns. It was not that she was
about to change her mind. Dots was as steadfast a woman
as one could hope for, and she was irrevocably faithful to
Boysie, faithful in her mind and in her duty, if not in her
body. She had not seen the orderly again. It had terrified
her. In her own way, she was so faithful that she was dull.
She read the column now to compare her choice of child
with the others. She wanted to be sure that she was about
to adopt the most disadvantaged child in Toronto. If she
had understood her motivations, she would have called
her decision to do so atonement.

She had not yet thought it was the right time to tell
Boysie about it. She felt that it would probably never be
the right time to tell him. But she lived through the dreams

of having little Jane in her home ("We will have to move out of this district. Down in here is not good enough, not decent enough to raise up children in. And Jane would need space, and") until those dreams became life itself.

She discussed with Bernice on the telephone just before she went to bed, in bed with the cat between her legs, what chances she had of making little Jane into a well-adjusted child. At first Bernice laughed at the plans she had for the child; but as Dots's determination grew into something like an obsession, Bernice too became more reasonable in her prejudice against physical and mental disadvantages (and indeed, this broad-mindedness surprised her, as she became aware of it), and tried seriously to comfort her friend, and at the same time, tried to steer her along a path of reasonableness. She no longer referred to Little Jane as "your invaleed." It was now Little Jane.

"How Little Jane feeling today?" she would now begin a conversation.

"Oh, not too poorly today," Dots would say, and anyone listening to their conversation and not knowing the facts would swear that Little Jane was already a part of the family, and was in bed beside her. But in more senses than one, Little Jane was indeed living in Dots's life. When Boysie was not at home she talked to Little Jane, as she used to talk to the cat. Gradually the cat became "You blasted cat," and Little Jane "my little child."

The day will come, Dots prayed aloud every night when Boysie was not at home (she prayed aloud for she felt that words directed above her head of consciousness were more easily heard if spoken), the day will come when I will have Little Jane. In the meantime, she placed a soft pillow, bought specially for Jane, beside her every night.

And because she was awake when her husband came in, at whatever hour, she removed it in time, before Boysie came stumbling into the lightless bedroom.

Bernice was breathless when she came over. She had hardly sat down. She asked Dots for the second time if she was alone. When she caught her breath, and was sure that they were alone, she held Dots by the hand and led her into the bedroom. Up until this time Dots didn't know what to expect. She had only said on the telephone, "You home? I have something to show you." And she had put the telephone down. Dots remained in a mild quandary of anticipation and torment: perhaps something was wrong with Estelle, although she could not think of what the problem was; Estelle was in good health and was happy, and so was her son. Could it be about Boysie? Could it be about the orderly? Had she heard something on the television about an industrial accident: recently, there had been many such accidents in Toronto; the weather was turning warm, and people were taking chances with their dress and with their luck. It could be . . . and she stopped at that point in the speculation; she had never really solved the guilt, nor could she face the repercussions of her crossing the street and sleeping with the orderly, and she never tried to see what she would have to see, through conscience and through the complication in her life, had her little flirtations with the man been discovered by Boysie. It was too difficult a thing for her to think about. She was not the kind of woman who could tackle problems in their abstract: she was well versed in seeing a problem, once it had become fact, right through to the end, but the end had to be seen as easily and as clearly as the problem itself.

Bernice told her to sit down on the bed. Dots's mind

wandered from the present dramatic situation in which her friend had her back now, years back to that other time when closeness and circumstance had found them sitting beside each other on a bed up in Forest Hill Village where Bernice worked at the time, and when the pressures in their lives and those same two factors, closeness and circumstance, had tumbled them, basically against their other sexual instincts, into an act of homosexuality. They knew then that their loneliness had caused it, just as their boredom and closeness in that boredom had driven them to perform an act they both detested. Again, Dots tried not to think about this. She closed it out of her mind and waited for Bernice to say what she had come to say.

"Child, I don't know if to call this coincidence, or just plain luck." Dots did not worry to ask her what she was talking about, for she knew that she would soon find out. It was just Bernice's way of saying important things. "You remember the conversation we had the other day?" Dots again refused to say anything, but she thought of Little Jane and of the orderly and of the disgusting way Llewellyn was behaving to Bernice. "I have it here, right here in my pocketbook." She fumbled among the many things in her pocketbook for what she wanted to show Dots, and when she could not find it, she emptied all the contents of the pocketbook on the bed. The cat jumped on a piece of facial tissue which was balled up, and which had lipstick, or blood, on it. Rouge, lipstick, an Afro comb, a photograph of Bernice, Estelle, Llewellyn and Estelle's son fell out too. "Here is the thing! Read this."

Dots took up the paper, which was clipped from a magazine, *Psychology Today* as the top of the page said, and read aloud. She read aloud because she always read aloud anything anybody asked her to read. With Boysie it was

197

the opposite. He had to be coaxed to read anything aloud. Dots was a worse reader than Boysie. Perhaps that is why she always liked to read aloud. She screwed up her eyes, pretending to be concentrating, that the passage was very difficult to read, that she was giving it all her mental attention. She read: *Sue, considers herself happily married. She enjoys sexual intercourse with her husband and usually reaches orgasm. However, just as she approaches the peak she imagines that she is tied to a table while several men caress her and touch her genitals . . .*

"Oh my God!" Dots gasped. Shame covered her face. Her mind went straight to the orderly's dirty sheets. She could not believe that such a thing as this could ever be printed.

"That is the same reaction I had when the lady I works for over in Rosedale gave this to me to read. What a shameful thing! I was so ashamed. I was so damn shame that I wonder why she would think o' giving me a thing like this to read. But I want you to read the *whole* thing before you talk again. I sorry that I didn't have the bravery to cut-out the whole thing, but I managed to steal as much as I could from the magazine. So, read it, and then I want to hear what you think. Start-back from the part 'bout the table and the various men."

However, just as she approaches the peak she imagines that she is tied to a table while several men caress her and touch her genitals "Oh my God!" *and have intercourse with her. It is a fleeting image; as she passes into orgasm it disappears. Dianne too is happily married. Yet she finds sexual foreplay with her husband more exciting if she imagines herself a harem slave displaying her breasts to an adoring sheik. While having intercourse, she sometimes envisions making love in the back seat of a car or in an old-fashioned house during a group orgy.* "Jesus Christ, Bernice! This could be true?" She thought again of the orderly's semen-stained sheets. *She likes to imagine being forced by one man after another.* "This blasted woman is sick!" *In one favourite scene she goes to a drive-in movie and is raped by a masculine figure whose face is a "blur."* "Bernice, my stomach can't take any more! It making me feel so guilty, just like if . . ."

"Read the blasted thing, woman. This is education. My lady says this is education, and I have confidence in her. Education . . . what a funny thing education is! It makes a man look so far inside himself, and the more he have, the further he could look, and with all this education, I swear blind it makes it more difficult for one man to trust the next man."

"That is what have me worried 'bout reading this. Education is a damn frightening thing, gal. Suppose Boysie was to see this, Jesus Christ, he would swear that one of these women is me! And he would want to know *why* I am reading things like this, all of a sudden."

"Read, read. Read and learn. And afterwards, we going discuss what you think. But first, you have to read."

Psychoanalysts, who treat many aspects of human behaviour as symp-symptoms of a path-pathology might conclude that Sue and Dianne were in dire need of help, "Be-Christ, I think so!". *Freud himself laid the grounds for such a diagnosis by declaring that "happy people never make fantasies, only unsatisfied ones do." A disciple of Freud's, Wilhelm Reich, claimed that fantasies during intercourse were an escape mech-mechanism, a diver-divers-diversionary tactic that helped people resist full orgasmic surrender. For both men . . .* "This is all?"

"No, wait. I tear-off a little more. Read this."

LOVER. Two themes were especially popular: being with another man — an old lover, a famous actor, a casual friend, and being overpowered or forced into sex by an ardent, faceless male figure. "You got any more?"

"Lemme see. I know I was in a hurry to tear it outta that magazine . . . maybe I teared out three pieces, I am sure I tore out three pieces . . . yes, here. This is the last piece. This piece I know I tore out because it apply to you, and me, to women our age. Read this last part. Read."

Elaine was one of a small group of women who reported no erotic fantasies. She was a bland, pleasant, conserv-conservative woman in her late 40s "Like we, like me and you, eh, gal?" *in her late 40s, who had been a bookkeeper before her marriage. She was the mother of four children and had no outside interests. Although Elaine had never had psycho-psychother-psychotherapy, she felt she needed it. She was happy as a woman and against men opposing her. Elaine's upbringing was strict and sex was never discussed. Her parents were very good to her and her two sisters. Elaine claimed that she had good communication with her husband and that they were good friends. She felt warmth and love during sex, but she rarely had orgasm.* "God!" Dots lost her breath. She put the small piece of paper on her leg. She held down her head, and said nothing for a while. Then, when apparently she had enough strength, she said simply, looking Bernice straight in her eyes, "You know, I never wouldda been able to admit this before reading this piece o' paper. But I don't have organisms, orgasm with Boysie, neither. You know what I mean? I have never come with Boysie. With that young boy, the orderly-man, is the *first* time that I ever came. It was a strange, frightening feeling. As if I was stealing. I always wondered what it would be like with him. I always

200

wanted to know if I was able to come. For a long time I felt I should find out. Now I know. But it is like stealing. But I have to tell myself, Dots, you are a married woman, getting near your mini-pause, so stop playing young." She shook her head sadly; from side to side, sadly.

"I have come only once before I met Lew."

"You have that trouble too?"

"You didn't know that, did you?"

"Bernice, you know, that women like we, like us, women from where we come from, don't discuss these things, not even to . . ."

"Nobody."

"Dark secrets, heh-heh-heh!"

"Women like us, women like you and like me and like Estelle, have so much inside our hearts that we *dare* not talk!"

"Yuh know, Bernice. I lay down here in this bed, beside o' Boysie, my legal wedded husband, night after night, and when he touch me, I feel that the devil touching me. And if, *if* I feel like in the mood for that foolishness, that *stupidness,* I have to imagine, as I tell you, that it is somebody else, like the orderly-fellow, even before it was really and truly the orderly fellow. And my God, all this time I thought I was the most sinful woman, the most sinful wife for imagining things like this. Not knowing that other women experience the same thing! And what is more, Bernice, it is written down in a blasted book. As you say, *education.* But as I say, the printed word. You can't beat the *printed word.* This is, therefore, *a very serious thing,* Bernice. You don't think so?"

"More serious than that, child. Blasted serious."

"Lemme finish-off this last piece, and then get you a drink, and we could talk some more. *She felt warmth and*

love during sex, but she rarely had orgasm. "Oh my God!"
She was not often in this mood for sex "Like me." *and
fatigue or children's problems affected her ability to relax
sexually. Elaine had few daydreams and no erotic fantasies. Women like Elaine were concil-conciliatory, un-
assuming, nur-nurture-nurturing, nurturing and affil-affil-
affiliative.* Dots said nothing for a long time. The cat
jumped on her leg near to her waist; she looked down at
the animal, lifted it off, and placed it gently on the bed beside her and Bernice. "Come, gal. We have to drink something before we talk more about this. This thing opened
my eyes to a lot."

"I tell you! Pour me a double, Dots; only a double could
take away some of the shame that I still feel after reading
this thing."

"You are a woman, Bernice."

"I wish so. I wish I could be like the lady I works for.
She and her husband discuss these things all the time, like
two friends."

"You think that I should show this thing to . . ."

"Boysie?" Bernice almost screamed her objection.
"No."

"Who, then?"

"The orderly-man."

"The orderly-man? Why the orderly-man?" Bernice
burst out laughing. "Dots, you are not telling me everything, man. Look, bring the drinks back in the bedroom
and let we sit down and really talk."

"You're the only person in the world that I would talk
this way to. I hope you know that."

Mrs. James did get Boysie to visit one of the black organizations in town, the Home Service Association, one

afternoon when he had nothing else to do. She had stopped pestering him about his social obligations. He felt somehow embarrassed that she should bring up this point, because before he met her he had regarded himself as being conscious of his social responsibilities in his community. But that responsibility did not include visiting organizations. It dealt mainly with writing letters to the editor. And his community was where he lived. But with his new car, and with the obtaining of three new contracts for cleaning office buildings on Bloor Street West, he soon became more involved in making money, and bit by bit he dropped his letter writing altogether, as he began to feel more uncomfortable among poor people like the Jameses. But he liked Mrs. James still, and his new financial position told him that he should go with her, see the depravity of the black organization's facilities and premises, as she said he would see, and come away without being affected by it. He was getting through, and no black organization had ever helped him. It was therefore *their* problem.

She took him along St. George Street, where he had worked years ago as a cleaner in the Baptist Church House, which was no longer there; and in its place was a luxury apartment building. He grew very nostalgic about this street, and he wondered whatever happened to Old Man Jonesy, the Jamaican who had given him the job, part-time, while he went back home with his wife on a twenty-one-day excursion vacation trip after working for twenty years. Boysie laughed as he told Mrs. James the story of Old Man Jonesy. "Now, you sweep this place clean, you hear, Boysie. And don't touch nothing in this place that don't belongst to you . . ." and Boysie told her about the all-night and all-weekend parties he held in the Baptist Church House, and of the morning the toilet overflowed and flooded the boardroom and damaged the mahogany table; and about Dr. Glimmermann, the boss, who had screamed and had lost his temper and his natural colour when Boysie told him he couldn't find the plunger because he didn't know what a plunger looked like. And they laughed as they passed the place where the Church House was, and when they turned into Wells Avenue, Mrs. James drew closer to Boysie, and put her hand on his thigh.

"You are something else." She kept her hand on his leg. Boysie did not know whether she was commenting about his leg or about his story.

It was a Friday afternoon, early in the spring, and the temperature was about forty, and many persons were on the street. As they got nearer to the Home Service, Boysie saw more people, mainly young people, in the park, playing on the green and white areas because the snow was melting and the grass was showing through. All of a sudden he became very depressed. He could see many children, dressed in heavy oversized red coats with dirty smudged white collars of something that resembled fur; he thought back to the old ladies who went each afternoon to buy their bottles of liquor and who wore mainly black coats with black or grey fur collars. He wondered whether this group of children was the beginning in time and place of those old ladies, whether this Home Service was the breeding home of the low-rental projects in the city, whether it was also the spawning ground for old ladies' homes and old peoples' homes.

"That's it!"

They were there. They parked on Wells, a street jammed with West Indians who went about their business with the easy pace and the silent dreamlike manner as if they were still walking under the sun. And the sun was shining

204

this afternoon, but it was not giving off much heat; so they wore hats made out of wool, and some of the men appeared to be aeroplane pilots by the black leather hats they wore with straps untied and flapping down in the windless afternoon, seeming to be on some flight of fantasy about their place on this springtime street in the new country in which they found themselves.

Boysie looked at them, and wished that they had never come here, that they would learn how to dress for the weather and not appear so conspicuous. Only the aeroplane pilot hats seemed to be keeping them warm, for they were walking about, some of them, in tropical suits. He was wearing his winter coat.

Mrs. James walked right into the Home Service Association building without even stopping in the vestibule cluttered with posters and amateur drawings of children and adults, proclaiming the "blackness" of the organization and of the members. All the posters advertised some meeting of "black" importance, and the drawings showed the powerful proud faces of black men and black women associated with something "black." There were many flags of red, black and green, and one sign over a door proclaimed, in case any intruder or visitor or organization member should not be certain, that BLACK IS BEAUTIFUL. Boysie looked at all these things very carefully, and when he had studied them all, he felt very uncomfortable in this building. Mrs. James was walking, just ahead of him, through a narrow passageway with a radiator in it, into the kitchen. A large, healthy black woman, her stomach making her look pregnant, stood like a queen over a large black pot which had steam coming from it. Her face was sweating, and she would wipe the water off her forehead with the back of her hand. The ceiling in the kitchen was falling down, and it looked as if the workmen had left before the job was finished.

"Well, bless my eyesight!" the woman said.

"How's things, how you feel?"

"You got it! You see me."

"Just walking through. You don't mind?"

"Sister, you're home!"

Boysie felt very ill at ease during this conversation. Neither of them felt it necessary to call either one by her name, and he wanted to know who this woman with the sweating forehead was. But it seemed as if to know, as if to ask, he would have to be a member first, or it would be an imposition, an exposure of his uneasiness in these surroundings. He wondered what Mrs. James was up to, for she had said nothing to him, really, of the reason for bringing him to this place. He wondered whether she wanted him to work here. The place was surprisingly clean, but clean in the way that a very old rundown house is clean: with the plaster falling, but around the broken plaster all cleanliness. The walls were painted by amateurs, and if not by amateurs, certainly with the cheapest kind of paint. Bumps were in the walls.

"How do you do, Sister James?" It was a man in his late thirties, who came out of a room, not really a room, but really out of one of the bumpy painted walls. He was well dressed, and Boysie did not expect this. He always thought that these militant black men who worked in these organizations were harsh and brusque and militant and threatening and violent.

"I am just showing the brother around. You don't mind?"

"Course not, sister. Show the brother round the place.

And I hope the brother would want to help us. We need part-time volunteer workers."

It was the first time that anybody had ever called Boysie a "brother." He did not like it. He did not at all like this assumption of closeness based on colour only. He would have preferred to have been introduced by his real name. In this black organization, walking up the narrow flight of stairs where the walls were again bumpily painted, but were clean, and where it was dark and with a strange odour, as if someone was sleeping in the building, Boysie wondered aloud in his heart why nobody in this place ever called anybody else by his name. It was the first time that Mrs. James had referred to him as "brother." Could she be doing this because of the circumstance, and not because of her conviction? There were lots of times in the past when she was alone with him in her apartment that she could have called him "brother," but she never did. Why wait until she was in a black organization headquarters to call him a "brother"? Perhaps she had just become black, or blackened, when she was around these black militants, who were always giving trouble and talking about a race war in the black newspaper, *Contrast*. It was too much for him to think through to its logical conclusion. Again he wished he had mastered the new language. So he stopped thinking about it, or rather had it wrenched from his thoughts, because he was at the top of a flight of stairs, in a narrow passageway, and Mrs. James was opening a door and motioning him to come and peep in.

She opened the door and pointed. At first all was darkness inside the room. But as his eyes grew accustomed to the darkness, he thought he saw bodies lying down on camp cots. His eyes became adjusted more, and he could make out that the camp cots were green, and the blankets on them were grey, as if they had come from an army that had been defeated by long marches and by longer battles. Everything had this strange odour, as if people were sleeping.

"Close the door. You don't want to wake up the little darlings."

"Wait, you mean . . ."

"The children sleeping. It's their rest period. Twenty children sleeping in there."

They tiptoed back down the stairs and paused once more at a door from which came the strange same odour. This time Boysie's eyes adjusted to these surroundings, these strange things happening in a city in which he had lived for so many years now . . . How many years I been here in this city without seeing these things, or even thinking 'bout them? . . . There were children in the rooms sleeping on army cots, or camping cots, and they all had grey blankets over them, and in the black corners of the room, perhaps it was at the head of the room, or at the foot, depending upon your vision or your perspective, was an oldish woman, waiting while the children slept, waiting perhaps too to see that they slept well, or that they would not like soldiers with dreams of defeat and conquests on their tired minds and bodies jump through the windows, thinking themselves to be birds or cannon or missiles. Boysie adjusted his eyes once more, but could not see the things Mrs. James was showing him. And he could not see why she was showing him these things.

"Take care, sister," the young well-dressed man said, as they were going through the front door. "Brother, *did you see?*"

Such strange ways of talking, Boysie noticed. And never

calling people by their real names. He wondered whether this was some conspiracy or some closer way of living that he had never considered before. And what worried him was that he did not crave it. It was too mysterious, too ritualistic, too tribal for him. That's it, he said, outside in the fresher cleaner air, with the only smell being the smell of spring and melting snow and grass trying to come alive. It was too tribal. It was like the antics and attitudes of all those West Indians at the airport, or down at the Jamaican patty shop, how they laughed and talked to each other, and slapped palms and laughed some more, even when nobody had made a joke. Or like all this thing about "Right on!" whenever anybody said anything important or relevant, which he could never understand anyhow. It was this closeness that bothered him, and made him feel left out, and inferior.

"Let's stop-off at the Blue Orchid for a drink. I need a drink." Mrs. James did not answer, and he did not object. "Why did you take me to that place?" he asked her, when the waitress, who was scarcely wearing anything below her waist, brought the drinks. "Nice!" Boysie said, not referring to the drinks.

"This is a nice drink, indeed," Mrs. James said. He considered her stupid for her answer.

"Did you *see* anything?" she asked him later on.

"But why did you think I should see it?"

"A man in your position should know everything, and should see everything."

"You mean those children sleeping?"

"That's only part."

He put his glass on the table. And he looked at her. On her face was not the answer he was looking for, so he looked instead at the scantily dressed waitress. She was more of a woman, for at least he could see the dimensions of her body and her mind perhaps, her intention. Mrs. James was too intelligent. She was too sneaky, too. Taking him to a place like that, like . . . "What they call that place?"

"That's a very important place, Mr. Cumberbatch." Why did she call him this now, after just having called him "brother"? "It was started in 1920. Served the whole community then. And still serving the community now." He did not understand this thing about the community either. Everybody nowadays was calling something a community, or a community project, or community aspirations. "Shit, when I was catching my royal arse in this place, there wasn't anything called a community. Community must be a recent word. What do you know about this community thing?"

"A man should be proud of his community, as a man should be proud of his African heritage."

"Wait a minute, just wait a goddamn minute, Mrs. James!" He even held up his hand to tell her to wait. He swallowed his drink off, and motioned her to do the same. She was taken aback at this. But she finished her beer anyhow. "I am taking you back to Apartment 101."

In the car, Mrs. James tried to make conversation, tried to find out what was the matter, but Boysie remained silent. He emptied his mind completely of Mrs. James, and of the visit to the old and sacred strange-smelling black organization building.

"Would you come in for a minute? I would like to talk to you."

Boysie nodded his head. He drove the car into the underground garage and parked it. As he was walking back to the elevator to take him back to Mrs. James's apartment, he saw a man dash behind a stone pillar. Boysie walked straight to the elevator. As he was about to enter, he glanced behind to see the man dart behind another pillar. He got into the elevator and tried to forget the man and the probable consequences of the man and the underground garage, and Mrs. James and black organizations; and he went instead straight up to his apartment.

The cat greeted him at the door.

"You goddamn cat!"

"Meeeeoooooooowwwww!"

"God!" Boysie felt it would have been better if this animal were not in the apartment with him. It made him lonelier than he really was, being only a cat, when he wanted a person, a human being, anybody to talk to, and help him explain some of the thoughts which were worrying him. He did not understand this "brother" thing that Mrs. James and the young man from the Home Service Association were talking about. He had lived his life, quietly and with a certain amount of success, and nobody had come to him before to talk to him about being a brother. He never had a brother; and there was no chance now that his mother would ever have a son for him to call "brother."

"God!" He had tried to live quietly and he was becoming successful, and in the earlier days when he and Henry roamed the city like two dogs looking for carrion, when he broke his back cleaning out all those offices in the Baptist Church House on St. George Street ("These people could really pull down and put up big-big buildings fast, eh?"), when the only person who ever helped him was Brigitte, his old girlfriend from Germany, herself once a servant for some rich Jews in Forest Hill ("Dots, my own wife, never as much as went down there to lift a blasted broom!"); not even Henry his friend had come to help him lift a garbage pail; he didn't see any black people in those days willing to help him with that work; but he had struggled, and had had to stomach a lot of insults from his wife when she thought he was a failure; and he felt in those days that she had helped him in the way she did in order to make him feel that he really needed help, that he was a chronically unemployed person, fit only to be helped; none of the West Indians with whom he used to play poker and throw dice had ever helped him. "God! I don't even want to be known as a West Indian. Being a Barbadian is good enough for me!" There was nobody with whom he could talk; and the things he had to talk about were simple things, things like "How's work, man? How's your car running these days? Do you like Scotch with water, or straight? What about the wife? She giving you trouble? Again? And how are your women, are they behaving themselves? And the children, are they learning good at school?" Such simple questions which a man needs to have answered by someone, preferably another man, but it could be a woman, too. But a cat! A cat? A goddamn cat? What could he talk to a cat, with a cat?

He went into the bathroom to pee. When he was finished he went into the bedroom. The bedroom was clean and tidy and bare and very much like a coffin. Dots did not even burn incense in the bedroom. And he felt that if he did not know the bedroom as the place where he slept, and slept very badly too, he would never know that a woman also used it. There were no perfume bottles, no lipstick, no shampoo bottles, nothing to tell him that he had a wife. And sometimes, if he were to be honest, he forgot that he did have one: Dots was now almost completely wiped out of the creative part of his life, and he saw her only as an assumed extra. She did not even make him get annoyed with her, she was so dull. He did not even have the anger in him to find another woman, and make her angry, or jealous. Jealousy was not what he felt any action of his would make her feel. She was just there, and he hoped that soon she would fade away. Or leave. "God, she is not even a goddamn pest!"

He looked at himself in the mirror, and he wished that it was a full-length one, so that he could see exactly how he looked. He had never seen himself from head to foot. Not when he was dressed, as he was now, in his three-piece suit. "How do I look to people? I wonder how I look to people?" He had never seen how he looked to people, and he wanted to know exactly how, now. He thought Mrs. James would be the only person to tell him, but she had come with this "brother" thing, and that had upset him. Who could he turn to for this knowledge? The strange woman who came out of the subway, he was hoping, could tell him; but he had grown tired of waiting for her, morning after morning, and he had nothing to go on which would tell him whether she was suitable. He saw her only from a distance, for a very short time, and from a height which had its disadvantages of perspective, perhaps, even, of seeing. "Cat!" He didn't even have the guts to strangle the cat as he had threatened to do. And looking at the cat now, and really seeing Dots, since the cat reminded him so much of Dots, an object in his house, no conversation, just an object with life in it, eating, drinking, sleeping and going to the bathroom; this cat, he could not even kill and get rid of from his thoughts. He had thought of talking to Dots. Many nights when he came home, after an interesting conversation with the Canadian young fellow, or with Mr. MacIntosh, who would have been working late and making money as he bent over the books in his office, or the night when he went to the Coq d'Or Tavern down-town, where many West Indians and black Americans and black Canadians always drank and danced, that night when he looked up for five minutes straight and saw for the first time how beautiful a black man who sang rhythm and blues could be, how the man moved like a tiger, how he twisted his face as if he was feeling the pain which were in the words of the song, how he snapped his fingers when he wanted the music to stop, or to grow louder as it backed his movements and his voice, and this man having the power to give orders, he wanted to share a little of this with his wife. But she was lying on her stomach, as if she was guarding her private parts from a rape during her pre-tended sleep.

He had entered the coffin-bedroom, dark and smelling of Dots's sleeping, a faint odour of the cat in the room, and the blanket wrapped tightly around her secured body, he wanted to be able to rip the covers off, and see, exposed before his eyes (and his eyes had not yet made up their minds how to react to her nakedness), he wanted to rip that blanket, sheet, pink quilted nightgown or housecoat off her body, and see what was beneath. And see what she would say. But he was too tired to do even that. She was like a very unattractive mannequin in his bed, except that there was something about the mannequin, its size and its smallness and its delicacy, which he did not associ-ate with Dots. Dots was a large, silent, sulking, black mannequin who talked only to the goddamn cat. "How do people see me, a man in my position?" He wished there was a full-length mirror in his apartment. He must remem-ber to buy one soon.

He had been spending all this time, all these long hours, working in order to make a better man of himself; he

214

wanted to be independent, to buy a house, to prove to himself that he could start from the bottom and reach the top. And it was all for nothing; it was all as if he had done nothing. His wife was not impressed; and those who were impressed were not the ones he wanted to impress with his success. Certainly he did not wish to impress the people over at the Home Service Association. And he had no intention of ever working in that organization as a volunteer. He could not work in such poverty. And the place was too close to those West Indians wearing the fliers' hats. He wondered what a man in his position could do. They, the West Indians, did not see him as a hero for writing those letters to the editor. Things like writing letters did not impress them so much as making speeches. His photograph was not one of the many hanging on the walls at the Home Service place, or in the Jamaican patty shop; and nobody thought seriously of him. He wished he could see himself as he was, even as others saw him.

He took off his clothes, intending to take a very hot bath. He liked hot baths. Every time he was upset, when he was disappointed in the strange woman, even after she had passed for that morning, when things were not going well for him, he would fill the bathtub and pour in bath oil, and soak and sink in the hot water, and he would feel very protected, as if he was inside something that loved him, something that was conscious of his success, something that protected him. He turned on the hot water tap, as he did always, and when there was enough, he would then run the cold water, because he thought he was better able to regulate the temperature of the bath he wished to take. He would spend up to thirty minutes in these hot baths, with a cigarette in his mouth, trying to empty his mind of everything, as he had been trying to do recently. Sometimes, when he took these hot baths, he wished he could fall asleep for a very long time, and never wake up. Never did he think of drowning himself, but more than once he wished he could just fall asleep, and that when he awoke, he would be somewhere else.

This afternoon, with his time for leaving the apartment already passed two hours ago, he was content to lie in the hot water, with his cigarette in his mouth, one eye closed against the biting smoke. He wished they would invent a cigarette that did not give off this biting smoke, when a a man who wanted to relax in hot water could just dream, and perhaps fade away.

The apartment door opened. It was closed very quietly. Boysie lay still in the hot water, imagining he was already fast asleep. The cat ran out of the bathroom when he smelled the person.

"Cat-catty-catty-cat!"

It was Dots. She put down whatever it was in her hands, and Boysie could hear her going into the closet that kept the coats and the overshoes. Then he heard a chair being pulled out, and he figured that she was in the kitchen. Soon, dishes and cooking utensils were put on tables; the oven door was opened, then the refrigerator door, and suddenly there was only the scratching of the cat. Dots was as quiet as a ghost in her own house. He wondered why she would remain so quiet in her own house. But he had nothing to compare her behaviour this afternoon with that of any previous afternoon. For it was seldom indeed that he was ever home when she came from the hospital. Still, something about how quiet she was bothered him. He wished he was the kind of man, now, to be able to fling the bathroom door open, and shout for her, and rip off her clothes and throw her into the tub. With him. But he was past that: he could not see Dots in the same bathtub of hot water with him. She was, after all, just a living object in his life now. And one did not do such personable, close things with an object, in spite of the fact that it was living. He wanted to be able to call her, and say even such a simple thing as "Dots, I'm still here." But it was past that, too.

He heard her go into the bedroom, and she closed the door behind her. After a brief period she was back outside. In the interim, he had heard the closet in the bedroom open. She's putting on her pink quilted housecoat now. She's already taken off her work dress. And she has taken off her shoes, and is wearing the old beaten-up furlike slippers which Bernice gave her for Christmas, three Christmases ago.

He decides to ignore her, for she is, after all, only an object in his house, and to go back to concentrating on his hot bath. He had become accustomed in that short time to her sound, and there was nothing he could do to make her come alive. For her to come alive, now, would be to destroy all the peace of mind, all the privacy, all the inward feelings he had about himself, and about his life. He would ignore her. He sank further into the water, and put the edge of the cigarette on the surface of the oily water, and then threw it into the plastic wastepaper basket under the sink. He closed his eyes and wished he was somewhere else.

The bathroom door was opened, and for a moment he wished it was not. He kept his eyes closed. When he opened them, Dots was standing at the sink, looking down at him, as if he had come into the bathroom after her. She *was* wearing the pink quilted housecoat, with the furlike slippers, and in her hand was her toothbrush.

217

He wished he was not there in the bathtub. He also wished she would take off her housecoat, and all her clothes, and come into the tub with him. But he knew she would rather die first. And in fact he wished, at that moment, that she was dead. Just dead. Dead dead dead dead . . .

For she had made him dead, had killed the spark in his ambitiousness, had molested all his dreams about becoming successful, and even his pleasure of listening to *floes and floes of angel's hair;* she had already killed him, for she had killed the way he saw himself. A man in his position.

She went out of the bathroom. The cat came in looking for her, and when she was not there, apparently knowing the hostility in the bathroom, the cat went out too. The cat went out as silently as Dots did.

Boysie sank himself further into the water, now becoming warm, and wished he was miles away. He wished he was in his car driving at a very fast speed, on a highway going across the border to Niagara Falls, into America, the States. He had never been to America, and he had promised himself for many years to go there, to see for himself. There were many things he had heard about America; but most important of the things he had heard, and had seen in the newspapers and on television, was the racial problem there. It was in America that he had first heard of this "brother" thing, and Power to the People and Black Is Beautiful. He had also heard about all the rich black people living in America, Sammy Davis, Jr., Harry Belafonte, and another man who owned the biggest magazine in the world, a man named Mr. Ebony; or was the magazine named *Ebony* and the man was the colour of ebony. If Henry was here, he would know for sure. Henry had never been to America, had never crossed the bridge that separated Canada from America, but all of Henry's friends before Boysie were Americans. Americans talked big and smoked cigars and had lots of money, in big fifty-dollar bills, in their pockets. He remembered that about the Americans he knew. The biggest car he had ever seen parked in front of the Paramount Tavern years ago had a New York licence plate on it. And it was driven by a black American, who had a shiny head, and lots of rings on his fingers, and who laughed as if he was the happiest man in the world, and who was very kind. Perhaps, he should go to America, the fountainhead of the "brother" thing, and find out some answers there. Just get into his car, which was not as pretty as the big black American's car, nor as expensive, and just drive, just drive, man, until he came to America, to New York City and to Harlem. All the best singers came from America, and all of the best ones he had ever seen or heard sing were black and were from America: and the way they talked, *Hey baby, that's heavy, heav-vee, ain't that a heavy motherfucker, baby, sheee-yit! like my man here is copping out, can you dig it?* Henry could do it better, because he knew America.

Hey, man, ammo gonna split from my old lady, just split, and slide on down to good ole New York – New York the big apple, my man! and ammo not gonna come back into this jive crib with this bitch, this bitch is killing me, man; like man, this chick I am hitched-to is something else, something else, you dig? Henry was an expert at this. He was still in the tub, with the water turning lukewarm like the tea Dots made and left on the kitchen counter for him, getting cold, with the top layers of the tea warmer than the bottom, just like in the sea back home in the early afternoon: you walked in the sea and your legs were colder than your hips; and once a fellow explained it to him this way: "Man, you don't know no geography? The sun hots up the top and it tekking a more longer time to reach the bottom than at the top, *hence!* Also, because the earth spins around 'pon its axle at a angle of twenty-three degrees, which make the sun do these blasted geographical things with we sea-water even down here in the fucking tropicks! *Understan'?";* but he preferred to compare it to Dots's tea and how she left it until it became cold, like a dead man's blood. And another thing about Dots: he should kick in her arse, just like the Americans would do it. *Man, this cat here, you see the motherfucker, well, this here be my man, my motherfucking man. He is a baaaaad-ass nigger! Always kicking ass. Kicked in his old lady's ass just yesterday, you dig? The bitch been uppity with my ace-boon coon here. And my man can't dig no house-niggers!*

Boysie began to experience strength coming into his body. The water was lukewarm. He was relaxed, and his dreams of America and American black men had given him strength. He felt like an American black man when he stepped out of the tub. Purposely, he left the tub unwashed. He was talking in his mind like an American: let the bitch wash the tub, you dig? But he did not feel so good about this. He was a tidy man. And, moreover, he did not wish to be so brutal with language. To be brutal with his language was worse than being brutal with his fists. He was not that kind of a man, and he felt in some strange way that, to be like those men, he would also be carrying a heavy responsibility, although the word "responsibility" did not come into his mind. He did not call it responsibility. He knew it by another name; but the name was not clear. He knew it better by a phrase, a feeling, that to be bad and black carried with it something which that badness and that blackness would take out of him, and he was too tired for that.

He took down a towel from the ring and dried himself. He still thought he should be man enough to have Dots undress in front of him; but that again carried with it certain responsibilities. He would have to admire her body, silently only; he would get an erection, and that would disclose his motive, even if his motives were just of the flesh (and he did not want to do that), for it was too great an exposure, too great an example of weakness. He could handle Dots and communicate with her better if he did not say a word to her. He felt stronger ignoring her. "A strong man is a silent man." Who said that? Mr. MacIntosh, or the Canadian young fellow, or Mrs. James, for it sounded very much like something to do with their philosophy; it also sounded like philosophy, which was what the Canadian young fellow always talked about.

If Dots was not home now, he could walk out of this bathroom, naked as a bird, and play his favourite record, which at this time was Miles Davis's *Milestones;* and he could even dance in the way he had seen some Americans dancing once at the Coq d'Or, and he could imagine that he was a great singer, and sing, or a great dancer, and dance, or something great, and be great. He could not even seduce the feeling to want to dance when Dots was around. He had built up a completely total existence in her absence, and she knew nothing about it. And this was not the time to expose himself to her.

Get out, get out, get out, a voice was telling him. He did not know whether the message meant get out of the apartment, from this seventh-floor boredom, or get out of the bathroom, or even get out of the country. But he knew he had to get out. It was dead inside the apartment. Here he was, a man in his position, and with a woman, a wife, in the apartment for almost fifteen minutes now, and this woman was so secure that she didn't feel she had to say one word to him, and had, in fact, not even opened her mouth to tell him, "You dog!" or "You cat!" Dots was now only a sound in his life. Perhaps, then, the message his brain was telling him was important.

Something on the floor of the bathroom, beside the toilet bowl, attracted his attention. He noticed it because Dots was a tidy woman: nothing was ever left on the floor in the entire apartment. He picked it up. Perhaps it had fallen from his own pockets. It was a piece of newspaper, folded into four. He carried newspaper clippings of his letters to the editor with him, just in case he had to show someone. He picked up this piece of clipping and put it into the pocket of his bathrobe. He would not have been able to look at this piece of paper once before, but now with his new strength he opened it expecting something, something which was unknown (it was this fear of things unknown, things that did not belong to him, things such as the letters he expected to find in his wife's drawers. He opened the folded newspaper clipping and read: *If the TTC is going to issue one dollar family fun passes, why not lower the fare for people who have to work on Sundays and holidays, especially nurses . . .*

Dots was sitting in the living room reading the newspaper. She was reading the Today's Child column. Boysie glanced over her head, and saw her looking at the photograph of a black child who was up for adoption. He moved away immediately, and wondered if his wife was going really mad. He thought of the children asleep in the upstairs rooms at the Home Service place, and he remembered the dirty blankets and the green army camping cots.

He wanted to tell her about the children he had seen sleeping there, but he felt the inertia again in his body, battling with the new-found energy and strength which he had found inside the warm bathtub of water. He wanted to go back into the bathroom and draw another hot bath, and he wanted to be able to do this immediately, without moving from this spot behind Dots, without changing his position. He wanted it just to happen. And he knew it could not happen, that he could not make it happen in the same way that he knew that he could not make his mouth open by itself and talk to his wife. He wondered if he was dying too; or if he was already dead, as she was. So he moved away and dressed for work.

Part Three:

The bigger light

B OYSIE SAT WAITING in his pyjamas and plaid house-coat for the strange woman to emerge from the subway station. He sat with the newspaper open at the stock market pages, resting on his lap, as the cat had become accustomed to resting there. He was just waiting, and not wanting her to appear, for that would cause him to have to get up and do something else. He had never before waited for her in his pyjamas. He wondered why this morning, at the same time as other mornings, he was still in pyjamas. There were other strange things he had begun to do. There was nothing strange in them when he first did them, but when he thought of them, and reflected on this previous behaviour, on the things he liked doing, on the things he liked listening to, he saw them as strange.

He was now a man of quite substantial means, a man who had reached what in Canada would be regarded as a grade four education: but one could not really make such a rough comparison between his knowledge of language in Barbados and that in Canada; and one surely could not conclude that because he had dropped out of school back there in Standard Three, when simple arithmetic was just included in the curriculum, that he was on the same educational level as a Canadian who had reached only grade four. One could not make those assumptions. For he was a man of some substance, respectable in his apartment building, well known by the most important stockbroker in the whole of Toronto, Mr. MacIntosh, one of his cleaning clientele; his bank manager called him often to ask him how he was getting along in his business, and whether he could do anything for him, "May I interest you in a demand loan, Mr. Cumberbatch?"; everybody who knew him, who met him coming and going, addressed him as Mr. Cumberbatch (even Mrs. James, whom he had stopped seeing on the terms that regulated their abortive relationship; she, too, started calling him Mr. Cumberbatch, as she had done when first he appeared at her door, Apartment 101, to give her the bag of pork chops and other pork products, because he was in those days obsessed by diets, like everybody in Toronto), and said behind his back, "A man in his position . . ."

He had everything he wanted in life in this country. He was solvent, his business showed a profit, his clothes were new and expensive, and he had the car of his dreams. He had recently installed a new stereo tape recorder, and he had the technician put in four speakers. The car was a small explosion of noise. When he wanted to he could listen to two speakers, or he could listen to all four. He had AM and FM and he had thought of installing a telephone, but he did not like telephones too much; in fact, he seldom answered the telephone in his apartment. But it pleased him very much that he could have these things installed in his car without thinking of the cost. He thought of installing a bar, and a television set (as he has seen once in a Cadillac parked in front of the Coq d'Or Tavern on Yonge Street, with New York licence plates), but he felt that that was too much show. Besides, he never allowed anybody to go near his car, and he never drove anybody in it. Mrs. James and her children were the only ones whom he could remember as having driven in the car. Yes, and Lew! But that was a short trip around the block to buy cigarettes and Chinese food. Boysie had not told Dots yet that he owned a car. It was something which he did not consider to be disloyalty; it was not that he did not love her, it was not that he did not trust her, that he was not aware of the principle of sharing in marriage; but he felt, quite bluntly, that it was none of her business. He could see himself having to tell her if he was still struggling, if she was still subsidizing him. In that case he would have to tell her, because he could see then that he owed it to her pride and to her feeling of superiority over him that he should be grateful, and tell her, and perhaps take her for a drive. His car was his car. To buy it she did not have to wear her nylons a day longer than normal; and she did not have to eat five months' dinners of hamburger meat, nor walk to work to the hospital. Life with her, and for her, went on normally, so his buying the new car did not touch her sense of material security.

"It is none of her fucking business," he said to the cat and to the newspaper. He was deeper in the habit of talking to himself, simply because he could not really talk to a cat. There was never anybody in the apartment with him when he wanted to talk, and he was not the kind of man to keep topics of conversation, things for discussion, on his mind, waiting for his wife to come home and join him in them. Dots was not that kind of a woman. She was leading her own life at the hospital, and in the telephone conversations, nightly, with her friend Bernice. And Boysie was glad that he at least had the sense to see that she had no intention of changing, so that he would come home (on those few nights when she was not in bed, with the cat asleep between her sprawled-out legs, both of them snoring), and she would make him a cup of coffee or hot chocolate, and say, "Well, darling, how did it go tonight? You must be tired as a dog. Let me rub you down." No, Dots was not that kind of a woman. And although he had hoped that she would turn out to be a woman of that thoughtful disposition, he eventually gave up hoping. Too much water was now under the bridge, and the bridge itself was crumbling. Henry had explained it to him once ("When a man meet a woman in the wrong kind of circumstance, frinstance, if the woman is the one bringing in the fucking bacon, and even if the man should become a millionaire, that woman, because she is a fucking woman, that woman will always say that she make that man into the millionaire he is today. That without her, he couldn't be a kiss-me-arse millionaire. And in the ten or fifteen years, that woman who might be working as a domestic for something like two hundred dollars a rass-hole month would argue strong-strong that without her money supporting that man, he couldn't be no fucking millionaire at all! Now, tell me, how in the name o' Jesus Christ, could you add-up two hundred dollars a month, multiply by twelve, and then by ten, or even fifteen, and come out with a fucking millionaire?"), and Boysie had refused to see it in his wife, because in those days he had had to love her, not in the way a lover loves a lover, not in that way, but with more feeling of obligation. He loved her in the same way that a thirsty man loves the hand that offers a glass of iced water.

Boysie had everything. But he was not happy. Perhaps, he sometimes told himself, as he sat on these mornings, listening to his music (he was back on "Both Sides Now"), and reading his newspaper, and waiting for the woman to appear, he had spent too much time making money. He was not a millionaire, certainly not; but he was well off. Money in the bank, so much that he never counted or checked his bank balance in his savings account; and his personal chequing account which was for bills and expenses in his home and his business was never overdrawn. He bought Canada Savings Bonds every month, and he had bought four houses within the space of four or five months; and these were now rented out. He never visited the houses, he never saw the tenants; his lawyer did all that for him.

He had been spending much time recently with his car: driving it to the same garage with which he had been dealing for years, having the mechanic check it over, tune it up, and look at the tires. He kept it always full of gas. It was washed and waxed every two days, although he was going nowhere, to no wedding, on no trip, never taking anybody anywhere in it (Dots trudged through the snow and blustery winds, and he kept the car in the underground garage); but sometimes he would get nightmares about the car, and regardless of the hour, he would get up quietly, put on his winter coat, or his raincoat, or remain in his housecoat (he had started sleeping in his housecoat, because there was no reason to be more naked than that in a bed with a woman who did not need the feel of his body beside her) and with torchlight in hand would check on his car. Once or twice, he heard some activity in the underground garage at that late hour, but he was never inquisitive. And all the newspaper reports and other apartment gossip about rapings and beatings and thefts in the garage never bothered him. He was not interested. He had closed his mind a long time ago against these things. He had closed his mind against the sleeping children in the Home Service Association place; he had closed his mind against the reports of young West Indians stealing purses from old women in the subway stations; he had refused to get involved; he had refused to listen to Mrs. James pleading with him to devote some of his free time in the morning on community work in the black community.

"I didn't know we had one o' them!"

"You are always joking, Mr. Cumberbatch."

"No, really. In truth!"

"Mr. Cumberbatch, where you been all these years you living in this place?"

"I have been in my apartment."

"Oh, go 'long!"

West Indians were coming and going; some of them were getting into trouble with the police, most of them were working, making money, making progress, gambling, running back to the Caribbean on holidays, some of them three times a year, and life was going on. He had thought of going back to Barbados once, for a vacation, but that idea soon went from his head. He had not even considered the reason for not wanting to return to Barbados. He began, however, to hate Barbados; not really hate it as he was beginning to hate Dots, not even for the same reasons. But he hated it, because you could say that he did not like it. And that is how he put it to anyone who asked him, "Why, a man in your position, with all the money you have, remembering that in Barbados, a Canadian dollar is worth two o' we-own, why you don't go back there and put up some beach houses and make some easy money offa the tourists?" And Boysie would just look the person in the eye without even changing the expression in his own eyes. But he knew that he was never going back. Not even to be buried in the warm soil of the land that had brought him forth. He did not consider it in these terms;

he did not think in terms of land and birth, and culture and warm soil. He knew nothing about soil. He was born in Barbados because he was not born in Canada. He was in Canada now. He had come here, he had suffered, and he had taken his licks, he had given a few (recently, to his wife), and he was content to spend the rest of his life here. He had applied for Canadian citizenship, at first as insurance against having to return to Barbados, or to go someplace else, and knowing that he could always return here in case things there got rough. But when he got it, when he touched the flimsy book with the Canadian coat of arms on it, he felt strong as he usually did when he got into the bathtub with the water hot, when he was in the apartment alone, and he could walk out naked, right through his apartment, and listen to his music without distraction. When he received his Canadian passport with the citizenship that went along with it, he felt this kind of strength.

All these things he had done without a plan. But as he would sit down on these early mornings, thinking. ("What you are really doing, Mr. Cumberbatch," the Canadian young fellow said, when Boysie, most uncharacteristically, told the young man what he sometimes did, "is not really thinking. Thinking is not sufficiently philosophical for what you are going through. You are meditating, Mr. Cumberbatch, and meditating is the most spiritual enterprise a man can get involved in, especially in a country as culturally barren as this one.") Boysie liked the idea about meditating. But he did not like the remarks about Canada being a barren country. Not *his* country. Nobody should say these things about his country. And he would have told the Canadian young fellow just as much, but his conservatism warned him to permit the young fellow to express his views without molestation.

Boysie's conservatism was being shown in other ways, more significant ways these days: his conservatism and the feeling of influence and ungrounded arrogance that went along with it. He had lived through many radicalisms: first Henry, then Dots, then Bernice and her young man ("A woman her blasted age should be looking for God, not man!"), the thousands of West Indians he was seeing on the streets everywhere in Toronto, walking around the place with all kinds of women on their arms, and not even ashamed or embarrassed to be seen in such exposure; and those at the airport, whenever he dropped in there to have his Scotch and watch the planes taking off for places around the world; yes, he had grown accustomed to radicalism, and it had not bothered him. He could stomach it, because he was a man "in his position."

His meditations, or his thinking sessions with himself, were not fitting into any kind of pattern or into any plan, at least not when he first thought out certain things he should do. The buying of the four houses was one plan. It was an investment plan. What else could he do with his money? He didn't have any children. He was still a young man. He was living well: buying new suits and shoes ("I won't be seen dead wearing those boots you want me to buy, young man. Shoes were made for gentlemen. Boots for old women and queers." The young man, who was very fastidious and very polite, lost a little colour and placed the five pairs of boots back into their boxes. Boysie bought the three pairs of shoes he had seen in the window, as he passed), drinking the best of Scotch, and wines with his dinner, which was usually alone, late at night, early in the morning, except on the weekends, when he had Bernice and her young man over to share his boredom. But if he could see the future when it began in the present, he would have known that his thinking sessions about life, about his life and about his wife's life, were bound to devolve into some plan. And the observer, Dots, and in some cases Bernice, would have sworn that he had been involved in devices. Devices. He had devised his plans to some peculiar conclusion.

He wondered how, sitting in his pyjamas, he had been spending all these months waiting to see a woman he had never seen close up. He wondered if he was not going mad, wasting his time in this diversion. And it was really a diversion. He hadn't known of any other man who sat every morning to see a woman pass. Now if the man had met the woman in a bar one night, and even if she had refused him, even if she had snubbed him, then he could understand himself waiting to see what colour of disposition her walk, the day after, would have: but this sitting all this time waiting for a woman . . . Perhaps the Canadian young fellow could understand this, and find some explanation in terms of philosophy! Henry was a man who could give a reason for this kind of behaviour too. Since it was not the kind of thinking about the strange woman that aroused his passion for her, since he was not in love with her, since he did not want to go to bed with her, he should have been able to talk about it to his wife. But would his wife understand? He felt she would not. But he had not asked her. It was his assumption, based on his knowledge of her, and her knowledge of the world, which told him that Dots would find something in the situation to laugh at, and then she would call Bernice on the telephone and laugh some more about it, and some more about "this blasted man going crazy, you hear me, gal. Going crazy as anything." No, Dots was not the person to entrust this sensitive thing to: and that was it, it was his sensitiveness, and the sensitiveness of the situation, and the entire sensitive embryo in which he found himself living.

Last night at the Coq d'Or he had seen another black American singer on the stage. "One thing about these black Americans, they really have style! Man, you should have seen that man up there, singing and carrying on, and looking so good that I wished I was a singer. I actually sat down there, with my drink in front of me, the same Scotch that I bought when I got there at ten, and I am a man who drinks four or five Scotches whenever I drop by there. They know what I drink, but sitting down there looking at that man sing that song, "A Rainy Day in Georgia," it's raining all the time, it's raining all the time. And then I saw what I was looking for all the time, it's raining all the time. He was free up there, he was so free that he looked like if the song was killing him, as if the song had him in chains, he was so pretty in the singing of it. But he was free, because it was a rainy day in Georgia, and a rainy day in Georgia is just like a rainy day in Barbados: you run out in the rain, bare-naked as you was born, and you open your mouth wide-wide and drink in the warm rain-water from outta the skies, and the barrel beside your house, under the drain, catches that same rainwater, and there is nothing better tasting than rainwater." Freedom the man had sung about, not the rains in Georgia. It was that freedom that Boysie found himself lacking all these years. This morning was the first time he had sat down in his own apartment, at this hour, dressed in pyjamas. Why hadn't he thought of doing that before? It was a good feeling. "A Rainy Day in Georgia," a black American singer, rainwater, and pyjamas were just like a hot bath in his bathtub.

My Dear Dots, I want to talk to you. Sometime. Your husband. He had written this letter to his wife some few weeks ago, he couldn't remember how many weeks; and he had put it on the kitchen counter where she was sure to see it as she came in to make her cup of coffee, and bring up "some o' this gas outta my stomach." But the letter had been removed. Could the cat have mistaken the name on it? He did not receive a reply from Dots whether in words or in attitude. And Dots never wrote letters to anyone.. He remembered the words he had written at work on his notepad which was attached to his wallet. He had wanted to tell her what he wanted to tell her about, but that would have brought about a conclusion, and he did not like conclusions, particularly when he was not certain that he controlled the conclusions. To have told her in that letter what he wanted her to know, that he was going away (not leaving her, for no one can leave Dots, Dots is a mere object that is living everywhere, and she would follow you to the ends of the earth, and molest your memory when you had nothing to think about, but the past of your boredom and its history and its growth), that he had bought a new car, that he had bought four houses, and had put them in her name; that he had made a will and had put all his money in her name (he did not hesitate to do this, he did not wonder whether she would outlive him, for he was certain that something in her, something in the way she saved energy by not making conversation, by not exerting herself in sex, by not doing things which one normally expected a woman to do, he was certain that he would die before her; not that she would kill him, no, Dots was not so cruel as that, even in spite of what he had been thinking about her. It was simply that he had resigned himself to her eventual widowhood, and himself to be replaced by someone else, and to be some place else, just before she inherited all his money), to make certain that her memory of him would not be discussed harshly between herself and Bernice. *"My Dear Dots, I want to talk to you. Sometime."* He thought of the letter. Should he have written, "I want to talk to you sometime"? And did the "sometime" standing alone frighten her? Or had she just disregarded it? But it was signed "Your husband." And Boysie knew Dots was a very faithful woman to him; the word "husband" would bring out her morality. She had never told him that she was not faithful to him; she had not told him that she had allowed another man to lift the dress-hem of her clothes in an act of love or even hate; she had not even told him, "I love you, Boysie." Dots never was so emotional towards him. But he knew that she loved him. A woman who behaved like Dots had to love him. And he felt she was faithful, and a faithful woman deserves something. What he had to give her he did not think she could appreciate; indeed, he did not know if he had anything to give her, except money. And he thought of the money because of the amount of problems it had caused them, early in their marriage, and the deep hurt it had caused him when she was the breadwinner. He wanted to tell her that he was tired, that he was dying, that he was fed up, that his life with her was like sleeping in a coffin, which their bedroom had become. He wanted to tell her all these things. And more especially, he wanted to take her back to that afternoon when she came unexpectedly early and found him in the bathtub naked, in the condition which would have demanded not much effort on his part, or on her part, had she been willing, when he wanted to rip the housecoat off her body and drag her into the hot water with him, not to drown her, but to drown her, for that last time, into an everlasting experience of love. But he could not tell her then, and it was no easier for him to report about that telling which was aborted by the noise and her sound and her presence. She was killing him, and he was tired waiting.

The strange woman comes out of the subway. She is wearing different clothes this morning. It must be the weather. Or it must be the time. In all this thinking session he has been in this chair only ten minutes. How time travels, from here to there, taking up space and places and dreams and life and death . . . but the woman wears this morning a yellow beret that flops down to the nape of her neck. Her winter coat, still brown, is open, *and he sees for the first time,* he sees for the first time the strength in her body, and in the colour of her dress. It is mauve. Her legs he can see now too, for the dress is short, although the coat is reaching the calves, or is it the knees? And there is the white shopping bag in her hand. It is flat, not bulging, so she must be carrying magazines or children's books . . . could she be a mother, or a teacher, or a nurse, or a baby-sitter . . . in this white bag. Her winter boots are the same colour as the coat. She is not wearing her sunglasses against the snow this morning. And he has a fair picture of her age. She is about thirty-five, but something about the arrangement of skin near the swallow-pipe tells him that she is probably older, or perhaps . . . she might be a woman who used once to be much fatter. She shows some emotion this morning. She wears the coat opened, and as if she knows that there is someone looking for her, someone watching her, someone who waits for her, she leaves it open until she is about to pass out of his sight, out of the reach of the desire in his sight (this morning is the first time he feels this way about her), and then she buttons up the coat, and disappears. He keeps this picture of her in his mind. It is a picture of a woman. He does not know what will become of her, but he knows that he has seen a change in her, and if she can change, then certainly he can change.

There was something about this morning which dis-turbed him. There was something in the way the woman walked, the emotion she showed, although he could not be sure it was emotion, since he was not sure she was aware of him, so it could not then be her emotion for him; but certainly he had shown emotion for her, and he had never done that before. It was not this emotion which both-ered him. But it was something else. He sat back down in the chair, and he tried to think. He tried to remember everything that went through his mind during his think-ing session; he travelled all over that space of mind and land, remembered the letter he had written to his wife and which she had not yet answered, he remembered the feel-ings he had when he listened to the black American sing-ing "A Rainy Day in Georgia" . . . that was something! He had called the song by the wrong name. It was not a rainy "day," it was a rainy "night," "A Rainy Night in Georgia." So he had been wrong in his comparison, be-cause nobody walked about on a rainy night in Barbados. The song was not fit, not suitable, the song could not be tied to his past and to his experience. He wondered whether he was wrong in seeing freedom in the singing and in the song as the black American sang it.

There is a great difference between a rainy day and a rainy night: between night and day. He had been wrong in his conclusions. That was why he could not afford to have said more in the letter to Dots without being there

240

to see her reaction when she read it, because she was capable of making conclusions, and he hated conclusions.

Was that why he had sat morning after morning waiting for the woman, and when she came he felt as if she had never come, because for her to have come, that would have meant passage from one time to another, and there was bound to be a conclusion somewhere: is that what a conclusion was; or was he just thinking stupidness? He had thought the wrong conclusion about his emotions for the black American singer; what else in his long life in this country had he seen and reacted to in the wrong way, bringing to a conclusion an incorrect beginning? The Canadian young fellow had a term for that. Boysie tried to remember it. There were so many things he had to try to remember these days. "Yes, I remember. The Canadian young fellow calls that a 'thesis.' Or did he say a 'diagnosis'? 'Diagnosis' is Dots's word, although she never used it with me."

There were things about his wife that he did not know at first, but which he hit upon by mistake; and the mistake would be made when he came home and found the radio in the bedroom still playing. He found out that his wife was a lonely woman. And she had never told him she was a lonely woman. He should have known. But he was not the kind of man to ask a woman, not to mention his wife, "Are you a lonely woman?" And she was not the kind of woman who talked, except it was to give a mild order (he had never given anybody an order in his life), or to report something, like, "Close the living room door, Boysie, I am sleeping. Dog tired, boy. This hospital work is killing me. And I am not getting no younger every day!" Or she would say, "I heard from Agaffa yesterday. She called." And she never told him what Agatha said when she called. Dots said nothing more than that. She was merely noise and sound and a presence.

But he came home one night and found the radio playing on a popular station, CHIN, which played sentimental music, music for lovers whose lovers are not present, music for persons whose hearts, broken by some circumstance or misunderstanding, should not be listening to that kind of music. He had known this feeling of loneliness. He had listened to *Both Sides Now*, and he had listened to Mendelssohn. Both had taught him loneliness. When he listened to calypsoes, he was merry during the playing of the tunes, he was alert to the words in the songs, but his mind never functioned, for the music was a drug, to be listened to more easily by another drug, liquor, and accompanied by vigorous dancing and swinging of the backside and by sex.

He had turned off the radio that night, late that night and early morning all wrapped into one feeling of loneliness, and he had remained awake, listening to her snoring, and to the cat moving from between her legs, in sleep, and onto the floor. The cat never slept between *his* legs. ("I wonder why? You goddamn cat!") He wanted to be able, through the quality of the relationship they should have had all these years, to have awakened her, and say to her, "Dots? Dots?" gently, with a soft voice, not requiring an answer; and to have her look up at him with those big bloodshot sleepy eyes, and say to him, "Boy, why you don't come to bed, nuh?" But he could not do it. He wondered if, had he the inclination to kill her, if he would stand above her bed, and wait so long? But that was a serious and stupid thought. He would never kill Dots.

242

He was worried about something this morning: something which had appeared to him either when the woman appeared, and which he did not see, or something in the journey of his daydreaming. He had miscalculated something in his long life, it could have been a mistake way back in Barbados (although he doubted that, for back there life did not take on the dramatic seriousness it was forced to have, in this country, as a factor of existence); or it could have been here in this country. He would have to take the long journey back, step by step, experience by experience, friend by friend (and some friends were already changed into enemies), he would have to look very closely at his relationship with Dots his wife, and see whether there was one iota which he had looked at and had not seen.

He knew he had to do this much; and he knew it because he had seen something new this morning, when the strange woman appeared with the small ruffle in her otherwise prim and unchanging appearance.

Janey, 4, is a cheerful invalid. Janey was lying flat on her back with both legs in traction when this picture was taken. They both examined the picture carefully and nodded their heads. Janey was indeed a beautiful little girl. *The position didn't affect her cheerful disposition and certainly didn't dim her sweet, warm smile.* "There aren't many people and very few women living today who would understand why you want to have a child like this, for adoption, in your home. They aren't many, child. Even me, as close as I is to you, had a hell of a time trying to understand what was in your blasted head when you showed me this clipping with Janey months ago. A lot of

243

time pass since then. And in all that time, I still don't know what to say." *But then Janey is used to splints and casts and bandages because she's had a lot of them.*

"Bernice, gal, people get used to everything. Anything at all. I know it would be something different if I had *born* a child like Janey outta my womb. That would have make it easier. But I still can't tell. What really worrying me is why I should be in love so much with this little darling girl. Probably, in a funny-funny way, she resembles me. She had a lot to bear and I had a lot to bear. The woman who borned this child should be ashamed of herself for giving it away. Such a beautiful darling!" *This darling was born with a long-name condition called osteogenesis imperfecta, known to laymen as brittle bones.* "Osteogennississ."

"Yeah, osteogennississ. Is that a thing that does come down from father and mother to son and daughter, though? Do you think that it is something in what people call the genes? Osteogennississ, Dots. That's a heavy burden for a four-year child to bear all by herself."

Dots felt the tears coming down her cheeks. "All by herself, Bernice. All by herself. A woman all by herself. Osteogennississ." *She has had a lot of breaks and will have more. The disease appears to have affected her most in the pelvic and leg area.*

"That means you will have to be careful when you are bathing her, and changing her, because she have osteogennississ, remember that." *She has had a lot of breaks and will have more.* "But that is a terrible break to have in life, though, you don't think so? Sitting down here with you, this evening, and looking at this child's face, I could see Lew, Llewellyn, that bitch. You know he came to me again last night asking me to lend him three hundred dollars to buy more books. More books? Asking me. A woman who haven't finished elementary school back in Barbados. And I had to think about that all night. He is a lawyer-student. I am a domestic. He is asking *me*. For three hundred dollars! Well, do I look to you like one o' them Canadian women who goes down to Barbados at the Holiday Inn place and Paradise Beach Club and let all them young mens screw them, and then turn around and give the men twenty-five dollars, Canadian currency? If I add-up twenty-five, if I add-up the twenty-fives that are in three hundred dollars, don't you see that Llewellyn would have to give me a damn lotta screws before he could pay off that debt? Don't laugh, child!" *She has had a lot of breaks and will have more. The disease appears to have affected her most in the pelvic and leg area.* "That means that she can't have thrildrens then, isn't it, Dots? The pelvic area? I am just like her, and I ain' got no osteogennississ. But osteogennississ on top o' that, in the pelvic area?"

Dots nodded her head, and some of her tears dropped on her dress. Bernice wiped them away. "It must be this pelvic-thing that make me like this child so! You see, it could happen to you before you born, then. And it could happen to you even when you born and think you are a big-big woman. Boysie never forgive me for my pelvic-thing. I don't think I am suffering from this osteogennississ, but one is as bad as the other." *Her legs are bowed and she will probably require surgery later on to have rods inserted in her legs.*

"But that would be painful, though. Won't that be painful for such a little child?"

The cat jumped from Bernice to Dots.

"I have seen up there at that hospital, the doctors in this country perform miracles. Doctors in this place are not like them hacks back home, some o' them, the minute they graddiate they done studying-up on the new practices and thing. We got some good doctors back there. But up here, they are miracle-workers with a knife! All kinds o' surgeries. But I am worried about this osteogennississ, and if it will break even more when they start operating on the rods. What you think?"

"You mean about the operation?"

"No. 'Bout Lew and the money he axed you for. Give him the money, Bernice. Give him. Give it to him. It is only money. You are in a position to demand much more in life. Give him. It would make him grateful. That is one thing I forget to make Boysie feel about me. Boysie isn't grateful for one blast that I do for him, because Boysie is independent. A woman can't live good with a man that is too independent. And to-besides, you don't have one blasted thing to lose, except . . . you know what." *Janey is luckier than some children,* ("You see, you ain't the worst-off woman in Toronto. They is some more worse-off than you can imagine.") *is luckier than some children with this condition because her arms, back and neck are healthy, and though at this time she is unable to use her legs, they are not seriously malformed.* "Answer me something, Bernice."

"I don't think I am woman-enough to be handing-out my hard-earned money to any man. In a few more months, that bitch will get fed-up with me, and I will need some more money to attract a new man, because no established man will . . ."

"Not that. I am not talking 'bout that. I axed you if you could tell, from the first time I bring-up this question to you concerning Little Janey, if you ever thought I wouldda do the same thing if Janey was a . . ."

246

"The same thing just ran through my mind, although I was answering your question as if it was 'bout Llewellyn and the money. I was thinking just-now to myself in those very-same terms: *because no established man, unless he was some elderly Canadian man, or an Eyetalian, or a German-man, would turn his head twice to notice an old whore like me, not at my age. But I would prefer a Wessindian man. Any day!* This is the only place in the whole whirl, where a woman have to really find a man. Back where we come from, a man finds a woman. Not here though. The shoe's on the other foot."

"You could break out, though."

"With what? You mean if I fool-round with a Canadian . . . oh! You know something, I was reading about that very-same thing only the other day in the papers. The numbers o' young woman in this blasted place who walking-'bout with VD and gonn . . ."

"VD? What the arse are you thinking?"

"You didn't just tell me I could break out?"

"I did."

"Well?"

"Well, *shite!*"

"I don't understand you at all, at all."

"You're a stupid bitch!"

"Oh my God, Dots, not that, don't say that."

"You are a stupid-arse bitch, then, Bernice! Stupid-stupid-stupid-stupid!"

"Well you really want to make me cry now . . . look how you making me cry."

"A woman in your position, forty-nine turning into fifty, mini-menopause licking-in your arse, and you tell me you won't give a young man three hundred dollars to keep him inside your pants? You have me vex-vex-vex as hell now. Here I am, sitting down with you, reading all this history about my child, about Little Jane, and you bugging me over three hundred blasted dollars, when only yesterday you your-very-self told me, and showed me your bank book with *thirteen thousand* dollars inside it! What the hell do you intend to do with all that money, after you pass fifty-one? Buy sperms with it? Eh? Buy a plastic banana? Eh? Buy a forty-year-old man? Eh? Look woman, read this blasted thing about my child, do! Come, read it, I want to hear everything about Little Jane . . ." *Jane is luckier than some children* . . . "Yuh read that already, Bernice!" *Just turned four, Janey is a tiny child with big blue eyes, blonde hair and fair skin.*

"Do you understand my question, now, gal?"

"What question, Dots?"

"About breaking out."

"Breaking out? What breaking out?"

"No young Wessindian man, going through to be a lawyer, is going to come smelling round you when you turn fifty-one, if you aren't that already. 'Cause you don't tell nobody your right age, you are frighten for your blasted age, because you lived your young-days so bad and so little that your old-days now taking a turn in your backside. Understann me? Now. That is what I mean by breaking out. Back home we does call it *brekking out*, meaning to leave something that you should be doing and doing something that you shouldn' be doing, like the Canadian man you talked about your-very-self. Breaking out, Bernice. Good Jesus Christ, breaking out. Breaking out."

"Do you want me to read on? I don't think I could live that way."

"Do you think that if this piece o' paper had say *with*

brown big eyes, knotty hair and Negro skin, that I . . ."

"Oh my God, Dots, don't bring up that now!"

"It has to be brought up."

"Not now, though."

"Read-on, then."

Though her physical development is naturally below average, she is fine emotionally and mentally — bright, alert, and happy, gentle, appealing, and loving. Janey is shy with strangers, but talkative, outgoing and humourous with people she knows. She is full of questions and loves the company of her foster sisters, just visiting or watching everything they do. She enjoys games and likes TV. Already she knows the alphabet which she sings. Sensitive Janey needs no more discipline than the occasional "no". She is upset by cross words or loud voices.

"I'll have to tell Boysie don't play the record player so loud, if the day ever comes."

Janey has been attending a clinic in Chicago where the treatment is free but not the transportation. Similar treatment is also available in Ontario.

"I have to tell . . ."

Dear Little Janey needs warm, loving parents.

"Dots, what do you think of this? Suppose I did give Lew the money, how would I know? . . . Oh, she's sleeping, poor girl. With all this thinking 'bout this girl, Janey, no wonder she can't keep her eyes open. What a woman this woman is! I know Dots will make a loving parent for this child, for there is so few people in the world today who have love in their hearts for anything, except money. It must be this country that makes a person fall in love with money more quicker than with a person. I am becoming as money-conscious as the biggest Canadian-born

Canadian! And to think. This damn little child with so much wrong with her, and she is smiling as sweet as ever in this picture. And look at me! Dots is right. It takes a real person, a real woman, to do a thing like what she is doing. Even to spend a hour over this child, even to read the story of this child. This whole case remind me o' Estelle and her little boy, Mbelolo. Mbelolo is growing so fast, that soon I could take him dancing with me, heh-heh-heh! And I worry myself over some blasted Wessindian lawyer-man, who when he get that piece o 'paper in his hand, when he graddiate, you think I will ever see him again? You think so, Little Janey? What would he be needing me for, when he could get a young woman to laugh-up and smile-up in his face, and take to his parties, buy a home for, buy flowers for, buy Valentine cards for, take to the movies with, here there and everywhere. All these is things a man never did for me in all the years I been living in this country, and Lew that bastard never even once asked me to a dogfight, and when he *does* ask me, he comes telling me some shite 'bout going *Dutch!* Dutch? Dutch, shite! I is a Barbadian! Or else I paying for the shot. I, Bernice, a old bitch like me, still having to pay a man to take me out? I don't need no man. I need a child who will be waiting for me when I come home, old and haggard from brekking my behind in somebody kitchen . . ." She looked at Dots and wished she was not sleeping. "Dots? Dots, I feel like, I feel as if I have the strength to do the things I see you about to do, if only I was a more younger woman, if only I was living in my own house, and not in a apartment, I would adopt somebody . . . if I didn't have to look after Mbelolo and look out for Estelle, or if I was back in Barbados . . ." *Dear Little Janey needs warm, loving parents who have the re-*

*sources — emotional, physical and financial — to cope
with her condition and to help her cope with it when she
gets older. She loves other children so there should be
brothers and sisters in her adopting family* . . . "Wait, I
didn't know this! I wonder if Dots know this. Dots, Dots!
Wake up! Dots you listening? I want to go in with you in
adopting this little girl. I can now see what you mean."

"We can't adopt her, Bernice."

"How you mean we can't adopt her?"

"Not in a mixed family."

"My God!"

"That is why I read this newspaper clipping every night
before I go to bed, and I pray every night for this child,
that nobody . . ."

"My God, Dots!"

"I tried, Bernice. I tried. I tried and tried. But not in a
mixed family." *Since much of her playtime, of necessity,
will be at home, her family must want to spend a lot of
time with her. To inquire about adopting Janey, please
write to Helen Allen, Today's Child, Box 888, Station K,
Toronto M4P 2H2.*

"But why are you doing this? I mean a man in your
position, I didn't even know black people in this country
had so much money in cash! and you giving all to your
wife? I have to explain to you, I have to advise you as
your lawyer, although I am not legally a lawyer yet, but
you understand that this is practice, and practice makes
perfect . . . anyhow I do the papers for you, I did the papers for you, and all you have to do now is sign them, so
if you would look down here, and sign just by that seal-
thing, yes, just there! you sure is a funny man, if you don't
mind me saying so. Christ! I wish I had half the money

251

you have, half, just half. And you know what I would do with half o' this blasted money you now signing-over to your wife? a woman who you don't even love, a woman who you don't know if she have, if she has another man . . ."

"Watch your fucking mouth, young boy!"

". . . anyhow, it is your fucking money, it is your bread, as the Americans say, and in this respect, and I respect the Americans a lot, but I must advise you that I think that as your counsel, even if I am not a qualified barrister and solicitor yet, even although I am not yet qualified to take this brief under the jurisdiction, anyhow, man . . . Lissen to me, man. For you to take all these Canadian Savings Bonds, three thousand dollars in bonds at how-much per cent, and for how-many years? . . . now this works out to, ahhmmmmm, Jesus-Jesus! Boysie, in my opinion . . ."

"You are a fucking idiot, Lew. You were born an idiot, and you will die a bigger idiot! It is my money, man. It is only money, anyhow, Lew, and a man in *your* position, with all the learning you have, and I envy you for that, with all that education, you are still a fucking idiot, *in my goddamn books*. This is my money. I am paying you five hundred dollars for doing something that my lawyer would do for nothing, and you are *advising* me? When you cash my cheque, I hope you will straighten your affairs. And even when you do, you will still have two hundred dollars left back. You can be a man on the two hundred dollars that are yours. Give Bernice the money you owe her. Give Bernice the money you owe her, and be a man. You are three hundred dollars in debt to Bernice, three hundred dollars in slavery to that woman. Don't ask me how I

252

know. But if I know, somebody else know, too."

"Guess!"

"Guess what, gal?"

"Guess, Dots."

"What, gal? Look, I am mad as hell, and I busy as anything, too."

"Guess who I see this afternoon?"

"Who?"

"Guess, I tell you! You won't believe."

"Look, Bernice, you think I have all day to spend on this telephone?"

"Guess who came up behind me, as I was stepping on 'pon the subway at Bloor, 'bout four o'clock this afternoon, coming back here to prepare for a party these people having tonight? And the person who came right up behind me, and touch me on my shoulder, and Lord! when I turn round, I couldn't believe my eyes, at all, at all, and I had was to hold on to my belly and say, 'Lord, *bless* my eyesight! I haven't seen you in years, in years.' Guess."

"Lew?"

"Lew!"

"Lew."

"That bitch? I took your advice and lend that bastard three hundred dollars, and I haven't see him since. Thursday gone is three weeks."

"Freeness, then."

"Funny you should mention him. I was thinking 'bout him only recently, and I had was to say how I don't see Freeness no more, not since he stopped coming to visit Estelle. One night he was here, and Mr. Burrmann came

253

to look for Mbelolo, and when Freeness see this big important man come in my humble place, well, Dots, you should have seen how Freeness changed colour. Freeness changed till he even changed the colour he have, then. And you know that it would take a lot to make Freeness change his colour, he is so blasted black already! No, it isn' Freeness, darling. I wonder whatever happened to Freeness, though . . ."

"He must be living."

"Or dead."

"You does see people often-often in this place for a time. And then, bram! they drop outta sight. Outta sight is . . ."

"Outta memory."

"Now, back home you born seeing a certain person, and you grow up with that person, you play together with that person, *Hide-and-hoop*, *Hobbina-bobbina-baby's-sneeze*, you play *Rounders* with a person, and when it is a moonlight night, you play *Thief*, or *Ship-sail-sail-fast-how-many-men-'pon-deck*, all during the corn season you play *London's Bridge*, all them sorts o'things you would do with a person who born in the same village back home with you. And you go to school and finish school, and then become men and women, and you see that person almost every day, and even if they moved away from where they was living as little girls and boys, you see them in the park at the Agricultural Exhibition, or on a Friday night listening to the Police Band on the Explanade . . . or on Christmas morning in the Park, Queens Park . . . you born and you grow up with a certain person, and that person is a friend for life! But in this place which you come to, as a adult grown-up person, a stranger, you could live next door to a person for years in a apartment building, and you think you could ask

254

me the name o' the whores living next door to me? I am sure they don't even know my name, neither. Except they get a letter for me delivered to them, by mistake by the postman-man. So, I am not surprised that you asking me what happen to Freeness. You remember the nurse-girl?"

"Who nurse-girl?"

"You know *who* I mean! The nurse-girl who was on duty the night we take Estelle down to the General Hospital to have the . . ."

"You don't have to feel 'shamed to say it, Dots. Say it. Say it, 'cause it gone and it past already. The *abortion*."

"The abortion."

"They giving-'way abortions now in this place. Anybody who find themselves with child could walk into *any* hospital, and say, 'Make me free again to . . .'"

"I know. I know. I work in one o' them."

"But guess."

"Not ahmmmm . . . but you didn't tell me who I mean, the nurse-girl, that is."

"Not Millicent!"

"Is she the one who came to Henry's wedding when nobody didn' invite her? And who was on Estelle's ward?"

"Millicent."

"Look Millicent, though!"

"Millicent, boy! I hear she married now to a nice German fella, and they living up on Baylawn Drive, up in Agincourt, the bitch, in a big house."

"Well, well, well, our girl, Millicent."

"What happened to those girls who was on the domestic scheme with us, when we uses to go down to Reverend Markham church?"

"You know I can't remember the name of that street! A person goes to the same church for three years, through winter and snow, fall and spring, summer too, in the days when we didn't have a bird to call a friend in this country, and all of a sudden, that part of our lives is like a book closed shut! Shut, shut, shut, tight, tight, tight, tight. What a thing life is!"

"If you wanted to kill me to make me call one o' them names, just *one* name, one name of a girl who was in the scheme with us, and who uses to go down to Cecil Street to those Thursday night cheap dances, or to the Hall on College, well, I would have to accept and face my fate."

"But who is this person that you axed me to guess about?"

"Agaffa!"

"No!"

"Yesss, girl."

"A-gaffa? A-gaffa! The A-gaffa we know? The same one who married we Henry? No, not she, not her, not the same A-gaffa who I blamed for killing-off Henry, poor fellow."

"May he rest in peace."

"Lord, have mercy."

"Poor Henry. Yuh telling me 'bout Agaffa, and how you saw her this afternoon."

"Did I say this afternoon?"

"I think so."

"No, man. It was recently."

"Recently, then."

"Yes, recently."

"Yuh know something, gal? We talking here 'pon this telephone just like back in the old days. You remember them days? The two o' we up here in this country, lonely! How I would sit down in my room and call you up, and you up there at the Burrmanns. And we would talk, and lick we mouth, take the world apart and put it together again."

"Humpty-Dumpty sat on a wall, Humpty-Dumpty had a great fall!"

"A great fall. A great fall o' loneliness. That is what it is."

"All the King's horses and all the King's men couldn't put Humpty-Dumpty back in one piece again."

"Be-Jesus Christ, gal!"

"Dots, you still there? I won't keep you much more longer, dear. But I wonder what time it must be now in Barbados? You ever, ever wonder about that? Or what the weather must be like?"

"It hot, gal. Hot as shite, too! Back there, now-so, you would be walking through the Lower Green bus-stand with a big basket in your hand, just come from shopping for supper for the missy, whoever you happen to be working for. Or you would be sitting down 'pon the Explanade we just mentioned, with some European-woman child, chasing the flies outta his face or from getting into his mouth! Or you might be home in your own home, doing something or the other."

"I was waiting for you to say I might be in my own home," Bernice said. "Or even married."

"In Barbados?"

"Or that I might be selling salt-fish and rancid butter from Australia, keeping shop in behalfs of one o' them thiefing merchants down Swan Street, or Roebuck Street."

"You are dreaming, gal."

"I wonder sometimes. I sometimes wonder." There was a pause in the conversation, during which there was heavy breathing. "I wonder, sometimes."

"Yuh know why you are dreaming? I will tell you. I had this woman for a patient once. A woman from the States. The minute she heard my accent, she start talking to me. She spends all her holidays and good times in my island. I don't grudge her for that. It is her damn money. And she told me she owns this big nightclub in Brooklyn, or New York, or the Bronx. They plays jazz. So she have the money to spend. But what really had me vexed as hell was the way she talked about *my* prime minister. That is where I draw the line. Just imagine. A little Yankee bitch like her. She could haul her self from all up in Amer'ka where there is the biggest o' race problems, and go down there in my peaceable country, and carry-on as if she owns the place. She is down there in kiddy-kingdom, and I am up here, me and you, Boysie, Henry . . . God bless his soul . . . the whole tribe o' us immigrants from back home are up here, and we can't pretend that we own a cement block in this country. That is what I mean?"

"What she did?"

"Did? Well, it is not a matter of did, Bernice. It is what she *thought*. And the thoughts that went along with the doing, which as far as I am concern, makes that doing even more worst than it was, if it had stop at the doing."

"Tell me what she say, then."

"Listen to this. This would change your mind about re-turning-back to that damn place, which we in times o' distress and loneliness and discrimination up here calls home. This damn Yankee woman told me, told *me*, that she have this big car, the English car, man, what they call that kind o' car that the Queen and Forbes Burnham in Guyana, and that little man from Grenada does drive 'bout in? You know that big powerful car? It is the kind o' motto-car which is the first thing a prime minister down there does think 'bout driving-'bout in, when he start feeling he is the leader of the people."

"Rolls-Royce? You mean a Rolls-Royce?"

"Thanks. She had one o' them. She told *me* that. She now sell-out every damn thing she owned in Brooklyn, and New York, and she heading down to Barbados to live. Well, there ain' nothing wrong with that. But hear this now. Listen to this thing now. This Rolls-Royce motto-car that she have, she intends to take to Barbados with her. And she ask me if I think, if poor-arse *me*, me a poor-arse black woman like me, think the prime minister would buy it offa her? Do you know how much millions o' we dollars that motto-car would cost? A car like that fit for a Queen to drive in *must* cost the taxpayers o' Barbados every penny that still remain in that country. Just to clean and polish that Rolls-Royce must cost a thousand dollars a day."

"Barrow would have more sense than that."

"Barrow? Who Barrow?"

"Barrow."

"That's what I mean? Who is this Barrow?"

"Barrow. We prime minister. Errol or Dipper, as they does call him."

"You don't know that I am living away so long that I didn't even know we had one' them, a prime minister. And by the name o' Barrow."

"And yet, you still had them feelings 'bout the Rolls-Royce motto-car."

"It is not a matter o' feelings, Bernice. It is the principle of the thing. As my ex-mistress Mistress Hunter would say . . . God bless her soul . . ."

"She dead too?"

"Not really. I just say so for so. But as she would say, we have to see things through the correct *sperspective* o' principles, always. So you see that when that Yankee bitch could leave Brooklyn or New York and go down there and cattawoul with a big important person like a prime minister, I am not talking about no ordinary person like a civil servant now. I mean a prime minister. A man like Trudeau or President Nixon, or the Queen. So when she could pick up her hot arse and wander down there and eat and drink with a prime minister, and then expect we prime minister to do what she wondered to me, as what she wanted him to do, Bernice there and then I write Barbados clean-clean offa my books. Barbados then becomes in importance just like a little town in the north o' Ontario. Barbados ain' nothing, ain't *neffing* to her!"

"Those is some harsh words, though."

The thruth, Bernice, the truth is always a harsh thing to speak, to hear and to listen to."

"Still."

"The thruth, the truth, or as we say, the trute."

"But, wait. You know how long we been licking our mouth on this telephone? And I didn't even tell you what I had to tell you."

"Agaffa."

"Yes. A-gaffa told me that she found out after all these years of asking herself who was really the person who wrote that letter to her, criticizing her concerning marrieding a black man, Henry. You remember? When the letter came? From somebody who didn't sign her name at all? And how the poor girl was upset, just before the wedding."

"Boysie told me 'bout it."

"Guess who that letter came from?"

"I had always thought that Henry himself had write that letter to try to get outta marrieding Agaffa. But I wasn't sure. From Agaffa's ex-boyfriend?"

"The mother."

260

"The mother?" Dots screamed the word through the telephone. Bernice was silent for a while.

"Her own dear mother!"

"That bitch?"

"That is a mother, sometimes. When she wants to keep tie-ing a girl-child. The lady I works for have a word for it. *Imbillical cords.* That imbillical cord is sometimes damn hard to cut off."

"I was thinking today that I wish I hadn' left the domestic scheme. No, wait and let me explain. Here I am as a nurse-aide, for years, and I still can't make progress in the things I want to make progress in. Now, just listening to you and listening to the whole conversation we having, and especially that last *sperspective* you mentioned. I remember during some class at the Doctor's when I was in training, that a doctor was saying something about this same ambillical cord. He was saying something that strike me as being funny funny funny. I wish I had the knowledge to really understand what a ambillical cord stands for, you know, the ins and outs. But it sound as if a ambillical cord is a damn serious thing. Ain't it the thing that does join-on a child to its mother?"

"It is that."

"And does connect life with death? Is that what it is too? I think that is what it is. Well, that ambillical thing is the *same* thing that is connecting my lack o' progress in being a damn nurse-aide to my progress if I had remained a domestic and had take classes at night school. And you know why I saying this? Boysie. Boysie has move-ahead o' me in this regards. Boysie has moved outta my life, through education. He isn't taking no night courses at night school, but I think he is learning *something*, some-damn-thing, to make him change so. It isn't the money so much that he is making. And he is making a damn lot o' that. More than I ever expect him to make. It ain't the money. I think it will have to be the *sperspective*. And the sad thing is that I am the person who first mentioned this sperspective-thing to him. But he is the first to use it. The same thing with you."

"Me?"

"You and Lew. You is a servant. And he is a lawyer-man. I gone. I going hang-up. I gone."

Dots was tired. She would come home from work and she would always be tired. She was working less overtime these days, but there was still this eternal fatigue in her body, all through her bones, and it limited the number of things she could do in the apartment. She thought of taking a tonic. Something like Geritol, which she had seen advertised on television when she would sit alone, with the cat curled up in her lap, waiting for the hours to pass, waiting for the television programmes to get more and more uninteresting, until eleven o'clock came when she could watch the CBC news, and during the most important part of the national news go into the bathroom to brush her teeth and to look at the black circles around her eyes, and come back outside into the living room just in time to hear "O Canada" being played, with the Queen riding a horse up in England and jet planes flying overhead, and she would always remember as they sped past her on the screen that two or three of them crashed at a Canadian National Exhibition some years ago; and then she would take the cat up in her hand, and go into the bedroom, and close the door behind her. And there she would spend her long time of night.

The cat would jump about in the bed, playing with the strings on her pink quilted housecoat, until it felt tired and purred itself to sleep in her lap, between her legs. And

Dots would turn on the late-hour radio programme from CHIN, with its West Indian music, black American music, and the West Indian announcer from Jamaica who tried unsuccessfully to talk like an American from the deep South. The songs would be of love and of lovers: of love that was not returned, and of lovers who had not looked back; and somehow, it would make her feel less lonely, probably because she was sharing an eternal arrangement with the countless women out there, some of them living in the lighted apartment windows surrounding her, on floors above hers, and floors below, to the right, to the left, in front and behind. So many people in one city, so many people so close to her, and she alone, at midnight in her apartment, with the cat and CHIN radio station.

She is ready for bed now. She gets up from lying down on top of the bedspread. Tonight the newspaper is still in the bed, folded and unread. She takes off her pink house-coat, and she is surprised that she is still wearing her nurse's uniform. "Forgetful?" she says, and she could have been talking to someone, or to the cat, or even to Boysie. She stands in front of the mirror on the wall, and she looks at herself, only for a moment or so, and then she opens her drawer where she keeps one of the two silk scarves which she uses for tying her head before she takes any piece of clothing over her head. Sometimes she would wear one of them when she is taking a bath. Or sometimes when she is vacuuming the living room. She combs out her hair, and braids it up, and ties the scarf back on her head. She pulls a hair out of her chin with a badly working pair of tweezers.

She walks to the clothes cupboard, which is beside her side of the bed, and she opens it, and hangs up the house-coat on a nail which she has herself nailed there. She unbuttons the work dress, takes it off, takes the housecoat off the nail, throws it on the bedspread, and hangs the dress on the same nail. She dresses and undresses behind this door of the cupboard when Boysie is in the bedroom with her, and she does it even when she is alone, with only the cat lying on the bed watching her. She puts on the housecoat. But she has forgotten something, so she takes it off again. It is her slip. Then she puts the housecoat on again. If she was going to take a bath tonight, she would have walked into the bathroom with these clothes on, as she does all the time. But tonight she is too tired to take her bath.

Still standing behind the cupboard door, with her cat watching her from the slits of his eyes, she takes off her brassiere, and as if she is uncomfortable with the eyes watching her, she puts on the housecoat quickly, and closes the cupboard door, and sits on the bed. She runs her hands up and down her legs, and the pantyhose comes off in her hands, like old skin. Once (Boysie was in bed when she did this undressing; and he said, "What the arse! You know what you remind me of? A fucking priest dressing in robes! Look woman, I am your husband, so why you are hiding behind that door when you are taking off your clothes, every night?") she spent the whole night sleeping in her housecoat and her work dress.

Tonight she merely takes off the housecoat, this time for the last time, keeps her panties on, and in her nightgown, the flannel one, gets into bed, under the covers, and continues to listen to the radio.

The lights are all burning. So she gets up and puts them out, one by one, all of them, except one which burns all night like a beacon to show Boysie the way between the furniture and the tricky centre tables, just in case he comes

264

home drunk again. Back in the bedroom she peels the bedspread off the bed, and folds it and hangs it properly over the back of a chair. She fixes her furlike slippers side by side beside the bed on her side, she cuffs the pillows on Boysie's side, and climbs back into bed. The radio is turned down, the lights are off in the bedroom, and she lies there thinking of Little Janey. The cat yawns and suddenly there is only the voice of a singer . . .

The mother of two testified yesterday that a short man with a silk sock over his head forced her at knife-point last December to have intercourse in the underground garage of her apartment building. Boysie held the afternoon paper closer to his eyes as he tried to remember a story of similar details which he had read months before. He was fully dressed, it was now one in the afternoon, and the strange woman had not come out of the subway yet. He was finding it difficult to concentrate on the story and on the subway entrance-exit at the same time. He had left his car parked in the driveway of the apartment building, the first time he had ever done that, and he was waiting. The cat was fed, and it was somewhere out of sight. He had been doing things which when taken individually would have suggested a rather disorganized mind and attitude, but when taken collectively could easily be seen as a carefully thought-out plan. But he did not worry about this. He just wanted to finish reading the story, and if possible, at the same time or during his reading, see the woman, and then leave in his car on the long drive he had thought of taking. He forgot which part he had already read; the story wasn't making much sense to him, so he began at the beginning. *The mother of two testified yesterday that a short man with a silk sock over his head forced her at knife-point to have intercourse in the underground garage of her apart-ment building. She identified her attacker as Caufield. The woman testified that she saw Caufield two weeks after the attack. He was entering a car at a shopping plaza near her apartment. She gave police the licence number. She told the jury that a man attacked her in the garage near the apartment. She gave the police the licence number.* "Did I read that already?" *She told the jury that a man attacked her in the garage after she returned from doing errands. She said he sliced her finger and threatened to kill her. She ran screaming up the stairway from the garage, she testi-fied. Her husband said she collapsed in his arms at the apartment with blood on her hand and face.* It was Friday, and he didn't have to clean offices tonight, unless he wanted to. Sometimes, in order to have a longer weekend, he would do his cleaning on Fridays, so that he wouldn't have to go to work until Monday night. But today, he thought he would remain at home, not all day . . . perhaps he shouldn't remain at home, he should leave as he always did, and just drive around the city, and leave for his trip on Saturday. But he couldn't do that because he had agreed to have a party tonight, just for the hell of it. He had not informed any of the clients he cleaned for that he was taking a trip, and he didn't worry about it.

Dots had agreed to the party. It was such a long time since they had had friends in to a party; and she thought it would do him good. It would cheer him up (although she did not tell him this,) and make the weekend seem shorter and more bearable. He thought of the shopping he had to do: liquor, food from the Jewish market, candles and incense (which, strangely, Dots asked him to buy) from the Cargo Canada store; and he had to call Bernice and Estelle, Llewellyn and Freeness (he had heard that

Freeness was living on Jamieson Avenue), and Agatha. Inviting Agatha was Dots's idea; but soon he warmed to it, for with Agatha present, well, after all, she was Henry's wife, and if Henry couldn't be present, then . . . and it was the first real party they had had since Henry's death. Boysie tried not to think of Henry, and he made an effort to concentrate on the story in the newspaper. *Her husband said she collapsed in his arms at their apartment.* "I read that already, didn't I?" He was losing his concentration. *blood on her hand and face. The 37-year-old attacker woman identified her attacker as being 5 feet 5 inches tall, of stocky build, and wearing a . . . and having a Scottish accent, and wearing a red plaid short-sleeved shirt and jeans. She said he also wore a mask, was in his early 20's and had well-tanned arms.*

He was losing his concentration, and thereby losing his strength, and his power over his patience was slipping away from him. He used to feel so strong when he was in the bathtub with the hot bath, when he would come out, and walk naked; he felt strong then. But this afternoon he could hardly read a short story about a woman who was raped, and rape was such an interesting subject with him before; he had discussed it with the Canadian young fellow who had given all the philosophical reasons why men raped women; and had reminded Boysie that during the Vietnam war, thousands of American GIs had raped millions of Vietnamese women; "It is just the way of life, philosophically speaking," the Canadian young fellow said. "Just as the American way of life, all their violence and all their wealth and all their power have become their philosophy of life." Boysie was intrigued. And he tried to look at his own life in a philosophical way, and try to see what interpretation, in strict terms of this philosophical

267

way of seeing things, was his waiting for the woman, his distribution of all his money to his wife, to a woman he did not love, and did no longer like, was not this also a philosophical way of doing things? But not to be able to read a short story about a raped woman, was this too such an importance weakness, if it was a weakness at all, that he could clothe it in this heavy interpretation?

From the last time when he saw her with her mauve dress exposed, he had realized that a very basic mistake had been made, and he had been searching for this mistake ever since. It could have been in the manner of his life, its style, its substance, its quality; it could have been in the way he treated Dots, and it could have been manifested (had he the eyes to see it) in all the parameters of their life together, in each smile (which was not very often) in each grimace, in each sneer and each harsh word and look; he had done very little, so he told himself now, to get to know her, but she was really like a deity, set there before him so that he would never really get to know her, just her presence and her sound and the noise she made; he was not meant to know her, and because he did not, it still grieved him and caused him to think that if he ever were to be happy another day with her, he would have to lift each brick in the structure of their relationship apart, each brick, brick by brick, from the very beginning of the foundation of mistrust, of jealousy, of inferiority on his part, and arrogance on hers, before he could ever be happy, and free. It was his happiness and his freedom, freedom like that of the black American singer who oozed freedom through voice and vapour, perspiration and smile, when he sang "A Rainy Night in Georgia." It was his happiness . . . his happiness.

That was it.

That is it.

His happiness, or rather his unhappiness.

He had not been happy since he knew Dots. He had not been happy, and he did not know until he had seen the woman the previous time, with her winter coat unbuttoned exposing the mauve colour of her dress, that he was not happy, for the colour of her dress was mauve. That was it! It was like peeling off a skin from a fruit, and the woman was the fruit. It was like his eyes which in sleep, in dream, would be clogged up by pus and cold and other secretions which would prevent them from opening; it was like in that dream he had when his wife was with the young man and the young man was doing something to her, and he was tied to his position, to his posture, helpless and observing, and the more helpless because he was a witness; it was like being unable to move from one spot to help someone like Dots, a wife, a woman, a woman raped just as the woman in the newspaper story must have felt when the man with the nylon sock over his head terrorized her movements and rendered them like the pillars of concrete in the underground garage, and the woman had to witness her own undoing.

Happiness.

He knew now how to be happy. He would be happy if he did not feel that he had to go to the Home Service Association place to breathe in the same spoiled air as those sleeping children in the army cots and with the grey blankets covering parts of their bodies (he should have sent some of his money to them: if he remembered, he would tell Llewellyn later tonight to do that); he would be happy if nothing, not even his being a "man in his position", for he did not have to be a man in his position: he could be a man, just a man; but it was Mrs. James who had decided for him, just as Dots and Bernice and Estelle and Llewellyn had decided for him, without having to utter a word of their intended dominance over him, "a man in that position," that he would go up to the same Home Service Association and be a volunteer worker. He did not have to dress as a man who cleaned offices, he could dress like a barrister; Alfredo his barber had seen that, and had said it; he did not have to live in a mould that people expected; he could wear his suits even in the morning when he was waiting for *her*: the woman, who has not arrived yet for the day, but he is not looking for her anymore. She means nothing now, for her purpose has been understood. And he should take the lesson from her appearance that morning, in spite of what she is, in spite of the fact that he has never seen her from any close and safe distance to judge character from the redness of her eyes, or from the clearness in her eyes, or from the movements of her lips.

He does not have to know her in this everyman's way of knowing, for she is not an ordinary woman; she is like a morning dream which he had, she is like his imagination, the object of his thinking sessions which bothered him until he was going out of his mind, living through a day of his life in the waiting seconds for her; perhaps she never existed, and he never did see her, for there is no one else alive who has seen her, and he could have imagined her. Only if Henry was here: Henry used to have so much wisdom about these things!

Boysie got up and went into the bathroom, and stood up and looked at the clipping of Henry's poem which he had framed and which he would watch while he shaved, or even at odd moments when he was not shaving. Dots had quarrelled about its appearance, but he had insisted upon leaving it there. Henry had such a love for roses, Boysie remembered. He wrote about roses as if roses were women. He wondered, should he give the strange woman a name, whether he should call her Rose. Perhaps her name was Rose. Rose and mauve. Have you ever seen a mauve rose? A rose could be mauve or blue, or a rose could even be a pickle, anything you loved could be a rose. Henry should have written a poem about happiness. "But this one about a rose is a nice poem and he has happiness inside it."

He was losing his concentration: he should get up right now and do the shopping for the party, perhaps call in on Mrs. James and see how she is, see whether she wants anything bought from the Jewish market (she has no money, but she likes pigs' feet and black-eyed peas and salt fish, a true Maritimer, Mrs. James!); but he shouldn't stop in, because he knows her needs, and he could easily just as easily buy them for her and drop them off at her door, at Apartment 101.

What happiness had he in his life after forty-nine years? A man forty-nine years old should have had some happiness. It was not the country; the country was good to him. It was all those noisy West Indians whom he had learned to tolerate but who were not good for the country, his country ("I must remember to take my Canadian passport with me, wherever I go, from now on"); it was the people like Llewellyn who thought they could purchase happiness by screwing post-middle-aged women, and borrowing their bodies and their money, Llewellyn in whom he had had so much hope. It was people like Mrs. James's son Michael who knew what happiness was because he had never experienced it. ("I wonder which page that little bastard is at now, in that book I bought him? How long ago did I buy that little brute that book?")

He should get up right now and leave to do the shopping. He should feed this goddamn cat before he left.

"Meeeeeoowww!"

He got up, and just as he was about to go into the kitchen, he saw the letter beneath the door. Somebody had pushed it there. Usually his mail, whatever it was, was in the mailbox just off the lobby. Perhaps this letter had been delivered at the wrong place, or a neighbour had taken it out of his box; after all, he was living in a low-rental district.

It was a special delivery letter. He picked it up, and for the first time since he had written the letter to his wife did he remember that Dots had said nothing about that letter in which he had asked for a time to be set aside to talk. She had said nothing. He didn't even know if she had seen the letter; or had read it. He saw this letter was addressed to him. And he recognized the Barbados stamps. "Strange!" No return address with name was on the envelope. It was addressed to him. He would have to read part of it at least (and his concentration was so bad this afternoon: what time is it now? He had forgotten to keep with the time) to find out.

Dear Boysie, Man! I bet you don't know who is writing this letter to you. Don't look at the last page, but read and see if you can find out the sender of this letter. All right? I trust you. And I bet you didn't know I was down here, in Barbados, all this time. Boy, this place is something else. The richest people are the politicians. I am thinking seriously about becoming a politician. And after the politicians, is the shop-keepers and then the people who owns hotels for the tourisses. After the politicians and the shop-keepers sell rotting pork chops and salt fish as dear as beef steaks, and the hotel people, comes the banks.

*Banks like peas. You could go in a bank, any bank, and
ask for a loan. You will get that loan if you intend to buy
a motor car or a frig or a stereo record player, or a bi-
cycle. But if you intend to open a shop of your own or if
you intend to buy land or a house spot on the beach, and
compete with the powers that be, well, forget it. Banks
down here are not for that purpose as much as for the
former. I have never seen so many people in Barbados
before with such big friges. And once I was up in the
country which as you know is a place where we uses to go
and drink rum like water, and which is the poorest place
in the island, relative speaking. But the biggest friges are
now in the country. I was visiting a friend of mine, a little
thing, as man! and she went to take out a Banks beer for
me, and the only thing inside that blasted frig apart from
two more Banks was a big big bottle of ice water. Now
tell me what you think that means? I don't want to waste
your time telling you all these things about the place, because I want to tell you something now that I see with my
own very eyes.*

*One night I was down at Paradise Beach Club, and I
was having a good time, cause as you know, I am a man
who travels with a lot of money. I was buying drinks for
everybody, civil servants who I think was making all this
big lot of money, but the minute they hear I'm in the land,
they come reminding me that I used to drink rum with
them in the Customs. Fucking beggars. Paupers. Well, we
was drinking Scotches like peas, and out of the blue, I
see this man with some nice-looking Canadian gashes, and
I know one of them, too. And when the man turned his
head, guess who that man was? Guess who that man turned
out to be? The fucking minister of Home Affairs! Man, I
was so vexed to see a Minister of Home Affairs drinking*

273

rum with the ordinary rank and file, that I start thinking serious about it. A minister of any government, particular a country like ours, should be a man who is heard and not seen. Well, when I saw that, I soon forgot everything about it because we were having a damn good time. Barbados means a good time. If you want a good time see Barbados. Well, I went up to the minister and shake his fucking hand, because I argued that if a stranger could do it, so can I, because I am a Barbadian. So we shake hands and he say how nice it is to see the fellars coming back even if for a holiday and spending money like water. He didn't say those exact words, but that is the feeling I got. Well, I didn't like that too much, because how he knows I come back here only for a holiday, and not for good. Because this is my country more than it belongst to tourisses.

But as you know, I am not too sure if I can really come back down here for good, to live. Not even if I can get some of this easy touriss-money, by building a little place with five or six apartments and come back and live off Trudeau and the Canadian Unemployment Insurance like the rest of the Canadians. But when I saw how things are down here, I decided that since I make the money up in Canada, and I can't live down here no more, I might as well come back up there and let the winter burst my backside. Later that same night that I meet the Minister of Home Affairs, I end up at a party given by a girl who we used to call by the nickname of Colleen. She was on holiday too. And she had this big party. Man, I have never seen so much rum, whiskey, Scotch, gin and vodka — you didn't know that, did you? That Barbadians drinking vodka nowadays! — and beer, and everything that we ate and drank that night and right into the next morning was imported from Overseas. And food? Boysie, there was

274

food like peas! And every politician in the House of Assembly, every man in the Cabinet and every diplomat that we have from Away was at this party. And the party hasn't finished yet. I am sure that somebody must still be at Colleen's place trying to drink up that liquor, as I am writing you this letter.

When I got home, two or three days later, because I was living as a touriss and I don't know up to now how the hell I did get home, or how the fellow who carry me home know where I was staying! But when I sobered back up, I had a bad feeling. And I had to sit down and write you this letter, which although it is long, I hope you won't mind listening to till the end. Because you are the only person I know in this whole world who would try to understand the kind of life that is going on down here, in the name of the people and of democracy. Every young person, the moment he has enough money, or pass the Cambridge School Certificate, which even changed its name nowadays to the GCE, well, he "leffing" Barbados. You remember that song that Sparrow used to sing? "Yankees gone and Sparrow take over now?" Well, in Barbados, the shoe is on the other foot. If you ever have any desire to emigrate back down here, even for a vacation, well, forget it. Go up North in Northern Ontario instead. The minute I come back, I intend to apply for Canadian citizenship. And if you haven't done that already, haul your ass down to the Immigration when you read this letter and take out some papers. The Barbadians who remain here don't want expatriate Barbadians who went abroad and made gentlemen and ladies out of themselves to return back here. Everything now is politics and black nationalism. They are even talking about going back to Africa, in ways that I can't understand. That in itself is a kind of revolution happening in this place. Everything is politics or Africa nowadays. If you want to become a millionaire over night, do one of two things. Enter politics. Or do like Harry, sell pussy to the tourisses. But praise God, Harry dead.

I am sorry to take up so much of your time. But there was nobody down here that I could have discussed these with, so I had to call on you. Look for me next Thursday. I coming back. By the way, the morning, or it was the afternoon, that I was leaving, I happened to see you going up in the elevator, but I didn't have much time to follow you up where you was going. I coming back. Yours truly, Freeness.

PS: I went to one poker game when I was here, one night with some civil servants. And when I sat down, the house-man asked me to show him four hundred dollars if I was going to continue sitting down at his table. Four hundred dollars. And he meant Canadian dollar bills, too. Is that saying something to you? How do these fellars get that kind of money? Everybody down here selling pussy? Then I saw a fellar raise another fellar four hundred American dollars (he counted the four hundred American dollars outta mere twenties!) on a pair of fucking threes! The pot that night had in about one million dollars. And two ministers in the government was playing, but I don't want to call no names. Everything that I telling you is what I see with my own two eyes. Another man might see things in a different light. I can only give you the light I see things through. But if you ever are thinking of coming back here to live, forget it. And tell everybody so, too. Unless you want to make money off the tourisses, and sell pussy, like the late Harry! I even heard that there was no Barbados Scholar this year. Do you know what that means? No Barbados Scholar in Barbados! F.

Boysie put the letter back into its envelope, and without making even a mental comment, he put it into his pocket and went through the door. Barbados had been out of his mind for a long time now. And, at least, he didn't have to call Freeness to invite him to the party tonight. He wondered whether he should bother to call Llewellyn.

"How many provinces there is in this country?" Dots shouted from the kitchen. Bernice had arrived early to help with the preparations. The apartment was tidy, and she was searching for records to play. But there was only one. The kitchen counter was full of food from the Jewish market, and it all had to be cooked. "How much provinces there is in this country, Bernice?"

"Yuh know, I never thought of that," she called out. And to herself, she added, "I never really thought about that. What a funny thing to ask me." She went on searching for more records in the place which she knew they were kept normally. "Where the records?" Dots moved from the kitchen and came into the living room. In her hand was a large slab of salt fish.

"You know how many provinces they have in this country?"

"Six?"

"Seven, ain't they? I think I heard a man on the television say there are seven provinces."

"Well, we can count them out."

"I wonder if they is really five, or six, or even seven."

"Well, to start with the one we living in, Ontario. That is one. Then there is Montreal."

"That's in Quebec. Ontario and Montreal, and . . ."

"Ontario, Montreal, if you say so." Bernice tried to concentrate. "BC, British Columbia, Nova Scotia . . . Halifax, that's where the man in the Conservatives comes from! Lemme begin again. Now, there is Ontario. Montreal, as you say. Nova Scotia and there is Halifax."

"I thought Halifax was a place, and not a province, gal!" And she laughed, as she would laugh when she was happy, when she had friends in her home, when she was listening to calypsoes and was dancing. "You know something?" But she did not bother to say it.

"I never worried my head about those things. I lives here and that is all I know. I makes a little money. I have saved for a rainy day when I have to go back to Barbados, and that is all I know."

"How long we been living in this country?"

"Ten years now, going 'pon eleven."

"Ten years?"

"Ten."

"Ten, eh?" Dots went back into the kitchen. Bernice continued searching for records. "You said that Lew coming over later? I wonder what happen to Boysie. He really went to town on this shopping today. I can't find fault with him for the way he shopped for these things. That man could trot when he wants to. He is a horse that could trot when he wants to."

"Where the records, Dots? We can't have no party without records. This place used to be flowing in records. I have had such lovely times here, and I want to make sure that Lew, when he comes over, have a good time too. Did I tell you that he paid me back the money? Every cent." Bernice waited to hear what Dots would say to this. She had taken Dots's advice and had lent him the three hundred dollars, against her judgment; but she was glad that

278

she had done it even before Lew brought back the money. She did not know and did not think that she ever would see him again after she had lent him the money. She decided to shout, "Did I tell you that Lew paid me back the money?"

"That's good."

Dots was becoming impatient. She had got home early, but she was tired and had had a rest before calling Bernice to come over and help her. The time was eight-thirty. Normally, she would have had everything prepared by then, and she would have been changed. But tonight she was feeling sweaty, and she wanted to have a bath. She also wondered where Boysie was. But she was not nervous enough nor anxious enough yet to start worrying. She knew he could not have gone to work, because she saw his panel truck parked in the underground garage. For some reason, she had thought of looking in the underground garage. She had never done it before. And now, she was wondering why she had gone down there, just to look for the truck.

"Who you think would know?"

"About what?"

"The number."

"I thought you would know, Dots. This is your house, isn't it? You ought to know where the calypso records are!"

"I talking about the provinces. Who you think we could ask about the number of provinces?"

"Lew would know. Or Boysie, he know so much these days!"

"Watch your mouth, gal! He is still my husband. Have

respect." And she laughed. "Child, what would I do without that man? He is good and he is bad." And she went back to give the cooking her attention.

Floes and floes of angel's hair, ice cream castles in the air . . .

"What the hell are you playing? Not in my house!"

Dots came out to find Bernice still searching for more records. There were none. The Judy Collins record was the only one.

"Where the records?"

"We had records upon records in here. The last time I looked, there was lots o' records," Dots told her. She started to think rapidly. Something was going wrong. She was beginning to feel strange in her own home. She left Bernice and went into the bedroom. She closed the door behind her. She opened Boysie's clothes cupboard and ran her hands along the suits, counting them, and then she parted them as one would part a window blind. She felt better. None was missing. And she sensed that her heart was beating less rapidly. But still, she went next into the bathroom, and flung back half of the mirror which served also as a door to the medicine cabinet. Everything of his was there. "What are you doing to yourself, Dots? What is happening to you?" *Feathered canyons everywhere . . . they rain and snow on everyone, I think of clouds that way.*

She came out of the bathroom and went back into the kitchen. "I had such a funny strange feeling a minute ago! Like something in the pit of my stomach . . ."

Bernice came into the kitchen with her, completely ignoring the music since it was not what she wanted to hear. And together they prepared the food. Then Bernice said, "I am

280

thinking of going back home. Maybe next year. Or the year after, the latest."

"What for, girl?"

"No reason."

"Sometimes I feel the same way. But I know I would have to go by myself. Boysie won't think of leaving this country. He's so successful."

"That's why he should go back. And take you back with him. The two o' you could be like king and queen down there. The place progressing, it is progressing. And with money that the two of you 'cumulated up here, man, don't you think you could open up a little guest house? The tour-isses spending money like water down in Barbados. I am going to get some before it is too late. Build me a nice home outta limestone. And I intend to open a little restaurant business and get some o' that touriss money."

"I can't help thinking that we should know the number o' provinces in this country. We been living here for so long, and what do we know 'bout this country?"

"I know who the prime minister is!"

"Who?"

"Trudeau! and he is a good-looking man too."

"Trudeau, eh?" Dots said and went off into a kind of a dream. "Trudeau. Everybody know Trudeau because he is Trudeau and because Trudeau is Canada. But I bet you that you can't tell me who is the prime minister o' this province we living in?"

"Well, I really never . . ."

"I wonder if Agaffa coming over tonight! It would be like old-times, eh? I sorry that Estelle decided to go to the country with Mr. Burrmann, but then again, it is her child-father. And she have to prepare the way for her child." She went into her dreamlike thinking, and then she sighed. "What I won't have given to get that child! Poor Little Janey!"

"The osteogennississ, though, Dots."

"Yeah, the osteogennississ."

"That's a hard thing."

"Osteogennississ. How are Lew and you making out now?"

"I going back home, I tell you. There must be some man down there willing to have a old woman like me. At least that old man would want me if only for my money. Money down there would mean a different thing to him, than up here to Lew."

"You seem as if you already left."

"My heart has left. I am only here making a little more, and straightening up things. But my heart is already there."

"But look at we two! You and me. Right where we started from. *Man*-less. You, waiting for Lew, but with your mind made up to go back home; and me, waiting for Boysie, as I wait every other night, alone. But what are we going to do? This must be the fate of women like us, you don't think so? Me and you." Something was in her eye, and she brushed it out with her hand. "You really feel Agaffa is coming? It would be so nice to see her again. I have to confess something to her. And beg her pardon for what I said. That is years now. But it is still riding me like a horse."

"Oh, she won't mind."

"Watch this pot for me. I going in now and have a bath and change," and she left Bernice. Bernice watched the cooking for a time, and then went to sit in the living room. Through the window she could see the entrance to the subway, and from where she sat afterwards she could see the hundreds of lights in the beautiful Friday evening. They were coming from the apartments which surrounded her like a sea. Heads moved in those which were near, and lighted shadows in those further away. She was happy. She was going back home, and her man (if only for the time being) was coming over. It would be like old times. She thought of the last time there was a party in this room, Henry's wedding reception, and she prepared herself for the fun.

Inside the bedroom, with the door closed, and with her clothes already taken off behind the door of the clothes cupboard, Dots was sitting on the bed. She was naked. That was a thing she never did. Even when she was in the apartment by herself, she never remained naked longer than it took, for a few seconds, before and after her bath. She was sitting now, in no hurry to put on the pink quilted housecoat, in no hurry to have her bath, in no hurry to move. It was as if she was too tired from her work at the hospital and was taking a coffee break in her own bedroom.

"*Bernice!*"

I looked at clouds from both sides now . . .

"*Bernice!*"

The screams took Bernice from her own dreaming.

. . . when every fairy tale comes real . . . so many things I would have done but clouds got in my way.

"What's wrong, Dots?" She was standing at the door. Dots did not realize that she was already in the room with her. Naked and still on the bed, Dots looked up at her, and smiled and said, "Let us have a good big drink. Go and mix them whilst I am in the tub."

Coming back with the drinks, which she set down on

the tiled counter beside the washbasin, Bernice sat on the edge of the tub while Dots wallowed in the scented bubble bath. And when the time came, she put her hand in the foam and rubbed Dots's back for her. She would have rubbed her front too, but the condition of Dots's skin, the way it had suddenly become old, and with no supporting muscles . . . "I used to bathe Estelle when she was a child," Bernice was thinking.

"You wish this was Boysie doing this, don't you?" Dots didn't answer. "And not only this."

"Why?"

"I sometimes lie in a bath for thirty minutes waiting for Lew to come. All the bath oil and perfume I using these days for that man! I hope he appreciates it."

"Gal, when that man of mine does come home tonight, and when this party is finished, and I get you whores outta my home, I have made up my mind that I am going to kill Boysie *tonight* with the best loving he's ever had!"

"Hurrah! Hurrah!"

"Kill him dead!"

"I could see that is what is on your mind."

"Bernice, I intend to kill him tonight, with loving. I've been too stupid. A woman my age, with not much left, and I am playing hard to get? That is arse. What am I getting vexed for? Wait, did you give me water, or Scotch? Pour me a real drink, gal! By the time the other guesses come, me and you are going to be stone-drunk. *Stone-cold-drunk!*" She laughed out loudly. "*Pissed,* as the Canadians say."

"Another drink coming up! Another drink coming up, ma'am." And playfully, as they once would be together, Bernice went for the drinks.

"You know something, I forgot exactly how to cook

split-peas and rice. Imagine that! I can't remember what to do exactly. But what the hell? When they come and they don't like it, they could go to hell. Tonight is my night. My night alone!" And they broke into their sensual laughter.

Boysie was satisfied with the speed the car was making. He had taken it up to over one hundred miles an hour, and it didn't shake. He was comfortable in it, and he was relaxed. He had stopped on the main street in the city and had bought three stereo tapes, *Milestones* by Miles Davis, Mendelssohn's *Midsummer Night's Dream,* and of course his old favourite, "Both Sides Now" by Judy Collins. He was playing the Miles Davis tape now. The horses in the tune were matching the horses under the bonnet of the car. He was driving, as he would say, at an easy canter. He had reduced the speed when he found out how fast the car would go. There was no hurry. There was no fire anywhere. He didn't know of any. He did not even know where he was heading, but he knew he was going to keep driving; and when the tank showed empty, or just before, he would stop, drink a coffee, a cup of black coffee, fill up, and drive on.

At the moment, he was heading towards Hamilton, on the 401 Highway West, which was the highway that led anywhere. It led out of the city, and he was glad for that. He had put nothing other than the three tapes into the car when he left after the market, and he hadn't even looked at a map. He knew somehow that he would find his place to stop; and when it came up against his headlights, he would know it was the place, and he would stop.

He was learning so much on this drive. All the towns he had heard mentioned on the CBC radio programmes:

and here was Hamilton, the home of the Hamilton Tiger Cat football team, with the black American guy who was the quarterback. That black man, the first black quarterback to take his team to the biggest football victory in the country . . . and the place he is passing now, where they grow grapes and make wine; for in his poorer days he had drunk some of this Canadian-grown wine. But the place slipped by him so fast . . . he cannot remember its name. But at least he has experienced passing through the town or the area or the fields, cut in half by the highway, and he knows. And this place, Barrie. Had he also passed Barrie already? It is showing now on the road signs. Barrie, the place mentioned every day, imagine, every day in the weather reports on the CBC. He wished he could remember all those other names, and the way the announcer read them: *"Barrie, Elliott Lake, Thunder Bay Region, cold with slight drizzle, and so on and so on . . ."* He should have written it down. "Where the hell is this Thunder Bay Region?" and he laughed aloud in his car, because nobody could hear him and wonder if he was mad or crazy, or talking to himself. Miles Davis had brought the quartet of horses into a gallop and Boysie found himself reacting with a dance in his seat, and his foot on the gas pedal. It was so beautiful. It was such happiness just to drive, just to see how long the highway was, as if the highway was a long long stretch of cotton, "Thread, they call it in this country, old man. Thread!" coming towards his headlights, and being threaded into them, without end, like a man in a plane boring his head through clouds.

He loosened his tie, and about half of the buttons on his waistcoat. His pocket watch glimmered against the light from the dashboard. He was doing fifty miles an hour. And it was now ten o'clock at night. He wondered what he had done so long in the city, why he had taken all those wrong turns before he got onto the highway, this highway that seemed to have been waiting for him for such a long time of suspended happiness and freedom. What had he done in the city all afternoon, all those other afternoons that it had taken him such a long time to reach this point . . .

Floes and floes of angel's hair, ice cream castles in the air . . . In the apartment, Bernice is dozing off on the couch in the living room. The glasses are set for the party. So are the plates and the napkins. The food has been cooked and the candles have burned themselves down and out. The last one explodes silently into smoke, and as if Dots is the only one to hear this gasp of life, or of death, she opens her eyes, shakes her head like someone caught sleeping in the wrong place, and she asks Bernice the time.

"Two."

"So late?"

"Well, it looks as if nobody ain't coming." She gets up and takes her plate, which she had used hours ago, when she became hungry from waiting, back into the kitchen. She comes back, like a woman disoriented, and takes Dots's plate too.

"Only me and you, girl."

"And Lew didn't as much as call."

The cat is sleeping. Bernice goes to the same window through which she had looked hours before, and around in the darkness outside and still surrounding she can see very little life. All the windows except a few have gone to bed. The night becomes old now, and the light in front of the subway entrance, or exit, is no longer burning. One after another, the remaining lights in an apartment across from her go out.

"What you say the time is?"

"The time, Dots?"

"Yeah. What it is?"

"The night old, Dots. Late."

"Yeah. It will soon be light, though."

Precisely, as she said this, Boysie reached the United States border. The Immigration officer nods to him, and waves him on. Ahead of him is more highway, and more music and more black coffee when he stops and where he stops. He can feel the bigness of the space around him, for he knows he has left one kind of space for another one.